CW01594148

The Promise of Joanaria

NR KAMPER

30130504673456

FANTASY

Copyright © 2018 NR Kamper

All rights reserved.

ISBN: 1987664884
ISBN-13: 978-1987664881

DEDICATION

For Lisa. Gone, but never forgotten.

For family. You may be far away, but you have always been there.

For friends and co-workers. You are all an inspiration.

For the wife. Many a night of editing, proofreading and continuously inspiring one another to do better.

But most importantly, to you, the reader.

CONTENTS

A Promise for Joanas

Many years ago, before the Empire of the Dragon Lords, there was a Kingdom known as Joanaria. Once a bastion of hope and knowledge, it was widely considered a symbol of humanity's golden age. But this glory was not to last, for Joanaria fell into ruins when an ancient evil began to stir within its walls. Hatred, greed and death plagued the lands, and entire cities were destroyed.

It appeared there was no hope for the people of Joanaria, except for a select few who had reached the outer lands. With nothing but the clothes on their backs, they begun the search for a new world to call their home. No one knows what became of them, but it is believed they found their new home, and their ancestry set the foundations for generations to come.

Today, the Joanarians are looked upon as a source of hope. Their story serves as a reminder that, even when darkness looms, a light can still shine through.

And darkness is looming now. Thias, Emperor of Joanas, is facing an uprising that threatens to shatter the alliances of the city states and bring about a great war, the likes of which have not been seen since the fall of Joanaria. As he prepares himself and his army to face the unknown, he can only rely on his faith in the legend known as the Promise of Joanaria to keep his spirits alive and victory within his grasp.

A Better Tomorrow

Thias woke with a start from the cruel nightmare that reminded him of his past. It always welcomed him without warning, but he had grown used to it with time. Instead of leaping for his sword or crying out for help, today he felt a contained sense of urgency within his consciousness.

The heat of the morning did nothing to ease his awakening; it had his clothes sticking to his skin and the smell of sweat tickling his nose. He looked ahead at the tent's walls as they quivered against the wind, and allowed the songs of the jungle to wash over him.

Damn that nightmare, he thought bitterly, trying to focus. It was always a challenge, but he tended to find solace in the memories of his wife.

'The doctor said you mustn't dwell on this', she would say. 'He said you have to concentrate on your surroundings when it happens, to ground yourself in reality. I told him you're just a big oaf who needs a good slap every once in a while.'

Thias smiled at the thought of her nagging. *I miss that silly old hag*, he mused.

He tried to sift through some old memories of her but, try as he may, his thoughts always returned to that night. He looked down at his badly misshapen hand with its missing thumb and grumbled. *Bastard Fallen.*

Soon enough the smells of cooked pork and stale toast began to filter through into the tent. Ordinarily Thias would never miss breakfast but, on this occasion, he refused to leave the tent without his proper attire. *An Emperor never enters his camp in nothing but his gown.*

As he dressed, he heard a voice call his name. It was his housekeeper, Edgar Crewe.

'Emperor Doncaster', he said. 'Are you roused and ready, Sir?'

Thias pulled the straps of his right gauntlet tightly, holding himself against the pain that crept through his bones.

'I'm just pulling together my armour', he replied. 'I'll be ready soon. If you insist on waiting for me though, tell me about the camp. Did we receive more men from the other kingdoms last night?'

'Not from what I have seen, Sir', Edgar answered. 'The number of banners has not changed. Yet I did hear the supply wagons carrying our next provisions arrived safely.'

Thias was not surprised. At this point, it would take the Dragon Bloods to get the rest of the Lords to rally behind him. It was typical for this country, yet his hopes were high for victory.

'Have we heard back from the scouts yet?' Thias asked as he strapped on his left gauntlet. 'And have you seen Commander Ouster on your travels?'

'I was in the Commander's sector before I came here. There was talk of a few hawks and sparrows returning but none of the riders. I did not think to ask the whereabouts of the Commander, so I did not hear what was discovered. Sorry, my Lord.'

'Not to worry, you're a butler after all. Not a messenger.'

'Yes, my Lord. Merek is going to pack up the kitchen soon. Do you wish me to wait for you?'

'Go feed yourself, my friend', Thias said. 'Be sure to eat your bread first though. I may steal it from you when I get there.'

'Very good, my Lord', Edgar smiled. 'See you there.'

With a chuckle, Thias inspected himself in front of his mirror. His breastplate seemed a little too high. *It needs to be perfect.*

He was too proud to ask for help with anything. When he lost his hand, he forced himself to learn to write with the other and would not accept assistance from Edgar. His sword, *Joanas-Star,* was specially built for him by the Capital's smithy, and it held a groove in its grip where he could slot his fake thumb. His swordsmanship wasn't what it once was, but it was enough to see him become Emperor of the Knights Republic.

Breastplate fixed, *Joanas-Star* bolted to his belt and the Emperor's helm under his arm, Thias left his tent and headed for the camp. He checked the tents for any sign of a new sigil, but nothing caught his eye. As he strode through the camp he was hailed by several soldiers, some of whom were heading out in full armour towards the eastern road. This was his first indication that some news had been shared.

He reached Merek's kitchen, hailed by Merek himself and the dozen men feasting at the benches. Edgar was sitting with a group of armoured soldiers, his grey moustache and beard dripping with the juices of his meat and his plate still holding some bread. He offered it to Thias with a smile.

Taking the bread and the last portions of meat from Merek's serving table, Thias sat down at a free bench and set his helm on the table top. The slices of roasted pig were chewy and refreshing, but the bread was stale as a rock.

Half way through, Commander Ouster called his name from behind. Thias turned to face him. He was glad to see his Commander's head held high with a smile burning through the recent news of his fallen brother.

'High spirits for a second day', he said. 'You're more a man than me, Ouster. Are you eating? Are you well?'

'No, my Lord', Ouster said, looking proud in his tight-fitting armour. 'But I am well enough for the morning. I can wait until you are finished before taxing you with the news.'

'I'm almost finished. Can't you speak it now?'

Thias wasn't afraid to talk while eating. He felt table manners were more damning than good during war.

'It must be said in private, have you at least heard about the Hobsythe?'

'No, what of them?'

Thias tried to loosen the last morsel of bread with the fat of the pork, bounding his attention between the plate and the gold-leafed eyelets of his helm.

'Well? Do we expect Kinas and his ilk to be late?' He stuffed the last of the bread into his mouth and took a moment to enjoy the zing of the juices as they ran down his throat. 'Or are they early?'

'They're early, my Lord.'

'They must be desperate to fight us', Thias said, as he stood up and took the empty plate to Merek's table. 'Judging by the number of prepared men I saw heading towards the east, I'd say they'd be here later today.'

Thias cleaned out his mouth with a sip of the tacky water on Merek's table and spat it out onto the mud.

'Does that sound accurate?'

'Yes Sire, if not during the night.'

'Nothing we can't prepare ourselves for', Thias said, wiping his lips and brow with a towel. 'But it makes you think, doesn't it? Why speed up now? Surely they would slow down. I know they're a race of halfwits but-'

'That's why I need to talk to you in private, my Lord.'

Ouster's face wore an empty stare. Thias' gut squeezed, and he began to feel the weight of his thoughts. He grabbed his helm and joined Ouster's side. *What could it be?*

'To the spike wall then, behind the shelters', he said, hand on Ouster's back. He led him across the trail to a small clearing between the spikes and the last line of tents.

'Tell me', he implored, checking for eavesdroppers. 'What is it?'

'The Hobsythe, sir. They're being flanked.'

'By whom? Who has the kind of power to push the Hobsythe?'

'According to the scout, it was an army of outsiders.'

'By what observation?'

'I don't know, it was just a sparrow. The bird keeper was adamant it said *invaders*.'

Thias' thoughts were running amok, but he remained

calm. After all, it wasn't yet clear whether the flankers were enemies.

'Have any of the other ground scouts returned?'

'No', Ouster said, rubbing the tattooed initials of his daughters on his neck as he looked around. 'How long do you think we should give them?'

'It doesn't matter', Thias said. 'Until we get better word, we should maintain the alert and keep up with the patrols.'

He heard his name on the back of Edgar's voice.

'Something is up – come on.'

Thias and Ouster returned to the trail and headed back towards Edgar. When they reached him, they were met by a crowd of soldiers. The leader carried an eagle, which held a message in its talons.

'Hand it over, let me see!' Thias demanded, taking the message from the bird. *By the Mother, be good news.* Unwinding the paper, he revealed the scribbling.

Eastern foot – Hobsythe line.

An army cutting through the shrubs and flanking the Hobsythe – Looks like a Dragon Blood army.

Leader's standard is the wolf-dragon of the Penance clan.

They were shooting at us.

Thias passed the paper to Ouster and grabbed Edgar.

'My tent. Pack my things and leave for the Capital right now.'

'Sire?' Edgar asked.

'Don't question me. Just go.'

With a nod, Edgar was away.

'*The Penance clan*', Ouster mused, folding the paper up and passing it back to Thias. 'Aren't they all thought to be dead?'

'Your brother's search parties found nothing', Thias replied, stuffing the paper into his gauntlet, 'We need to re-think our strategy, the numbers aren't clear and…'

He was interrupted by the distant cry of a Hobsythe war horn from the east.

'Get your armour and your hides to the field now!'

Thias took a second glance at Ouster's armour as the soldiers dispersed into the camp. He had his jewel-encrusted sword and dagger, with only the helm missing from his armour.

'Do you need to get a helm?'

'Captain Carnac has my spare', Ouster replied. 'I'll pick it up when I see him.'

'Very well'.

Thias could not help wondering what the Penance clan's survival meant for him. Its last leader, Jack, was a friend who shared the burden of the night which haunted his dreams. If he were leading the army, there would be hope. Every member of the Penance clan, except for Jack, hated what Joanas had become and what the Knight's Republic had done to it. Prayer would be the only solution if it came to an invasion.

The Joanarian war bell broke Thias' train of thought as it let out its call and prompted the camp to erupt into another torrent of orders and shouting. The pace of the soldiers slowed as more formed in, forcing Thias and Ouster to the centre of the trail.

'What is our strategy, Emperor Doncaster?' Ouster asked, puffing as he ground to a halt. 'Shall it be the same formations?'

Thias considered his answer carefully. The news had his plans in shreds, particularly if the invaders were to charge while they were still dispatching the Hobsythe. He needed a better tactic than waiting for the Hobsythe to come to them.

'If you are suggesting something', Thias said, 'then say it now.'

'Well, instead of waiting', Ouster said, 'we could do what we did in the war with the Dragon Bloods.'

Thias stopped. *That's brilliant,* he thought to himself.

This would give us the chance to dispatch the Hobsythe before the second army is upon us.

'That's good', he said. 'When we reach the flag-bearers, give the order. We need to do it exactly like we did there.'

'And the flankers?'

'Use the shield turtle until you can better assess their numbers', Thias answered. 'I think I can persuade Jack to stand down, but if it is anyone else it may be hopeless.'

Thias put on his helmet and jogged to his position behind the front three lines. When he had surveyed the edge of the jungle the day before, it was filled with the calls of song birds and primates. But now it was silent and he could see the shadows moving closer towards the clearing. One such shadow was very near to the open and, as it stepped out, it revealed its carrier. It appeared to be a Hobsythe Commander, carrying the trophies of his war.

The man-sized lizard sank his webbed claws into the undergrowth when he was only a few paces from the trees. He proudly wore the crown and matching breastplate of the last Emperor, along with a skull around his neck. The plate's sigil, the silver songbirds of the Ouster clan, were scratched beyond recognition. *This must be Kinas.*

The belief was reinforced by the lizard's current weapons of choice; a spear of the East and a Great Eastern scimitar, strapped to his back.

Thias nodded to Ouster, who whispered the new orders to the local flag-bearer whilst the army prepared for battle. He thought for a moment about diplomacy as the flags relayed the orders across the army, reminiscing about the times before the War of Sanctity, when the Hobsythe had their own state and representative in the Knight's Republic. There was even a Hobsythe Emperor at one point. But man's lust for power and the racial tensions destroyed that Kingdom, and far too many wars were fought since then for petty reasons. The aftermath of Sanctity forced the Hobsythe from their homes and into the jungles. *Years of prosperity and friendship gone in a month.*

Treated as if they were nothing but rats.

'The orders are relayed', Ouster confirmed. 'We're ready when you are, my Lord.'

'He hasn't called his army yet', Thias replied as he studied Kinas' demeanour. 'We can't have them stay in the trees like that. We need them out and dispatched before the flankers catch up- dispatching in halves will be better than one simultaneous attack.'

'We haven't had confirmation of the flankers' numbers yet, Sire', Ouster said, 'If they are all Dragon Bloods, there could be thousands of them.'

'I'm still hoping its Jack. I'd be happy with a rabble led by an imposter if not. If they are Dragon Bloods, do you think they are acting on orders from the Dragon King?'

'That's my concern, my Lord. His efforts to get the Penance clan in Joanas in the first place would be for nothing if he ordered them to attack us like this. It wouldn't make sense.'

'Very true', Thias said, caressing *Joanas-Star's* hilt. 'Whatever happens, do not forget how much greater a man you are than your brother. I am proud to have you by my side, helping me clean up the mess he made.'

'It is my honour and it is my father's honour. By the Mother, I hope Cain is a better man in death than he was in life.'

Thias had no more words for Ouster, so he returned his attention to Kinas. The Hobsythe was now holding a stare of a thousand needles, his upper teeth resting above his lower lip as if biting away a decision. With the stare held, he bashed the butt of his spear into the earth like a drum.

Thias watched as the other shadows moved through the trees.

'Here we go…'

With a set of rustles and a chorus of whistles, the Hobsythe line showed itself. They crept and crawled through the undergrowth and into the open, as if they really were lizards. But Thias, and likely his men, knew better.

Many dug their claws into the bark of the trees, elevating themselves over the heads of the foot soldiers. As the rustling of the leaves and branches settled, Kinas inspected his line and spat towards Thias' army.

'Where is the human army, pond scum?' he demanded, smashing his spear against his breastplate. 'You look like servants to Kinas. You should go back to your houses and await Kinas' conquering.'

Thias was impressed by Kinas' confidence, yet intrigued by the fear on the other Hobsythe's faces. Their legs twitched as they awaited their leader.

'He sounds friendly', Thias said to Ouster, keeping his tone low. 'Ready the archers.'

'Yes, my Lord.'

Thias turned to the rear flanks. He watched as Ouster raised his hand and shouted the order across the heads of the army. The flag bearers of the squads flapped their charge across the lines, allowing the several hundred longbowmen to prepare a volley. Thias waited until the unsettlement amongst the Hobsythe escalated to worried whispers before he addressed Kinas.

'Kinas Kirk! It doesn't have to be like this; there is an army flanking you. I know you know it, and I know your people know it. Fear comes in many forms, even for you. Tell your people to put down their weapons, and they can run for their safety unharmed.'

'Fuck you and your safety!' Kinas retorted. 'Give Kinas the Capital, and your families will suffer quick deaths.'

'Why in the Mother's name does he want the Capital?' Ouster asked.

'Who cares?' said Thias, speaking loudly enough for Kinas to hear him. 'It's not an option he's getting in this lifetime. We'll just have to take them all down.'

Ouster turned his back to the rear flank, and lowered his arm with a shout. The arrows were released, and they rained down onto the enemy lines. Thias counted only a few fallers from the trees, with even fewer receiving an arrow. The surviving Hobsythe peeked out from behind the old wood giants, chuckling nervously.

'Shall I send another volley?' asked Ouster.

'Give it a moment', Thias replied. 'Have the archers wind and load the crossbows, then continue firing arrows. We can't wait a moment longer, that army will be upon us soon. Fire the crossbows when they charge.'

Thias slotted his metal thumb into *Joanas-Star's* hilt, and pulled it from its holster, allowing it to gleam against the sun as he toted it into the air.

'For Joanas', he cried.

'For Joanas', his front line returned.

The swordsmen drew the swords from their scabbards, and began to march forward. 'Don't forget, Ouster', Thias said, 'follow our plan.'

'Yes, my Lord', said Ouster. 'Just hold out for as long as you can.'

'And in the name of the Mother, find your helmet!'

Thias followed the front lines as they marched. The weight of his steel felt heavier with each stride, and he could hear the reeling of the crossbow twines. *I'm not a coward.*

The lines were slowing. Thias looked to the drummers marching at the flanks and, like clockwork, they began to play the beat of the Joanarian March. He controlled his breathing as his mind started to rupture with thoughts of pain, suffering and torture at the hands of the Hobsythe. *I'm not a coward.* Another volley shrieked over him and he shrank his head into his neck like a tortoise. *The Emperor of Joanas is not a coward.*

The volley did little damage, yet Thias could see the Hobsythe were growing even more uneasy as they began to fidget. He knew what their charge would be like and how ruthless they would be. Hobsythe left no quarter for men anymore, not since the atrocities and the uprising.

Since they looked desperate to survive, it may be an even more brutal attack. He raised *Joanas-Star* again.

'Soldiers. Who are we?'

'We are the children of Joanas', replied the lines. 'The hand of the Knight's Republic!'

Thias fixed his eyes on Kinas, who seemed amused by the demonstration. However, his comrades were slow to join him with their own cackles, as their fear was a mistress who couldn't be ignored. *Stop laughing and make them charge. Make that leap, please. Do it. Come on – charge.*

Kinas wiped the hysterical tears from his face and raised his spear over his head as another volley flew into the treeline. With a long battle cry, his front line came running out into the clearing. They sprinted towards them like wild cats, blades in their mouths.

In the distance, Thias heard Ouster give the order to fire the crossbows.

'Halt and kneel!' Thias called to his army.

The human line stopped and dropped to their knees. The bolts flew straight into the flesh of the Hobsythe runners with a set of cracks and a flood of screeches. Thias and the line cheered only once and then returned to a standing defence, greeting the surviving Hobsythe with spears to their guts and swords to their necks. The line held strong. With bloodied helms and weapons covered in entrails, they strode over the fallen with a huff.

Thias could tell Kinas was not pleased. Even though he had taken bolts to his chin and his leg, he was now approaching. He held a mean gaze as he closed the final gap between himself and the humans, backed by a full charge of Hobsythe.

'Secondary attack', he called.

The swordsmen made their dash towards the Hobsythe, holding their lines as they covered the sprint to the tree line. Thias quickened his pace to stay in line with them, glad to be as fit as they were. He let out a long battle cry, and gleefully listened to the voices of his men as they drowned his into the sky. With a loud set of clangs, the two armies met and began to battle, showering the air with blood like a summer's eve dance.

Thias took quick and controlled breaths as the sweat raced down his back. His mind fought the fear as he approached the crush zone, trying to make contact with a Hobsythe.

He found one, and it came at him with a morningstar and a long scream. He denied its attack with a duck, countering with *Joanas-Star's* cross to its face and a follow up stab in the rib. He turned away from the Hobsythe as it moaned and fell to its knees. *The Emperor is a beast.*

Although excited and proud to still be capable, he needed to find Kinas. He heard the roar of another Hobsythe coming for him. This one had a sword, and was a step ahead of him with his attack.

Thias brought up his right gauntlet. *Shit.* The shock of the hit rattled his bones and sent pain down his arm, but he was able to turn the attack around by thrusting *Joanas-Star* into the creature's neck. The strike covered his arm and breastplate in a shower of blood, and he forced the Hobsythe down into the dirt.

He flexed his sword hand for a moment, then pulled out *Joanas-Star* and proceeded to scan the surroundings for his next attacker. He remained calm, keeping his eyes level with the heads of the Hobsythe. None were visible through the cracks in the lines and Kinas was nowhere to be seen, so he shadowed the nearest swordsman and helped him take down his mark. Swiftly, he cut off the Hobsythe's sword arm as the swordsman jabbed his blade repeatedly into its stomach. With a quick word of thanks, he sent him on his way and watched as a clearing began to form. At the opposite end of the clearing stood Kinas.

Thias watched as Kinas thrust his spear into the nearest swordsman's throat, ripping a chunk of it out as he pulled away. He then clutched what remained of the man's neck and tossed him aside with a snarl. With a brief look at

Thias, he smeared the man's blood onto his face with a satisfied grin, then threw the spear like a javelin into the neck of another soldier. He spat, cricked his neck, and pulled out the scimitar. The sight of the steel crescent as it danced made Thias uneasy but, with his duty still calling to him, he approached Kinas with every ounce of courage he could muster.

Thias' plan for Kinas haemorrhaged suddenly when a Hobsythe jumped on his back from behind. The shock made him drop *Joanas-Star* and, in that moment of dread, his courage vanished quicker than the sword. But he wasn't giving up. He smashed both his hands against the Hobsythe's arms as they scratched against his armour. Between the desperately drunk spins of his struggle, he realised Kinas was now walking towards him, preparing the scimitar for a meal. The Hobsythe were also beginning to surround them, the one on his back clawing at the leathers around his neck.

The Hobsythe forced him onto his knees, grabbed his helm's eye sockets and prised at them until the helm was off. This gave Thias a full view of Kinas, who finished his approach with his scimitar ready to be fed.

'Emperor!' Ouster called from the rear.

Thias felt the Hobsythe behind him seize up. The hands holding him down let go as another bolt flew straight into Kinas' shoulder, shocking the beast enough to make him fumble the scimitar. Thias took his chance. He secured his grasp around the scimitar's hilt, and bounded up from his knees to plant its point into Kinas' pelvis. Using both hands, he pushed the blade higher into his body.

Kinas let out a traumatic squeal as Thias rose to his eye level, letting the warm Hobsythe blood soothe his hands. He watched as Ouster's charge mowed down every Hobsythe left unbeaten in a victorious mash of axe and blood. Four spearmen appeared from both sides of him and planted their spears into Kinas, two under his arms, two into his hips.

'The last Emperor and I warned you of this, but you didn't listen', Thias reminded the defeated leader. 'Now your people's fate lies with the Mother.'

'Fuck your Mother', said Kinas in a struggle, spitting blood onto Thias' face. 'Fuck Joanas and its people. Fuck the promise of the Old Kingdom.'

Thias pulled out the blade and watched Kinas squirm as it cut away yet more flesh in its exit. The four spearmen pulled out their weapons, letting him fall backwards into the earth with a thud. Kinas let out a final rasp before his eyes closed and his last breath choked into the air. Thias threw the scimitar to the side, making peace with the lost hopes of a Joanaria with the Hobsythe and accepting the need to have the last of Kinas' blood flow onto the earth like rivers across a wasteland. *There's still hope for us. There is still hope for men.*

The soldiers cheered and raised their weapons in celebration, but Thias himself refused to rejoice at the passing of a small dream. Ouster soon found him, and he did not hesitate to thank him with an embrace. Although the jubilation was great and the relief was strong, his dread still reminded him of what was to come.

'Get them into their formations, Ouster', Thias ordered, as he began to search for *Joanas-Star*. 'And try and find my sword for me.'

Ouster acknowledged him and shouted out the orders. He pushed the men into boxes of fifty swords, twenty spears and ten bows, and scattered each turtle across the field leaving ample room for cavalry and chariots. Thias couldn't have been more impressed with Ouster's command, or the discipline of his army. However he hoped this wasn't the end and he could still restore Joanas' peace. He heard Ouster call his name, and when he turned to face him, he was relieved to see *Joanas-Star* in his grip. But before he could take the sword, the afternoon air shook with the long-winded trumpet of a Dragon Blood horn.

The mood of the soldiers mirrored that of the Hobsythe before the battle, uneasy and frantic. Thias watched as the stragglers disappeared inside a mass of shields and spears, leaving only himself and Ouster.

'The soldiers are ready, Ouster', he said, slowly taking *Joanas-Star* as the pounding of drums rang in his ears. 'I need you in one of those formations.'

'Begging your pardon Sire, but not yet', Ouster said. 'Let me see what we're up against first.'

'Very well. But I want you in one the moment it's clear.'

The horn called again, and the endless clanking of a thousand foot soldiers began to drown out the beats of the drums.

'Hold easy gentlemen, and stay calm. Keep your thoughts on your charge and your wits at the tips of your weapons.'

'My Lord', Ouster said. 'To the north!'

Thias turned and watched as a heavy line of spearmen, clad in armour darker than the shadows of the moons, slowly spilled out into the field. Amongst their ranks were the standards of the Penance clan flapping in the breeze. They had begun chanting their war call in a tongue Thias recognised but could not translate.

'Is that what I think it is?'

'The Dragon Tongue?', Ouster asked. 'Yes, it is.'

'Emperor', called a soldier from the nearest formation, pointing to the south. 'Look, over there.'

Another line of spearmen was marching parallel to the first, with the same pace and the same chant. Thias' mind filled with worry once again. Their numbers were huge and both lines were still growing. He looked to the trail heading into the jungle and saw a set of heads bobbing to the trot of heavy cavalry.

The first to enter the clearing was a Joanarian stallion, a towering adult Storm Trotter with a mane as dark as the beasts of Thias' dreams and eyes as empty as the cloudy night. The rider was donned in black armour and his face hid behind an iron-gated helm.

Striding to his left was his standard bearer, wearing only leathers. He held the banner's pole against the Storm Trotter's saddle, allowing the sigil to dance with the lowly winds. Their horses stopped ten paces from the clearing, permitting the host's heavy cavalry to spill out in two lines behind him.

'Commander Ouster, if you were needing any better time to get into formation, that time is now.'

'Yes, my Lord', said Ouster. 'The Mother is watching.'

Thias heard a soldier greeting Ouster and telling him that they had his helmet. He could not help but laugh.

'Indeed', he said, trying to find any notable features on the leader. 'My scouts told me you attacked them?'

'Not all of them', the leader replied in a broken and artificial slang of Joanarian. 'They were distracting the Hobsythe's retreat, and spooked my horses. But it was not our intention to kill them.'

'Only the birds returned though', Thias said, watching the leader as he dismounted his horse. 'What did you do with the men?'

The leader turned to his standard bearer and whispered something in the Dragon Tongue, before returning his gaze to Thias and moving closer to him.

'They're quite safe', he said. 'But I find it interesting that you decided to greet us like this – swords drawn and shields up.'

Thias tried to read his body language, hoping to see something in his memories of the sessions between the Dragon Bloods and Knight's Republic. *This could be Jack, but he had more respect for us than he is displaying now.*

'We had no clue who you were', Thias said, looking at the lines who were still marching towards them. 'Or what your intentions are. You haven't even given me your name, but judging by your standard and the way your tongue carries Joanarian, you must be a survivor of the Penance clan.'

Penance stopped mere paces from Thias, giving him a fuller view of his face. The skin was young and fair, so it couldn't have been the patriarch, Stanley. The eyes were a darkened green and the hair a silver blonde. Judging by his freshly shaven eyebrows and the fringe dangling around his eyes, it may have been Jack? Or Edgar? *Oh Mother, please let it be Jack.*

'I see you have slain the Scourge', Penance said, looking at the body of Kinas with an approving nod. 'It must have taken some incredible wit to subdue him.'

Thias tried to identify the voice as either Jack's or Edgar's, but found it difficult to differentiate between the two sons. There was something not right about all of this. The way Penance's cavalry stood before him, looking poised and ready to attack. Plus, the voice seemed peculiar for a Penance. The Dragon Bloods were proud and the Penance clan even prouder, yet this one's voice sounded somewhat distant.

'The Scourge?' he asked, referring back to Penance's observation. 'Is that his name now?'

'No, it is what the Morre call him in the Dragon Tongue. Kinas Kirk, the Scourge of Joanas.'

The way he said 'Joanas' suggested it was Jack. But the dread still burned as the lines marched and the heavy cavalry looked ready for a skirmish. Thias could not falter like this, so he pulled his wits back up and willed his bravery into his mouth.

'Are you Edgar or Jack?' he asked.

'Forgive me', Penance said. He slowly pulled off his helm to reveal his long, silver hair. His frown and the daunting sockets of his eyes revealed the secret.

'Thank the Mother – it *is* you Jack', Thias sighed with relief. 'Can we talk for a moment, like old times?'

'Of course', Jack replied, throwing his helm onto the floor. 'I'm always in the mood for chatter when I have

Thias Doncaster in my presence.'

Thias caught a glimpse of a scar running from Jack's left ear down into the recesses of his armour. It was new, and he supposed it could have come either from a scimitar or from the very large katana he was pulling from his holster.

'There's no need to draw your sword here', Thias said, sheaving *Joanas-Star*. 'We're allies. You guided the Knight's Republic and reminded us how it felt to live in peace. There's no need for that kind of formality with us.'

Jack's eyes followed the katana as he moved it from hand to hand. Thias was suspicious of his intentions but, being the hopeful Commander that he was, he wished to keep the conversation going.

'Jack, please', Thias begged, offering him his hand. 'We have such history together, you and I. Swords are only for strangers. Did the Prince send you these men?'

Jack scowled.

'I have no business with Drake O'Neil', he said. 'But my business is with you.'

It was clear that his efforts had been in vain, but Thias could not retract his offer of peace now.

'Why just business?' he asked. 'I'm not just the Emperor, I'm Thias Doncaster. Of Winter-Haem? Surely you remember me? We held court in the Capital when Cain Ouster was Emperor, and we trained together with Drake in the earlier years in Centra.'

'*We* trained together – with Drake?' Jack repeated, as he turned towards Thias.

'Yes', Thias said, 'I beat the both of you in the final test.'

Jack smiled. With a hopeful laugh, Thias offered him his hand once again…

But he could not shake. His arm was gone. A bleeding stub was all that remained.

'What are you doing?' Thias cried out in pain.

'I am restoring Joanaria to her former glory!'

Thias' body ruptured as the sting of Jack's blade coaxed his mind into a paralysis. He fell to the ground, the agonising pain blinding him. Then, as he slowly began to drift out of consciousness, he heard Jack's voice taunt him one last time.

'You didn't beat me, Thias.'

The earth cradled his broken body. The army encircled him. And then Thias took his last breath, leaving the world behind and taking with him the sacred Promise of Joanaria.

Come ye to all who fallen,
To life's bitter fate,
Open arms on an endless lake,
To the Promised Land,
Where the Children of Joanaria,
Rest their spirits make.

Letters of Late

Gromwell lowered the parchment and peered over at Drake.

'This is definitely from Jonathan Ouster?' he asked, stumbling over his words. 'The insignia and the writing are his?'

Of course it is – I have seen more letters from Joanas than you have, Drake thought to himself, but he held his tongue and merely nodded.

'I've never known a human to address us as the Morre before.'

He inspected the letter again, rubbing his chin as he did so, and then passed it back to Drake.

'What do you think about the bird?'

Drake looked at the Silver-Tailed falcon perched on the window sill. It was freshly groomed, well-fed and apparently oblivious to their suspicions, although it had a tendency to scowl at them.

'It looks like an innocent messenger to me', he replied. 'And although he insists on calling us Dragon Bloods in the courts, Jonathan respects us enough to call us the Morre when he needs our help. What is wrong with the bird?'

'They've all been Silver-Tails. Even the ones from your father. They also don't understand a single word of the Dragon Tongue, and the convenience of that is unsettling.'

He's right – He's always right.

Gromwell shooed the bird away with a hiss and watched as it flapped into the night. He then turned back to Drake, focusing on him with a stare that would make a human feel cold and unsettled.

'Even your father knows better than to send Silver-Tails. Their range is shorter than the sparrows, and half that of the Snuggle-Tails. These messages, as legitimate as they appear, are being intercepted.'

'Why would anyone want to intercept our messages?'

Drake could not bear to look into the middle-aged Morre's eyes for longer than a pace's worth of passing.

'There's a number of reasons', Gromwell answered. 'Not even magic can reproduce this kind of calligraphy, even if the owner's family is threatened. It could be to get us to act at a desired time.'

'But I want to lead the armies to the Eastern Shores right now. Were the Hobsythe ever known to pick fights with the Morre?'

'There could be some ill feeling towards us after the war', Gromwell suggested, leaning against the window sill. 'There's a reason the Knight's Republic only swear in their Emperors in times of war. Without an army to lead or an enemy to fight, Cain and his crown came down hard on the Hobsythe.'

'Stanley Penance encouraged it, and Jack did very little to stop it. By the Torre, a fool would see the Penance Clan's disappearance as a coincidence. The Hobsythe did it and that's a fact. At the very least they have ill feelings towards the Morre, but they are not smart enough to intercept our messages like this. It has to be someone else.'

'Like another member of the Knight's Republic?' Drake asked.

'Like an imposter, yes', Gromwell said.

His jewel-like eyes locked onto the letter in Drake's hand.

'Show the letter to me again', he demanded, snatching it. He read it once more and mused over the words briefly before continuing.

'Whoever they are, they are not consistent. The Penance Clan's disappearance has been longer than half a year and, according to this, Cain marched a day before he discovered the uprising was happening.'

'Do you still have the other letters?'

'I do', Gromwell replied, folding up the letter and stuffing it into his shirt pocket. 'I will raise this with Jefferson and Bartarian. We need to think of a plan to bring this up with the navy.'

'Will I find the three of you in the mess at breakfast?' Drake asked.

'For certain; the talk of the stewards is that it is a full breakfast', he answered, opening the door to leave. 'There will be none the following morning.'

'Why?' Drake asked, stopping Gromwell before he could make his exit. 'What is happening at that time?'

'Laura and Tiana Rivera wish to discuss the state of Joanas with the town, but we can leave the other details until the morrow. Goodnight, my Prince.'

With the door shut and Gromwell gone, Drake settled down on his bed. He thought of Laura Rivera speaking to the fishermen and traders about war. *She'd be a laughing stock. The Morre wouldn't even take her seriously.*

He dwelled on the idea of sailing to Joanas as he blew out the candle on his side table, but it quickly became a folly. Firstly, his father had not allowed it yet, and secondly, even if he had the will to go, no one would follow him. A wave of sadness engulfed him as he remembered. Just like Laura, no one had any respect for his command.

That very thought opened the floodgates. He cast his mind back to his departure from Morkor, where the soldiers had cursed his royal right to the banner. Their disgusted looks had made him feel small and unworthy. Deep down he knew their disdain for him had merit, but he'd grown tired of feeling sorry for himself every time he dwelled on it.

He flipped onto his side and pressed his face into the pillow, burying the bad thoughts. However, it wasn't long before he'd fallen asleep and dropped into that all too familiar dream he'd hoped never to see again.

***

His eyes were focused on the firelight, watching as each

lick quivered into the night sky. The burning needles and cones atop the logs gave off the scent of a dank forest flower, with a hint of toasted sap and bark. The fire lit up the clearing in front of a brick cottage, and three faces danced within its light. The bald and badly scarred Elder to Drake's left never blinked nor moved his eyes, but he mused with the legends of the three moons that hung overhead. The two boys to his right were silent. One played with his long, silver hair, and the other would occasionally rub his outcrop of brown hair with a grunt.

All remained calm until the Fallen's call was heard. Drake's blood thickened with fear as they all stood to attention and the rest of the Fallen hailed out over the trees.

'They're coming', yelled the Elder. 'Keep your swords sheaved. Drake – get the water and douse the fire. You two – come to me.'

Drake looked for the pail of water in a frenzied scramble. He found it sitting at the foot of the nearest tree, perhaps fifty paces from the fire, but it seemed to creep further away the longer he stared at it. He hesitated, then ran to the bucket, picked it up and turned to the campfire.

'Behind you!' the silver-haired boy shouted.

Drake's dread grew fierce as he turned, and when he saw the Fallen's oily-thick mane and tasted the smell of wet mould, he froze. The creature's big, yellow eyes dug into his soul, and its growl rumbled through a set of slimy fangs.

***

He awoke, his forehead dripping with sweat. Rubbing the dew from his face, he turned to the window and looked out at the mist-coated streets ahead, his thoughts still plagued by a sense of doom. However, it wasn't long before he was greeted by the smell of baked bread and roasted salmon, and he knew right away he couldn't miss out on this breakfast even if it did mean facing the other Commanders. Thanks to his speed and agility, he was dressed and in the Mess Hall within minutes. He found the three middle-aged Morre sitting together on a bench near the northern door.

'Good morning Lords Gromwell, Jefferson and Bartarian, may I sit with you?'

Bartarian, larger but significantly stronger than the rest of them, stopped eating and looked up at him.

'I need good reason to allow your royal arse to fester over my breakfast, boy.'

Drake bit his lip and looked to Gromwell for support. The old pig's greetings were almost ceremonious, but he still found it hard resisting the urge to fight back.

'There's no need to be so harsh, Karl', Gromwell scolded, slapping his back. 'Where else is the lad going to sit?'

'He can eat in the stables for all I care, as long as it is not here.'

Jefferson, opposite Bartarian, cleared his throat.

'Edward is right, Bartarian', he said, 'You're such an ignorant ass. Leave the boy alone and let him sit.'

He signalled for the attention of a steward.

'Sit Drake, this salmon is delicious.'

Drake sat down beside him and exchanged a quick glance with Bartarian. The Morre gave him a look so sharp it could have shaved his beard.

'Keep to your bloody self and I will keep to my own', he grumbled, returning to his food.

A plate full of salmon, eggs and beans was placed before Drake, along with a flagon of foaming liquid. Although content with the delicious smell of the freshly-roasted fish, Drake was unsure about the drink, as it appeared looser than the ale he was served during yesterday's evening meal.

'It's still Joanarian Ale', Gromwell assured him. 'It has been loosened with ciders from the apple orchards.'

Drake looked at him, the disappointment evident from his frown.

'The town is down to its last barrels- just be grateful they used apples. The townsfolk are so used to the ale that they'd quicker taste a bastardisation then any of our imports.'

'I quite like it', declared Jefferson, holding his flagon with a proud smile.

'That's because you're as ignorant as they are', Gromwell said with a chuckle. 'If I wasn't so parched I would go to the Vengeance of Dunfife and enjoy the sugar of our homeland. But as my mouth is drier than the Navurian Desert already, this smut will have to do.'

Bartarian allowed himself a small laugh, but still refused to look at either of them. Drake tasted the ale. He expected a burning trail of fizz to run down his tongue, but instead was greeted with an aftertaste worse than a Navurian whisky.

'By the Torre!' Drake exclaimed, slamming the flagon down against the table. 'It's nasty!'

'The more you drink it the less your stomach wants to hurl it back up', Jefferson said, slurping at his flagon with widened eyes. 'That's when it really tastes *good.*'

'Never mind him, lad', Gromwell said, 'How was the night for you?'

'I had a nightmare', replied Drake, 'It was the same as the one I had before we left Morkor.'

Gromwell stopped eating, and scanned his face.

'The wolf-men?'

'I don't know why you call them that. All I see of them is their eyes and their fur. They are the Fallen, true, but they could be anything.'

'You'd best keep hunting for the truth behind them. I stand by my word when I say it's the same wolf-men as those that attacked Soule. Given that it was around the same time you went south, you'd permit me to believe you had a part in their disappearance.'

Gromwell had told Drake about the Fallen's raids when he came home, and he had never let him live down the fact that his mother and father feared for the worst. They'd sent him with search parties across the Morkor Hinterlands, south into the mountains of Gaul, past Soule and even down to the coast of Citadel. Although he pretended that he didn't care personally, he'd taken any opportunity to remind Drake about the Fallen's disappearance ever since his son passed.

'Does Drake's silence mean we can change the subject?' Jefferson asked. 'I'd prefer to talk about the ale again than those bastard creatures.'

'Forgive me, Jefferson', said Gromwell, 'I forgot.'

'It's alright. We ought to get down to the matters at hand and tell him about the letter from the King.'

'You got a message from Father?' Drake asked. 'What did it say?'

'Indeed', confirmed Jefferson. 'You have the letter Edward, show it to Drake.'

Gromwell reached into his jacket pocket and pulled out a scrap of paper barely the size of a horse's foot.

'Comparing the letters', he began as he tossed the scrap to Drake, 'there has been some meddling with time for sure. This new one proves it. It's like your father sent it before Lord Doncaster travelled to the Capital.'

'That was twenty days ago', Drake said, checking the signature at the bottom of the parchment was indeed his father's. 'Are you sure it isn't caused by the birds' flight path?'

'We are dead certain of it. Just read the letter and see for yourself.'

Dearest son,

We keep getting reports that the Hobsythe are moving further westward, and Cain Ouster has called the Western Kingdom's Lords to Negura to answer the threat. But we have heard nothing from you.

Have you obeyed my request? Are you still there? Please may it be so; I need your eyes and ears for the times to come. The Kingdoms have not been this desperate since the War of Sanctity. I fear there is something else going on that they either don't know or won't tell us. I trust you this far my son, please try to write back as soon as you receive this.

Your mother sends her love and hopes you will be back with us soon. The urgent matter of your future Kingdom needs to be discussed. We will convene with the Dragon Council to find the quickest resolution of this dark time.

All of our love and blessings,

King Sepherance.

Drake dropped the letter onto the table.

'This is more delayed than Jonathan's letter', he said. 'We have to do something about this. We have to stop whoever is doing this.'

'It's not really about stopping them delaying the messages, Drake', Jefferson corrected him. 'It's about what they are hiding. What it is we don't even know yet. Surely Edward discussed this with you in your chamber last night?'

Drake's stomach began to sink. Somehow the Commanders had already figured out his intentions, and worse, Gromwell was looking as if there was something he had forgotten to mention.

'I didn't tell him about that part.'

'Which part?' Drake asked, staring at each of them in turn. 'You're not thinking of doing that, are you?'

They can't – It's against the Crown. He said stay here until he said so.

'That would be treason. He would have me exiled.'

'He wouldn't dare', Bartarian sneered, crossing his arms. 'Stop testing the runt, just tell him.'

The three of them leaned in closer, Gromwell grabbing Drake's shirt to pull him in over the table. The Commanders took a few precautionary glances around the room before Jefferson continued.

'The truth is that the army is ready to go right now', he whispered. 'They can't live another day knowing the Joanarians are suffering, let alone some of our own.'

Drake's thoughts came to a standstill as he realised the implications of his words.

'So you are planning to set sail for Joanas?'

Jefferson grabbed his hand and hushed him.

'Your voice is carrying. Be careful what you say here, these people may enjoy our company, but it only takes an ear that knows the Dragon Tongue to ruin our plans.'

Jefferson nodded towards the southern wall where a cloaked figure, staring right at him, slurped loudly from his flagon.

'Don't stare at him! Do you recognise him?'

Drake stole a glance at the stranger and caught his eye. The flagon was down and his mouth, straight and stern as an old hermit, seemed ready to bite at him.

'I can't say I do.'

'Captain Weir. The only naval officer in Joanas-Sorrow who has the influence we need to rally the entire fleet to our cause.'

'That's Captain Weir? What is the problem? The fleet is going to help us, right?'

'Wrong', interjected Gromwell. 'The sailors are loyal to your father's command. They don't care about what happens on land. All they care about is what happens at sea, and what they can do for the crown. Weir is no different, except that his loyalty is set in stone. He will be the first to raise the alarm at any proposition which goes against the crown. His deeds at sea, and the enormous amount of respect he commands, make him our only hope of getting to Joanas.'

'This sounds like a lot of effort to get a few ships to

Joanas. Couldn't we steal some ships? Can we not at least buy our way there on the human caravels?'

Gromwell shook his head.

'To steal a Centurian ship against the King's orders is treason', he said, looking at Weir like an uneasy mouse. 'Finding human caravels in a place like this will either be extremely expensive or a fool's folly. We must win Weir's blessings.'

'If we did get the sailors on our side, wouldn't we all be stealing the ships against the King's orders *anyway*?'

'He's right Edward', Jefferson pointed out. 'What makes you think we won't be exiled for this?'

'Because the Prince will be involved', answered Gromwell with a smile. 'Won't you Drake?'

Drake's pride began to swell.

'Are you asking me to be your leader, against my father's wishes?'

'Don't act stupid lad', Jefferson said. 'Before we do anything, we need the sailors on our side. Look at it like this. Weir only bows to a royal command, and you are royalty. You are the only Morre in Joanas Sorrow he would listen to, and therefore the only Morre that could change his mind.'

Drake chanced another look at Weir. He looked more like an outcast than a legend but, considering he was the only living legend left, the outcast look suited him.

'How do I go about this?'

'By the Torre, he's Captain Weir Drake! Shadow him. Watch his drills at noon', Jefferson said. 'Ask one of the servers what he usually gets up to. It isn't that hard for a Prince to speak to an honoured soldier, is it?'

'We don't really care how you do it Drake, just do it for us', interjected Gromwell, drinking his last fill of the ale. 'You'd gain respect in the army regardless of what happens as well as the soldier's loyalty. Right Jefferson?'

Jefferson nodded.

'It's simple enough to achieve. Give the Morre what

they want, and they will respect you', he said. 'What they want, as it happens, is to get away from this shit hole and bash some Hobsythe skulls. Agreed, Bartarian?'

Bartarian looked at Drake with a stiff upper lip.

'It'd be hard to convince them that you're still the royal tit afterwards. But don't expect anything different from me. I know a pig's errand when I see one.' He got up with a grunt and trundled away into the city.

'Never mind him, Drake', Jefferson reassured him, clapping his shoulder. 'You are going in the right direction. See you both later on.'

Gromwell nodded with a smile, and waited for Jefferson to disappear after Bartarian before addressing Drake.

'Are you sure about this?'

Sure as anything. Anything to show them. Anything to get my right to command.

'Yes. By the Torre I've always wanted respect.'

'You could have had it by now if you didn't act like some spoiled child.'

Drake's face dropped.

'Don't look at me like that. You understand your problem better than me. Far better than that oaf Bartarian. I like the idea of you redeeming yourself, but are you sure you could face your father when this is done?'

'Edward, I'm ready. I'll do it. I'll take whatever he throws at me.'

'Even exile?'

'Especially exile.'

Gromwell smiled with a nod. 'Good. I'm glad.'

He looked at Weir, still gorging on the fish and beans.

'I suggest you wait for him to leave, and follow him. Don't be late for practice later.'

'I won't.'

Gromwell's bench let out a large groan as he stood up. Drake was pleased the Commanders trusted him with the task, but Bartarian was going to be a problem. *As bloody always. Nothing new there.*

Drake drank the last remnants of his ale. As he sipped on the bitter foam his thoughts ran into overdrive. *What words will I need to use? What kind of conversation will I have to start to get him on my side?* He considered all the conversations he'd had in his life, lining them up one by one in his mind.

How about the way he convinced the Navurian council, still young and very fresh with power, on *not* invading Joanas as retribution for their crimes? No, it wouldn't work on Weir. Weir was a naval officer, not a politician. He didn't abide by a certain set of creeds. The sea was his creed, the sea by way of his King.

How about the many girls he had courted? Certainly not. Women and men were different beasts entirely, and Drake had not tamed the latter with regards to Morre-folk. Besides, Weir seemed far too intelligent to submit to word play and charm.

As his time as a Dragon Keeper resonated in his mind, he began to consider all of his training and the endless conversations he'd had with his teachers, neighbours and friends. He remembered how he wasn't treated specially, and how his tasks and efforts were as strong and powerful as any Morre's, if not harder. But training and experience were as unrelated as cider and ale. The only viable way to convince Weir was by convening a need to save the Penance family, perhaps dreaming up a lie about Jack or Stanley asking for assistance.

Drake was so deep in thought that he almost didn't notice Weir hovering over the end of the table like a prison guard. Upon realising, he was startled, but took control of the situation by raising a finger of patience and pretending to finish his ale. As he took a final gulp, he slammed the flagon on the table and wiped his stubble clean.

'Damn that is very fine ale!'

'It is bull's piss, even without the cider', scowled Weir. 'They serve finer bastardisations in the poor districts.'

He beheld the table and the flagons left behind by the Commanders, proceeding to inspect them with a slow stride. He grabbed one of the empty ones, Gromwell's if Drake recalled correctly, and made the remaining ale dance with the sounds of slushy disgust.

'I think they agreed.'

'Who?' Weir froze and glared at Drake as he spoke, soon turning into a stare best left to the wolves. 'Did you know them? I didn't know them, but they seemed to want to talk to me.'

Weir slammed the flagon down, causing ale to splatter over his hand.

'You aren't *peasant* enough to tell convincing lies, my Prince', he said, pulling a handkerchief from his gauntlet. 'May I sit?'

Drake looked at him like a lost kitten as he rubbed the ale off his hand. It was as if Weir had fished the lie straight from his sea of thought, cast it on a bigger line and caught the rest straight from his mouth. All he could do was nod.

Weir sat with a clunk of his armour. In doing so he revealed a golden-white breastplate embossed with the etchings of his house's sigil, the sword-wielding, flying dragon-fish.

'They are your friends. And perhaps your only friends out here. Well, I'm not so sure on the brute Bartarian, but Gromwell especially. But that's irrelevant. You were all staring at me, and you were all concocting some kind of plan that involved me somehow. What was that plan?'

'We were talking about our orders. Err – your orders. We were discussing what would happen if you were to sail for Joanas.'

Weir let out a loud and thundering chuckle. *He's mocking me,* Drake thought to himself angrily. *So much for loyalty.*

'That's a good joke', Weir said as his laughter subsided. 'Tell me another.'

'I don't have time for this. I am not some child. I've

told you what we spoke about, what else do you want?'

Weir pulled off his hood and revealed his face.

'You haven't told me though. You gave me another lie. Amusing, though it might have been, it still detracts from the fact that I'm not an idiot. You did talk about me, and about Joanas, but it wasn't about me going to Joanas, was it?'

'I don't know what you're talking about.'

'There it is again. A lie so obvious it makes you look more like the pompous, entitled idiot I keep hearing about. Where is my Prince of Centra?'

'I am your Prince, and I am telling you the truth.'

'That is the same lie, only told differently. I have important matters to attend to, and I can't have you sticking your nose into them when it suits you. We can try to be truthful with one another, or you can scurry back to Gromwell and tell him you're a failure and you won't be going anywhere.'

Drake settled for a moment and allowed Weir's words to wash over him. He balanced the Captain's convictions and history upon his judgement. *His loyalty must extend to me in some way. I must tell him the truth.*

'How long do you think my father will keep us here? The Hobsythe are winning Weir, don't you want to do something?'

Weir lowered his stare and moved his lips into what appeared to be a smile.

'That's what we really spoke about. We were talking about finding a way to help Joanas.'

Weir relaxed. His forehead was dry of sweat and his eyes were clearer than the sun's rays that shone into the hall. The immortal legend was receding, and the humble Morre was beginning to show his face.

'Better, my Prince. I could imagine the whole conversation was about getting transport, provisions and supporters in the fleet? If there were any difference to your conversation, please correct me.'

'We didn't get as far as provisions. The Commanders need transport, and for that they need loyal followers in the fleet.'

'Strange. It is no secret the only way to get that kind of support quickly is by getting my permission. I never quite understood why. All I can guess is that the navy respects my judgement.'

'I may be naïve Captain Weir, but I understand why they respect you. I also know why Joanas-Sorrow leaves an entire port ready for you in every season of every year, just in case you decide to land here with your ship. You can't expect me to have no understanding of that, and what you did with the Grand Duchess in the war.'

'That honour should have been my Captain's.'

'But it isn't. You had the command, you pulled the manoeuvre. Do you remember what it was like to land on the docks of Fugula after what you did?'

'I try not to. Those were the kind of moments that reminded me of the secrets of Sanctity. The things they didn't tell the historians.'

Weir scrunched up his lips and looked away from Drake for a moment, before returning his gaze with moistened eyelids and a frown.

'In the build up to the war, she was part of the slaver interception group. After we had become infamous to the old countries, the slavers, at the sight of our colours, would kill their catch to teach us a lesson. Worse, when the Council heard about this, they decided it was more economical to destroy the ships at first encounter. Instead of finding the bodies of the slaves, we now had to listen to the screams as their ships burned and sank. What we did for Joanas-Sorrow was just a pinprick against the memory of a season of horror.'

'Do you not think the Joanarians feel the same way? Consider the country before all of this mess started, they were moving on so well since Sanctity. Stanley Penance helped build that.'

'Stanley only helped the larger realms. He was drunk on the Promise of Joanaria, just as Ouster was. By Stanley's hand, the smaller states and kingdoms were left to destroy themselves or be destroyed by the larger ones. It is no secret that Stanley, by his influence, caused the Hobsythe uprising.'

'What about Jack then? He did far greater good than his father ever did.'

'It was an unorthodox way to handle such an unstable economy, but by the Torre did he bring the Kingdoms closer together.'

Weir smiled for a moment as he thought on this suggestion, but his expression soon returned to a frown.

'But Stanley's damage was too great, and by then the Hobsythe were drunk on vengeance. Drunk on Ouster and Penance blood.'

'Don't you at least want to know what happened to Jack and his part of the family? We may not be able to save the humans but at least help me try to save our own?'

'They could be dead already.'

'Maybe they are, but they deserve a proper burial and their deaths would need to be investigated. I don't think we would need to look any further than the Hobsythe. We could even hold Stanley to his crimes.'

Weir considered Drake's proposition for a moment before standing with a sigh.

'You have an interesting way of looking at this situation. We're on this planet for six hundred years, the humans for little more than two hundred. It's important to look after each other in times like these. Don't make me regret helping you.'

'So you will help us get the navy to side?'

'Yes', Weir replied, pulling his hood over his head. 'But don't expect us to wait on the eastern shores for you or keep quiet when your father realizes what we are doing. We'd rather betray a new friend than lose our right to the seas.'

Drake stood to meet his gaze from under the hood. 'That is an acceptable risk.'

'I'll remember those words. I'll be in the meeting tomorrow, it seems we have much more to discuss with the townsfolk now than we had originally planned.'

Weir slowly bowed; the first sign of respect Drake has seen anyone give him since he left Centra.

'Until then my Prince, farewell.'

Drake's pride danced as the Captain headed towards the north exit. His walk was a skilled militaristic stride, with perfect spacing between each step and very little movement in the upper regions of his body. He acknowledged the guards and servants as he passed them, clapping and laughing with them as if good friends. This broke Drake's expectations of a legend wide open. *Living Legends don't mix with commoners, do they?*

As his mind loosened its grip on his bewilderment, he began to feel concerned. Concerned what his father would do now that it was officially happening. Concerned for the Morre, who were now becoming something more to him than bullies and traditional old farts.

Drake soon yearned for a distraction. He walked the Southern Sprint as he had multiple times before over the course of his stay, through the markets that sold huge baskets of Alcadian Trinkets. He took note of how little Joanarian artefacts there were now and how, when he did run into any, they were set at an outrageously high price. The Southern Sprint was full of commoners who neither knew nor cared who he was, and this was what he liked the most. *Good folk – Minding their own business.* He followed the Sprint until it reached the gate of the water gardens, a place where he spent most of his time whilst in Joanas-Sorrow. A place where he could be alone with his thoughts.

It was essentially a farm, born from the only bay on the island and surrounded by a mossy-stained palisade. The walls were in the process of being replaced, with a tower of scaffolding and fresh stone reaching around the southern side. The farmland itself, at least two sprints wide, was tended by the women of the town. Whenever he visited, Drake would sit and dangle his legs in the waters of the bay, where a line of thick, slime-tainted grey blocks protected the soil against the unsettlement of the water.

Drake had jumped into the water yesterday. It came up to his waist before his toes were comfortably set in the sand, but he didn't feel like swimming today. Instead he settled his eyes on the great wooden palette that separated the sea from the bay, and the waves that leapt well above its height before crashing back down in a glittering shower.

I did well today.

The palette clacked against the railing and spat into the bay, seemingly proud of Drake's achievement. He wanted to go out there and bask in the rain of the waves; that way he could feel the appreciation and hear the clatter of the palette's approval much more clearly. But he wasn't dressed for swimming, so here would have to do. He bobbed his legs in and out of the water, just as he did in the river Morkor.

He remembered how it felt to be tickled by the slow waters from the snows of Gaul, as they made their snaking pilgrimage to the western coast of Centra and became one with the sea. During the several years within Morkor before his deployment he would ask the river questions and seek its advice. It would merely slosh and tickle his feet, but it soothed him and calmed his nerves.

Drake smiled at the memory. The bay was nice, but it did not have such an effect. It did not hide the memories of his mother and father summoning him to their endless meetings, nor did it help him forget the time wasted shadowing their business every day on the run up to the deployment. But it'd do. *There's not much one can do with such business, anyway.*

The palette belched, this time with little more than a mist and some streaks of fresh wetness falling down its back. It was a poor attempt at comfort, but an attempt nevertheless. His thoughts stumbled upon the last talk he had with his mother and father, the talk of his betrothal to one of the high ladies of the Morre. *I should have the right to bed whomever I want.*

He spat at the thought of a stranger in his bed, looking up at him ready and willing to be mounted. *What if she were as ugly as a horse? How would I bring myself to finalise the marriage?* Such a question hardly seemed worthy of answering- even the palette seemed to scoff at him for thinking it. His thoughts then turned to Gromwell's shadow, which would linger over him every time he got a little too close to someone. Every time a chuckle or a smile would gleam from a lady's face. He looked up at the palette, which clanked towards the sea as it was sucked against the outer rail. *Is there a chance I could choose whom to marry, when I am King? Could I overthrow that stupid law?*

The palette made its answer with a powerful clang and a good shower of salt and spit billowed over the wall. The bastard was laughing at him.

'You must lead the high life if your family lets you sit here', remarked a woman's voice from behind him.

Drake lifted his legs from the water with a heavy splash. The lower half of his chaps were heavily soaked, making him look as if he had been standing in the bay the whole time.

'In chaps, no less', she continued with a chuckle, 'Whoever you are, you aren't very well dressed for an outing with the bay.'

Drake's eyes found the maiden's face. Her blue eyes studied him and her lips wore a shallow smirk. Drake stood and shook his chaps, allowing a small cloud of water to douse the mud and bricks.

'It is only a bit of wet, Madam', he said. 'What has the 'high life' got to do with wallowing in the bay?'

He tried desperately to loosen his chaps, but they would not co-operate with his wishes. He gave up and looked back at her, imagining the critique forming in her thoughts. But instead of rolling back her head and laughing, or pointing up her nose and skulking away, she merely shook her head and transformed her smirk into a warming smile.

'I'm not a 'Madam' yet sir. I'm just a Lady under the shadow of my mother. I can't be honoured with the title 'madam' yet.'

'Nor am I a 'Sir'. Well, you could say I am, but I am not worthy of one. Does a 'Sir' paddle in summer waters like he did when he was a child in the waters of the river of Morkor?'

'It depends which Clan you come from. What is your name?' she asked. 'That is if the Morre before me has been honoured with a named Clan?'

An interesting thing to say. The palette agreed. The concept of a Clan not being named wasn't new to him, but he had never met a Morre who was not part of a named Clan.

'Drake of Morkor', he replied. 'I came here several days ago with the Imperial Fleet.'

Between her alternate glances at the bay and him, she seemed concerned by the group that was heading in their direction a sprint away.

'You are Drake of Morkor? Does that make you the Prince?'

Drake considered telling the truth, but feared what may happen if she knew.

'I am not the Prince. Drake is my Clan's name. In honour of the Prince. My first name is Thomas.'

'Clan Drake is a new one to me. But Centra is a very big place these days. I suppose, since I have your name, I should tell you mine. It's Laura, from the Clan Rivera.'

The Dragon Keeper of Joanas-Sorrow. The very same.

'So, you are a Lady then, Miss Rivera?'

'I am merely a Lady in training, Master Drake. This is my first assignment as Dragon Keeper.'

She looked at the group again, now half a sprint away.

'Are those your teachers then? I mean, you seem awfully interested in them.'

'You could say that in a way. That is my mother and her companions.'

Drake peered into the line of bushes, where the small harem were walking the line towards them. He recognised Tiana Rivera at the helm, conversing with the maidens of the garden. *She looks well, considering what she has been through.*

'Mother came here to shadow me for the meeting tomorrow, but she has been shadowing me ever since she and the army got here. She wanted to say hello to the gardens at least once whilst she was here, which explains our presence. But it doesn't explain why you're wallowing here. Again.'

'You've seen me here before?'

'Twice before – you were better dressed. The last time you were swimming, and it would have been rude of me to spoil your fun. I had to see who you were, and what you were really up to here. So, now that I have you, why are you here again, Thomas?'

She seems very defensive of this place. What is she hiding?

'Can't a Morre just wallow? Think about things? Resolve some bad thoughts and moods?'

'Umm – As long as you aren't harming anyone or breaking anything, I don't see any wrong in it I suppose. Does it help?'

The palette roared an intervention, but Laura seemed unaffected and unaware of its words.

'It does in its own way. The waves help me think. Sometimes I squeeze in a conversation with the palette, see what he thinks of things.'

'He?' She looked at the palette with a chuckle, just as it sucked up some pride. 'That seems very entertaining.'

'It's a good way to distract yourself. Enough to forget about the current affairs anyway.'

'I may try it.'

She nodded to the palette in approval, smiling daftly as

if mocking it. It spat at her, but with little effort.

'I'd need it to stop thinking about this meeting tomorrow. It looks like instead of just settling the town, I now need to settle the Imperial Army.'

'Indeed, rumour has it they would do something drastic.'

The palette was not pleased to hear Drake blurting out the secret. Drake's mind was in agreement. *What was I thinking?*

'Why would they do that? What are they planning?'

Drake cowered from Laura's attempts to study him, but he could not conceal something he had already partially revealed. Feeling like a slave to her questioning gaze, he reluctantly shrugged.

'Why would they risk treason?' She barked the question at him, which made even the palette appear nervous. 'Isn't the army under orders from the King, which moves to me in his stead?'

'We keep receiving news of the Hobsythe uprising escalating beyond the humans' control. We haven't heard from the Penance clan since they were reported missing, and the Emperor has led his first army into the Dapple Lands. It's not an uprising any more, my Lady, it's a war that is at the tipping point of the country's demise. They won't harm a soul in Joanas-Sorrow, but they do not care for your orders at this point. They may even sail for Joanas.'

Laura loosened her lips and relaxed her stare.

'Maybe it has become a war, and maybe they do need our help. But I can't just let the army deploy against the King's orders. He'd punish me and my mother for letting them go. Not without a good reason at least.'

'But there is good reason.'

Tiana called out for Laura. She looked behind and answered the call, requesting a small amount of time to finish what she was saying.

'I will need to talk with the Commanders about this.'

'No, please don't. They'll kill me if they think I told you. Can't we talk about it instead?'

'You're just a Knight. Well… That's what I gathered after what you have told me. What makes you think you'll make any difference towards my duty as Dragon Keeper?'

Drake descended into his cave of creativity, searching for another suitable lie.

'I may serve under them, but I am more of a friend than a lower officer to them. I know a lot about their opinions and the reasons for their decisions, including why they are getting impatient. Please Laura?'

Tiana and her group had stopped, and the High Lady was looking impatient.

'Fine', said Laura. She acknowledged her mother again by raising her hood over her hair, and began to walk away. 'Be here after sunset, when the farmers have gone home.'

'I shall be. Thank you and goodbye Lady Rivera.'

'Goodbye Thomas.'

The palette celebrated.

She wasn't what I imagined her to be at all, Drake thought. *I very much look forward to tonight's meeting.*

Letters of Laura

The evening meal was a roasted Centurian pheasant, with side dishes of Navurian potatoes and Fugulian oranges. The beverage was a choice between the sickly Joanarian Ale and the unknown taste of Draberian Wine. Naturally many chose the wine, including Drake.

'So, tell me lad', said Gromwell, between chews. 'How did you convince Weir that going to Joanas was the right thing to do?'

Drake looked at the Morre, his pride and self-confidence bubbling over like a cauldron of achievement.

'He seemed already convinced', he replied. 'I just pushed him in the right direction.'

'Indeed', muttered Bartarian. 'You did a good job boy, but I'm still waiting to see you demonstrate some worthy qualities rather than the usual shit.'

'Enough of that, Karl', Gromwell scolded, 'Let Drake enjoy his dinner without having to stomach your mood for once. He deserves that at least.'

Bartarian grumbled. 'It isn't merely a mood if it's true, Gromwell.'

'That's not of our concern right now', said Gromwell. 'Let's act more like humans for once and forget what should or shouldn't be said. Let's pretend to scoff and drink until we are fat and merry, dancing with the pigs and wondering why we woke up with the serving girls.'

Bartarian almost choked on his wine as the table let out a small laugh. Even Drake was amused at the thought of being drunk and foolishly-happy. However, he soon remembered the meeting he had promised Laura, and began to nurture the idle thought that she may be interested in him for more than just his alleged connections.

'Have you always had a way with words, Edward?' Jefferson asked. 'Or was there just a strike against your helmet during training?'

Gromwell thought on the question for a moment, looking down at the now fleshless pheasant leg on his plate.

'I couldn't tell you personally', he said. 'But maybe Drake would know. He practically grew up under my wing.'

All eyes turned to Drake as he slowly picked up his flagon. The wine served as comfort as he delved into the library of his memories.

'He was a stern and serious master before Sanctity', Drake mused. 'But he seems to have lost his manner in the shock.'

'I thought it would have been the opposite', said Jefferson. 'Besides, he seems very serious outside of the occasional outbursts.'

'He's done very well considering what happened to Walter', added Bartarian. His words brought a sudden chill to the table. 'But I suggest we shut up about it.'

Gromwell, with a smile, patted Bartarian on the back.

'Thank you, Karl. I'd much rather leave the matter like that for now.'

'I'm sorry for your loss', said a fresh voice.

All turned to look at the source. It was Weir, with his cloak gone and a young falcon perched on his right shoulder.

'Captain Weir', said Gromwell, as he shook his hand. 'Glad you could join us. But what brings this little fledgling to the mess hall?'

Weir did not look happy. His frown dominated his cheek bones and his eyes were staring into the distance.

'This brave little bird has brought us a message.'

Weir pulled a rolled-up piece of parchment from his right gauntlet and handed it to Gromwell.

'Is it serious?' Gromwell asked as he untied the rope from the paper. 'Who is it from?'

'It's very serious. We have brought the cast-off forward because of it. We leave the morning after tomorrow.'

The faces of the Morre fell, and they all turned to Gromwell as he scanned the message.

'It's from the Lord of Segura', Gromwell said, 'It's dated two days ago, noon. Emperor – 'Emperor?' – Doncaster has been slain.'

'My efforts to convince the Admiral that we needed to sail on Joanas were made very easy thanks to this letter. After a brief discussion, he was insistent on leaving.'

'But what happened to Cain? Since when did Doncaster take the imperial oath?'

'Let's agree now that not only are the messages being delayed, they are being lost.' Weir looked at the bird briefly as it studied each Morre's face with a bent neck and a pair of beady eyes.

'If we are to gauge how fresh this letter is, then we need look no further than Kristen here. She is a Centurian Snuggle-Tail.'

Drake studied the bird's extended tail, with its white contours and feathers which resembled a spear tip on a small mat of brown.

'Can we assume that she also speaks the Dragon Tongue?' he asked.

'Yes', replied Kristen in the Bird Tongue, with a click of her left talon and a short chirp. Drake examined the bird's feathers and posture, trying to find weakness in her composure.

'You do understand why we'd be sceptical of you', he asked. 'Don't you?'

Kristen looked at Drake, bobbing her head and rustling her feathers as if upset with the question.

'I understand why. The Silver Tails are the messengers of the east. This is not I.'

'You understand us well', said Gromwell, stroking Kristen's back. 'Do you know what is happening to the others when the messages are intercepted?'

'No', she said. The sudden dip in her neck and shiver of her spine told Drake that she was genuine.

'Did you face any resistance, at least?' he asked.

'No. The winds from the East were strong enough for me to get high. You must trust me.'

Drake looked at Weir, who was lost in his thoughts with his eyes fixated on the table.

'Weir?' he said, capturing his attention. 'What is to happen at the meeting on the morrow?'

Weir paused, causing Drake to feel disconcerted. He was concerned the Captain was struggling to answer, but the silence was soon broken.

'Tiana Rivera expects the Commanders to speak for the Morre. She said there were stirrings 'of a cast off' during her visit yesterday, but I was under the impression we were not to tell anyone of our plans until the day of our actual cast off?'

The Morre fell silent, lowering their flagons. Drake watched as they scanned one another, probing for hints of betrayal. Bartarian's eyes soon fixed upon him, causing his throat to swell and the back of his neck to simmer with the fear of reclusion.

'Have you tweeted to someone boy?' he asked.

Drake crushed his seething thoughts, and shook his head. Weir reached forward slightly, his hands upon the table, his mistrusting stare burning into the back of his skull.

'So, uh- we weren't supposed to tell anyone before that?' questioned Jefferson, to the relief of Drake's heart. He looked confused and very worried, with clouded eyes and a quivering lower lip.

'You blundering idiot', snapped Bartarian, clanking his flagon against the table, 'Who did you tell?'

'I might have mentioned it to some of Rivera's hand maidens.'

'No doubt the ones you have been bedding each night?' Gromwell asked.

'I only meant to tell one of them', Jefferson stuttered. 'But the other two were pretending to sleep and were actually listening.'

'You delude me Tony Jefferson', sighed Gromwell. 'There are times I wish you would settle down with one of your exploits like the rest of us. At least then you would babble to only one person rather than half the fucking town!'

Gromwell turned to look at Weir and Kristen as he gulped down the rest of his wine. 'Thank you both. We'll discuss the meeting in the morning before it starts.'

'What about Drake?' Weir asked.

'What about him?' said Bartarian. 'What soul would listen to his words or take him seriously? The boy is best left in the back with the other rejects and miscreants.'

The words bit at Drake as if they were a pack of small dogs. But it wasn't long before Weir sent them scurrying away.

'That boy is your future King', he reminded Bartarian. 'He's also the Morre that will take the brunt of his father's wrath. He is worthy of the decency you refuse to give him, and it would be wise to grant it to him whilst at sea. Good day to you all.'

Weir let the shock bleed from Bartarian's face before bowing in Drake's direction.

'We shall discuss it on the morrow, my Prince.'

***

Drake was soon away into the humid night. The Commanders were keeping to themselves following Weir's scolding and, although his pride was dancing as he ran down the streets, he felt sorry for them. *Will they resent me after this? Or are they just shocked at the way Weir addresses me?*

His thoughts drifted towards Laura as he approached the gate to the water gardens. Thinking about their conversation and the way she held herself did not make him louder or clumsier than usual; in fact, it calmed him. When he reached the gate, he squeezed through the opening, nodding to the guard as he did the night before.

She had not arrived yet, but he soon had his feet into the water. The cotton pants he had changed into before the meal turned a dark brown as the water seduced them with its power. He greeted the palette with a smile, and the palette rattled in response. The ripples of its voice made the three moons dance on the water. He began to think about Laura, and let out a small smile as he recalled their earlier encounter.

The palette snarled in disagreement, but he was already away. He fell deep into his thoughts, his mind creating hopeful pictures of romantic intimacy. Growing hot and restless, he started to smile.

The palette was having none of it, and it let out the largest derision Drake had seen it release. A shower of water hit him, splattering well beyond the bricks and into the mud. The palette had got him good, reminding him of his duty. *Ill-tempered bastard.*

He looked to the living moon, Allora, and begged her to release him from the shackles of his destiny. She, unlike the palette, said nothing, instead choosing to dance on the ripples of the bay. Drake could not help but feel hopeless. *If only I really was Thomas Drake. If only I had a simpler life and could marry the Morre I wanted. I wish the Torre would stop this, and allow me something useful for once.*

'What good is a Morre-man if he cannot marry the one he loves?' he asked.

He allowed Allora, Mobius, Titus and the palette some time to answer him. The moons did not reply, and the palette went back to spewing pitiful mists in the far darkness. They had left him, with no sign of life beyond the sounds of his beating heart and the pounding of approaching footsteps.

'Are your parents from the more traditional side of Centra, by any chance?' asked Laura, as she approached.

Drake turned and nodded at her. He noticed that she was wearing the same cloak as before, but she had let her hair down. It was now moving freely like a veil of black silk.

'Have they found you some suitors yet?'

'I suspect that they have my Lady, but they have not yet told me', he said. 'I hear a similar tradition is favoured by your clan, with the exception that it only applies to the ladies of the family?'

'You are half right', she said, studying the reflections of the moons with an empty glare. 'We have to marry human Lords – luckily we get to choose them ourselves. Does your family at least let you pick one from a group?'

'They said they'd allow that. I have let possible suitors run through my mind as I have tried to cling on to some form of hope.'

'Hope in what?' She sat beside him and looked to the sky. 'You sound like someone who is rather entitled, Thomas.'

She breathed in deeply. Her eyes closed and her body lurched forward as if it were the first time she had been allowed to breathe in such a way.

'We should be thankful for what we are given by the Torre. To call any of their gifts hopeless is selfish and stupid.'

Drake's mind cared little for the scolding. He was still enjoying her company, but he did not wish to come across too keen, so he turned away and watched the ripples as they fled from his legs.

'You should try hanging your legs in the water. After you get used to the cold the water begins to relax you.'

Drake watched as she took off her cloak, revealing a simple dress and shorts perfect for the warm night. Her left leg was first to test the waters. It hesitated as her toes skimmed the surface and her breath caught in her throat. But, once both her legs were submerged, she relaxed and began once again to draw in the night air.

'How do you feel?'

'It is relaxing. You're not such an entitled fool after all.

But is it anything like the river at Morkor?'

Not at all.

'The river is better because the current caresses your feet, and the silts help with any aches from the heavy training.'

'Did you just have training then?'

'No, but even if I had this is more for seclusion. It is mainly to get away from all the people to just enjoy my own company.'

'What's wrong with the people in Joanas-Sorrow? What about the Commanders? Aren't they your friends?'

'The company is fine. It's just there isn't a lot to do here besides eating and training. The Commanders are irritable most of the time and I'd rather not make a scene for all the humans to talk about.'

'That's quite smart. Are the Commanders irritable because of what they are planning for Joanas?'

Drake realised that he had lost himself in the conversation and almost given away too much of his true personality. However, she seemed so immersed in her own relaxation that he may have got away with it.

'It is mostly because they want to sail to Joanas, yes.'

Drake's eyes could not stop studying her. The interview for a potential suitor had begun, and his eyes were now beginning to feed his imagination as it wandered deeper into his fantasies. As he came to his senses, he quickly averted his eyes and looked back towards the water.

'What do you think about it?' she asked.

'I haven't even told you why yet. Why would it matter how I felt about it?'

'You seem like the kind of Morre that doesn't take sides easily.' She turned to face him, keeping her legs in the water. 'I genuinely want to know how you feel about sailing to Joanas against the King's wishes.'

He reminded himself of his cover.

'The Prince has endorsed it, and I have no thought about it.'

'You can't expect me to believe it is that simple.'

'Why not?' Drake's eyes returned to her. 'What is so hard to believe?'

'Every Morre has feelings, Thomas. It's important for us to talk about them. You don't have to hide from me.'

Drake began to fear for his cover. However, he kept up the facade, hiding his identity behind his squinted eyes and stiffened jaw.

'So what about my feelings? We came here to talk about what the Commanders are planning.' He quickly turned away from her and focused on the moons dancing against the water. 'I'm just a Knight, remember?'

A long, silent moment passed before Laura spoke again.

'It is your parents, isn't it?'

'Why are you so interested?'

He did not move his eyes or his head to address her, but he could see her in the reflection still looking at him, her eyes studying his form and her hand a few paces away from his.

'Maybe I am interested in you because you aren't the usual grunt. Maybe I don't just want to find out the reasoning behind the Commander's decisions. I'd like to get to know you better, Thomas. Aside from acting like you deserve more than what is given to you, you genuinely seem like a Morre I'd be a fool to forget.'

Drake's lips released a smile, but his eyes remained fixated on the water.

'Well – It is my parents.'

Drake allowed the lie to sculpt and develop another child before throwing it out into the world.

'They are extremely loyal to the crown, and I'm afraid they would beg to have me exiled after this, even if I was following orders.'

Laura's hand reached out to his shoulder and caressed it. Her touch was soft, calming and very uplifting.

'I think you are one of hundreds Thomas, and you

shouldn't be afraid of that. No mother or father would exile you for following your honour.'

The lie spoke some truth. Drake genuinely feared his father's wrath and his mother's look as if he were a child again. They may not exile him, but they would probably shadow his every move until he was crowned.

'If I were part of this, my mother would do much worse.' Laura began, hand still on his shoulder and eyes pressing for his attention. 'She'd send my uncle to take over my duties and marry me off to one of the Lords in Draberia.'

The thought of marriage to a human must have worried her because she retracted her hand and looked down at the water. Her eyes looked lost and concerned as they darted each way across her reflection.

'There was only one Draberian Lord that I thought I could have loved and married.'

'What happened?'

'He passed in the War of Sanctity.'

Drake could not hold back his stare for a moment longer. He gazed at her as she studied the waters.

'I ended it before he deployed. I was only nineteen and he twenty-five. We were so different when it came to Sanctity it broke my heart.'

'I'm sorry. I didn't mean to probe.'

He put his hand on her upper arm. He relished the smoothness and the warmth, but his own understanding of what it might have felt like to lose a love to the war was enough to derail his imagination.

'I fought in that war – I lost a lot of friends.' *Tommila – Biggs – Jamil. All of them long gone and buried. Strange I still feel sad, after so long.* 'I might have known him.'

'It doesn't matter.' She allowed herself to look at him, her eyes glazed with what must have been the push of memories into the night's air. 'I miss him more as a friend than a love now anyway.'

Drake nodded with a smile as he slowly removed his

hand.

'Do you believe what they say about the Morre and our mortality?'

'No. It's a legend told by the elders, nothing more. We're as mortal as the humans, and the only thing that makes us different is how long we live.'

Laura took hold of a silver pendant which hung from a chain around her neck, and caressed it with her thumb as she gazed at the fortifications protecting the bay.

'My father believed that we were special.'

Drake realised what she was talking about, and immediately threaded his memories and readings of Sanctity's events together to form a picture.

'So that explains why you and your mother were here, and why you were so defensive about the bay. I didn't think. I'm sorry.'

'It's alright. I should really talk about business rather than the tragedies in my life.'

'Business can wait, Laura.'

He allowed his eyes to meet hers, his heart aching as if he were channelling her grief.

'I've always come here. I like seeing the farms and the flowers. My father always loved seeing the farms on the Draberian hillsides. We used to walk through them together when I was a child, talking about the old times as if it were just a day before.'

'What about your mother? Does she regularly come here too?'

'Whenever she can, but it's never about the plants or the flowers. It's always about my father's sacrifice, and what the people owe him.'

'So you don't see it as a mark of thanks?'

'Of course I do, it's just I don't like remembering him and this place that way. He thought Joanas-Sorrow was never going to survive the War, and he almost left the town to die because of it. It's now twice the size it was, growing its own food and rearing its own animals, all thanks to him.'

'How would you have him remembered, then?'

'I don't know. Maybe erect a huge statue in front of the keep like everyone else does. I'm sorry. I came here to talk to you about Weir and the Commander's plans, not fuss you about who I am.'

'Then ask me about them.'

Laura took a moment. She looked away and studied the waters, before turning back to him with a serious expression.

'Why are they willing to defy the King, Thomas?'

Although put off by her sudden shift in tone, Drake put his thoughts about her to rest and used the information he had to feed the lie further.

'There is an imposed latency of the messages from Joanas and Centra. At first it was a simple worry, but then they received another message just before I came here, and it wasn't purposefully held back. It basically said Negura had fallen, with two Emperors slain. It's all the convincing they needed.'

'So, in theory, they're sailing because they feel that the King would sail if the messages arrived in their intended times?'

'I hadn't thought about it like that.'

'Of course not. You're just Thomas Drake, a grunt.'

They both looked in the direction of the keep as the night bell rang across the darkness.

'We should end the night here', said Drake.

'You're right.' Laura pulled her legs out of the water, playfully allowing some of the wetness to splash onto him as she stood up. 'It was a nice evening, Thomas. We should do this again sometime. Maybe when there is less business to attend to?'

'I'd like that very much, my Lady.'

She stood. Her eyes locked upon him and she gave a tiny smile. Drake took her hand without a single thought, and kissed it. The palette belched up a fury, but he paid it no heed. Laura threw her cloak over her shoulders and tip-toed towards the gate. However half way there, she stopped and looked back at him.

'It's locked!'

Drake stood up and shook the wetness from his legs before running over to join her at the gate. He grabbed the lock, feeling the coldness of its prison engulf his mind.

'Can you climb?'

'Help me up and I should be ok.'

He pushed her feet upwards so she could grab the wooden post and perch upon it. She leapt down, stood on the other side of the gate and leaned against it, facing him.

'Will you be ok?'

'I'll be fine, my Lady.'

She looked towards the keep, before returning her gaze to him and taking hold of his shirt. Her touch was gentle but full of intent. He had no choice but to surrender.

Although the kiss was brief, it was enough to make Drake's emotions explode. It felt as if Laura had broken into his personal interview room, thrown water over his face and told him he had already made his decision. The palette was missing, and the moons held no care at all. Her wave goodbye and disappearance into the shadows were enough to convince him that he needed to see her again.

Hearing movement in the west, he decided it was time to cross over to the other side of the gate, and he did so as easily as Laura. As he landed and extended his right foot onto the cobble of the road, he was met by two clenching hands of a quickly-moving shadow, which pushed him with an unnecessarily large force against the wooden wall. Drake's back hit the hardwood posts with a great thump.

The aggressor's face was revealed from the thick, baggy hood. It was Gromwell, and he looked very displeased.

'Now who by the Torre was that?'

Drake did not answer. Gromwell smashed his back against the wood for a second time, forcing him to face him.

'You've been courting again, haven't you?'

Drake grabbed Gromwell's wrists as they pushed against him.

'I was only sitting at the edge of the water garden enjoying the moons.'

Gromwell slammed his back into the wall once more before releasing him. He took a few steps back to gain some distance.

'You are a liar. You haven't stayed there that long. You were courting someone.'

'What is it to you?'

'What is it to me?' Gromwell poked him with his mailed finger. 'I am your guardian, and whether you like it or not I am supposed to keep you from the women you've been courting.'

'By my father-'

'Yes, by your damned father!'

Gromwell noticed the window of the dwelling facing the wall light up. He quickly grabbed Drake and dragged him to the rear where no windows sat in the plastered wall. The light shone for a few moments, and a heated exchange between a man and a woman rang out into the night. The man soon convinced the woman to return to her bed, and shortly after the light vanished, allowing them to continue their exchange.

'You are to be married in the next year! What am I to say to the King after I promised him there were to be no girls?'

Drake lowered his head to hide his frown.

'At least tell me who it was so that I may keep some shards of my honour?'

'It was Laura Rivera.'

'Torre deliver me. That is the last maiden I'd hoped you'd court. Please tell me it was just testing the waters?'

'What does it matter? I'll be married soon to some pureblood I may not even love. At least grace me with the chance to enjoy myself before I am thrown into my duties?'

'I'm trying boy, but you're making it harder. Don't fall for this one. Not now, not when we are to meet with the town council tomorrow. Think of what it could do to the both of you.'

'I don't believe in that nonsense, remember?'

'Well you should.' His tone remained quiet but sharp. 'It can kill you, and her. You are to end any inkling of it on the morrow after the meeting.'

'Can I at least say goodbye to her?'

Gromwell thought on Drake's plea for a moment.

'In brief, you say farewell in public with my shadow behind you, following you.'

'She can't know I'm the Prince.'

'So, you are lying to the poor girl now?'

'It's not like that. Her mother is here, and I don't want her thinking I'm only interested in her to get some satisfaction.'

'So, you are interested in her. Fine, I'll just be your Commander. My words will be brief but to the point. You say goodbye and then you're done, and you part ways.' Gromwell sighed and straightened out his dangling, brown hair. 'Don't test my patience. I'll happily blow your cover if you try anything foolish or romantic. Hold that thought, I'd happily embarrass you by making Tiana aware of this canoodling as well as the King. Do I make myself clear boy?'

'Clear as always, Edward.'

Drake looked down at his feet, searching for his lost soul as it retreated.

'Good lad.'

Gromwell opened his reach to Drake, allowing him to join his side. They moved into the clearing and onto the road which led back to the keep.

'If we stay out any later, Tiana will see to it that we are both flogged.'

For the Children

The Hatred tickled Jack's senses, flooding his blood with the relentless energy of anger and terror. It was the kind of energy he had thrived on ever since his re-awakening, the kind that fed his body with the confidence he needed to remain calm and above his wits.

He closed his eyes and listened to the buzzing words of the souls as they spat tainted energy into his body. Amongst all the curses and regrets he listened out for one specific soul, which would bring with it a particularly nasty set of ill wishes. No sooner had he felt the soul's presence in his hand than he heard a muffled hiss, followed by a series of curses in the Dragon Tongue.

Like the thousands of others he had collected, Jack ripped the soul from the Afterlife and dragged it into the mortal world, where its body lay before him in a pool of its own blood. He approached the body, plucked Cain Ouster's crown from its head and sent the writhing, purple-black soul into the body with a long blow. The body shuddered and groaned as it rose.

'You're certainly not running now', Jack said, closing his hands around the crown and taking a step back. 'Are you, Kinas?'

Kinas opened his eyes to behold Thias Doncaster's army, slaughtered like cattle. Jack could see the woe drifting across his torn form as he took in the sight of Doncaster's head on a spike and the mass of Hobsythe bodies piled up behind it.

'Kinas should be dead', he gasped between coughs. 'Why do you persist in maintaining Kinas' life Fallen One?'

'You're important to me', Jack replied. 'As are your people. Tell me – what did you hope to achieve if you successfully took Negura? A fighting chance, perhaps?'

Jack read Kinas' thoughts. It seemed the Hobsythe was disturbed by the notion that his life, or his people's lives, had merit. But regardless, the relief was warming his heart.

'It matters no longer', Kinas said. 'The other man-scum are hiding in their forts, afraid to unify against anyone. The Knight's Republic is finished. The shadow is beginning to fall on Joanas, and Alcadia, for ever. Do what you will of Kinas' people Fallen One, it makes no difference anymore.'

Jack admired Kinas' use of words – *The Shadow over Joanas*. But he had soon heard enough and took back the Hobsythe's soul, returning the body once more to its death. With a flutter of his hand he returned the soul to the Hatred, but not before leaving his mark on it so that he could call upon it later. Cain's crown still in his grasp, he turned around and looked over the fields where he had butchered the last unified army of Joanas. A forest of mutilated bodies was strewn across the greenery, set against the backdrop of flames.

His company of the Fallen and their horses had joined the rear of the northern march, led by his companion, Sirius. Only the mud goblins remained on the field now, collecting trinkets from the bodies of the men and dumping the Hobsythe into a pile ready to be burnt. Jack spotted five mud goblins heading towards him, dragging with them a lifeless man covered in dirt and blood. The group was led by a plump but tall goblin, who held in his hand the scimitar of Lord Montfort of the Halos lands. *The beast must have inherited it from Doncaster.*

'We have Commander Ouster, sire', said the leader, raising the scimitar over his head with a toothless smile. 'He is still alive.'

Jack approached them. He noticed that Ouster still had his armour on, and a battered helm barely clinging to his scalp.

'That's no way to treat a Commander', he said. 'Stand him up before me.'

The goblins dropped Ouster to the floor and fiddled with his armour as they tried to pull him upright. They were barely tall enough to support his shoulders, so had to rely on each other to get him into a sitting position. The hardest part, pulling him upwards into a standing position, was executed well aside from a few mishaps (one of which resulted in a lost arm). However eventually he was up and beginning to awaken. Jack pulled off his helmet, clearing his face of the feathers and silk of his house.

'Traitor!' Ouster exclaimed the moment he saw Jack.

He tried to swing for him, but his grogginess caused him to tumble to the floor instead. The goblins giggled at his misfortune, especially when he revealed his muddied head to them. Jack crossed his arms and looked sternly at the leader, who was still grinning with the others.

'This isn't some kind of joke', Jack said. 'This is a Commander that has just lost his army. He is owed more respect than the butt of your stupidity.'

'Get him back up', the leader ordered.

The goblins hushed and proceeded to move Ouster over, mumbling and fidgeting as they did so. Due to his awareness and rapidly returning co-ordination, the second pick-up was a lot more difficult. More mud-limbs were lost, and there was one goblin that was unfortunate enough to lose a head.

Ouster was proving to be a stubborn beast. Whenever the goblins thought they had him on his feet again, he would push back against them. Eventually he tumbled through two goblins, breaking their frail bones and tearing their muddied flesh in a few wailing screams. He began to laugh at himself as if still a champion, and pushed away the leader with a spit.

'Must I do everything myself?' Jack sighed, shaking his head in disappointment. 'Get up and look at me, Lord Ouster.'

'Never!' Ouster pushed himself up onto his knees and spat at Jack's boots. 'Traitors do not deserve a man's audience.'

Jack rolled his eyes, and began to unbuckle his right gauntlet. The goblins still able to retreat did so before the bare skin was revealed. Feeling the Hatred flow into his nails, he channelled the energy through his claw towards Ouster. At his whim, the energy of the souls pulled the Knight into the air in a web of lightning.

'That's better', he said. 'Forgive me, Jonathan. These goblins are useless for taming captives. The mud makes them weak and the bones make them fat and stupid.'

Jack could detect Ouster was in great pain as the zaps of energy tore through his body. He could barely move or make a sound, yet he held firm against the bolts as they jumped across his armour and body. Accepting Ouster was now under his control, Jack brought him closer.

'I have two reasons to spare you, should you wish to grant me your hearing?'

Ouster tried to speak, but his whole body was rigid and his words could not escape him, so Jack lowered the power of the bolts running through his hand.

'W-why?' Ouster asked.

'Pardon me?' Jack drew closer. 'It sounded like you were trying to ask me something?'

'Why did you spare me?' Ouster's teeth chattered as he spoke.

'Like our friend, Kinas over there', Jack replied, 'I have plans for you.'

'What plans?'

'I need some information from you to start with. The second purpose is still in planning, depending on how you react to me.'

Jack clasped his hand, cutting off the flow of power. Ouster flopped to the floor, lying across Jack's boots for a few moments before he pulled himself up.

'What kind of information would I have that would serve you?'

Jack took a step back and kneeled as Ouster pushed himself up onto his knees.

'I want to overthrow the Dragon Throne. You know something. I can see it scurrying across your mind like a little mouse.'

'Then what's stopping you from taking it and being done with me?'

'The second part of my plan needs you alive.'

Jack grabbed Ouster's face and looked into his eyes. He tried to extract the Lord's thoughts, but his soul was too strong. Eventually he gave up and pushed Ouster to the side in frustration.

'I can't take the thoughts of a fighter, even if he wanted to give them up. I guess you will have to tell me willingly.'

'I won't let you have it. I can't wilfully betray the Dragon Throne. Not after this – not after your treachery. What has the Throne done to you? By the Mother, they're your people!'

'You know it has done many things to me. My Clan, besides the O'Neil Clan, was the most important family in all of Alcadia. It's been half a year since their disappearance, so where were their search parties? Where were the successors? Why hasn't the King come here yet in full force? Why must the humans act in their stead?' Jack looked at Ouster and smiled. 'All of these things are questions which Centra have answered poorly, if not at all. I want to see it all burn, just as you do, deep inside that Joanarian heart of yours.'

'You mistake me for wishing ill of the Dragon Bloods' Kingdom', Ouster said, his eyes holding against Jack's stare. 'You're worse than the Hobsythe. I can see why they ran from you now.'

'I was hoping you would be uncooperative anyway. Uncooperative men have much more to lose.'

'Best get used to that then. Cut off my cock and feed it to the ravens. I still won't be telling you anything.'

'I like your spirit, and for your sake I wish it were simple.'

Jack looked up at the mud goblin leader and nodded. The goblin leapt up and hit Ouster's head with the sword's hilt, catapulting him back into unconsciousness. He was then loaded and tied to a cart by a pack of the Fallen, where Jack hoped he would be comfortable during the ride to Negura.

Jack would catch up with him. His plans for the bodies scattered across the earth weren't quite finished. As with the Eastern Kingdom's armies, he filled the air with the Hatred. Its presence, like a dark fog, covered the bodies and the mud goblins as it worked on the dead. Any mud goblin remaining inside was to be consumed by the Hatred; their mud and flesh used to fill holes and wounds in the bodies of the reanimated dead. Jack's fourth army roused and formed up into a set of squares before him, their spears, swords and bows held high. They proceeded to follow him to Negura, the Capital, where Sirius had led the second and third armies to conquer before his arrival.

***

Standing half a day away from the battlefield, the city was built from a huge rock oddity. It stood above the farmlands like a beacon, with an organised mass of windows and etchings carved into its body. This tower was the Necromancer's dream, and although his nature was cruel, the tower itself had served its use well after Sanctity. The walls surrounding the city, however, served no purpose. So Jack had Sirius smash them into rubble, exposing the houses and businesses mimicking the stone tower. They were all surrounded by a thick mist, and a very impressive column of smoke spewed from the pinnacle of the stone tower itself. *How beautiful. The throne room had better be intact.*

The second and third armies were marching through the city towards the west, and the first army was still pillaging and establishing the new order by the time Jack arrived. Keeping to appearances and respecting the farmland, he and his new army passed through the only part of the wall that remained untouched; the Eastern gate.

Jack didn't remember ordering Sirius to spare the gate, but as he studied it, it seemed to bring a chill to the surroundings. Like a broken memory – something to unsettle the survivors. More importantly, the main road to the tower entrance went through the Eastern gate. Maybe Sirius was thinking economically. Maybe he knew there'd be little time to clean up the mess before Jack's arrival. *How thoughtful of him.*

Ouster's cart had waited for him at the inside of the gate and Ouster, now awake and aware, remained silent against the lines of captured onlookers. Jack took a sense of pride in their cries as he walked his great beast of a horse through the city. The loss of hope was the beginning of a torrent of feelings that served his powers best.

Jack stopped his horse and Ouster's cart at the great arched entrance of the tower. With a click of his fingers, two of Ouster's own men, now the Fallen, untied Ouster and helped him to the floor. They accompanied him to the square where the great spiralling ramp leading to the old city began, and where Jack would take over his care.

The lines of black columns surrounding the hall were vandalised with the blood of the innocents, much to Jack's displeasure. He'd hoped they wouldn't touch it, but old habits were hard to shake. The spiralling ramp into the dungeons had inherited a light brown colouring with a great deal of muck around the edges. Jack had no interest in taking Ouster down there – no. Instead, he guided him up the ramp into the murky squeezes of the old city.

Jack watched his minions scurry between the many doorways, caring little for the messes they had made or the bodies that were festering. As he ascended, the familiarity of the city began to fill his mind as the rooms and the businesses became larger, with the vandalism showing no quarter.

Benson and Crandall, one of a few businesses Jack once had a stake in, was laid to ruin. Its desks, once filled with Joanarian tender, were now beaten to splinters. A single mud goblin had collected most of the money in the centre of the clearing, and was swimming in the coins like a giddy little fairy. It took no notice of the movement outside, not even of Jack. *Cheeky little bastard.*

The great residences near the peak of the city were now only hosts to piles of burning wood and plaster. Their hall-facing windows were smashed out, and the views inside were dominated by struggle after struggle, ending only in fire, every single time.

One residence had the entire hall facing wall stripped away, the carpets torn up and the furniture ejected, possibly through the windows facing the outside. Its fire burned the hottest, and its smoke roared up through the chimney and out through the holes that were once grand vista windows. This residence belonged to the Emperor, and the ill feelings had taken care of it down to the last panel.

However, in a wave of relief, one place remained unharmed. The Throne Room, best known as the Knight's Republic's council chamber. One chair for every major state, 15 chairs in all, one of which was for the Emperor. Jack cared little for reciting their owners in his head, they would all be dead anyway. But he could not help but notice the state of one chair, which looked as if it had been thrown at a corner in anger and smashed into pieces. It must have been the Lord of Ponte's chair – A Hobsythe, no less. *Believed to have been owned by Kinas' father, well before my time.*

Formerly, this chair had been a spot for jesters and fools, with the occasional angered phlegm towards the end of Jack's reign as Dragon Keeper. The start of his misfortunes. Cain must have flung it at the wall in a temper. No doubt after hearing about Montfort's defeat at the hands of the Hobsythe.

Jack turned his attention to the Emperor's chair, whose wood was etched with carvings and stories of the countless wars in Joanas' history. At its left side sat the Emperor's meeting chamber, just as it was before his undoing. *Advising Cain – Advising him and warning him of all of this. He only ever seemed to listen when it suited him. Ignorant buffoon.*

He caressed the red cushion of the Emperor's chair mockingly, ensuring Ouster could see him.

'That doesn't belong to you.' Ouster spat, as Jack made himself comfortable.

'Of course it does', Jack returned, crossing his legs and rubbing his back against the velvet with a smile, 'What was that law? 'He, by vote or upper hand alone?' You could say I am here by popular vote – what say you over there?'

Jack's minions, the Fallen and the one fat mud goblin, thundered a *yes* from as far below as the hall would allow.

'Come, sit in your chair, Ouster. Let's pretend as if nothing had happened.'

Ouster held his stance, and his sneer. *As perfect a representation of honour as I have ever seen. Or just denial.*

'Pity. But no harm done.' Jack ordered his minions to unbind and take Ouster to the Emperor's meeting chamber. 'I'll be there in a moment. Remove his armour and bind him to one of the chairs.'

Jack took the moment to enjoy the throne alone, calming his soul against the brunt of his memories. It wasn't always debates or arguments with Cain that stirred him; sometimes it was just parties and weddings. Emma always loved the weddings, and so did the girls. With his hand supporting his forehead against such hurtful memories, he let out a smooth, long-winded groan.

'Excuse me, sire', came a voice from the other side of the room. 'My Lord Emperor?'

'I'm not your Emperor', Jack replied, keeping his eyes on his feet as his memories began to fade. 'I dislike the title. I may come to enjoy this chair, but the title itself speaks too much of the old ways.'

'My Lord, then', the voice said. 'What is your command?'

Jack looked up to see the leads of his new fourth army

packed into the front half of the hall. They looked at him like a handful of curious kittens. He smiled to himself, he had forgotten they were still there. They must have filled the tower with all manner of swords and spears.

'March towards Winter-Haem', Jack ordered. 'Join your brethren in the sacking of Joanas. The Commander out there, Sirius, will tell you what to do.'

They all bowed, turned, and began to march on the spot. It took them several minutes before they started to move, and the clanking of their armour echoed through the tower before the dull ambience of the pillaging took over. The large mud goblin from the battlefield, still holding onto the scimitar, was the only creature that remained, standing by the door like a confused guard dog as Jack studied him.

'You're a very strange mud goblin', Jack said, rubbing his chin in thought. 'Aren't you?'

The creature seemed startled when Jack spoke to him. He lowered the sword and began to search the hall for another being, before realising and pointing to himself.

'Yes, you. You're twice the size of the others, and twice as fat. But you carry that sword around like a trophy. How many of your kin did you cut apart to get it?'

'Dozens milord', the goblin replied, lowering his eyes and holding the scimitar closer to his breast. 'They wouldn't let Grigor have it, they said Grigor was too fat to use it properly. They said Grigor was better off with the Fallen. But Grigor showed them. Grigor showed all of them.'

'Indeed', Jack said, waving away the Fallen carrying Ouster's armour. 'That scimitar belonged to the Lord Knight that once sat in that chair.'

Jack pointed to Lord Montfort's seat. It held no special carvings or drawings, and it was made with the trunks of sea-soaked palm trees. The wood was bleached and held several cracks, but it told the Eastern shore's story better than any of the others.

'Should Grigor give master the sword, milord?'

'No, it's yours, and you should keep it', Jack replied, watching as the mud-goblin's eyes glazed over with happiness. 'If you serve me well, I may even let you sit in Lord Montfort's seat.'

Grigor danced like a little girl in response to Jack's promise. Although he felt somewhat strange about making somebody happy, he knew he needed to keep a fresh approach with his minions else they'd rally against him. But the mud-goblins were safe. They were stupid and very simple, and Grigor was no exception.

'Lord Montfort was one of the few that sided with me when I confronted Cain and his crusade against the Hobsythe. Much good that did him, hey Grigor?'

Grigor shook his head.

'Still, he was a good man, with a healthy family. Those scaly bastards treated him no differently.' *It might have been worse – like the kind of revenge one exacts towards a friend who couldn't support you in your time of need.* 'Good riddance to them and their leader. We owe that much to our friend Ouster, if anything.'

'What made the scale so spiteful, milord?'

'What indeed.' Jack consulted his memories. 'My fool of a father had a hand in it. I saw that the moment I realised my family was gone. He was more interested in pleasing the Lords than holding his honour. But it was definitely the humans, or should we say Cain and his ilk, that made them that way.'

'What did they do milord?'

'The more relevant question is, what didn't they do?'

Jack sighed away his concerns over Grigor's curiosity. It was a relief to have something in his light brave enough to ask a question, let alone be in his light to begin with.

'The Hobsythe were barely different from the humans once. They wore fashionable clothing and had Lordships and states of their own. Then, after Sanctity, it all fell apart. Some manner of blame game, suspicion, politics. Enough to light the fire of tyranny and separate the Hobsythe and humans. Make them hate each other.'

'Add that hate to famine and the countless raids of Hobsythe villages and you find yourself in the situation that brought on Cain's rise to power. Cain spared nothing and drove them out into the Jungles. But here we are. We know the rest.'

A member of the Fallen had joined them. It was one of the guards from the Capital. Sirius must have left him to undertake Jack's main desires.

'And who may you be?'

'Master Sirius tasked me with finding the beings you requested, my Lord', the guard said, holding an expressionless stare. 'They await your summons in the upper dungeon.'

'Very good', Jack said, turning his attention to Grigor as he stood. 'That will be your first task for the day, Grigor. Follow this Fallen into the upper dungeon and bring the catch to me.'

Grigor smiled and nodded before following the Fallen out of view into the old city. Alone again with his thoughts, Jack decided to be a good host and join Ouster. Entering the Emperor's office with a calm skip and a smile in the Commander's direction, he slammed the door shut and began to take off his armour.

'How did it feel returning here under my banner? Were you expecting anything?'

Ouster held his stare. He seemed calm and very much aware of his surroundings, even if a little injured. Jack's eyes studied him, trying to gauge the purpose in remaining silent. As he removed his helmet, he detected some stirring in Ouster's feelings.

'Why have you brought me here, of all places?' Ouster asked, as Jack settled his helmet on the desk. 'I used to speak to my brother and Lord Doncaster in this office. Aside from the few splinters of rotten wood, this place makes a very poor torture chamber. This place is designed for meetings and drunken parties.'

'Ah – thank you for reminding me', Jack said, reaching into the desk's cupboard for a bottle and two cups. 'How about some wine?'

Ouster remained silent. A reminder of his courage and duty rang in his head as he watched Jack pour the wine into the cups. Jack approached Ouster, untied his right hand, and gave him the cup, before returning to his own chair and placing his feet upon the desk.

'What is the purpose of this?' Ouster asked, studying the liquid for a moment. 'It's well turned, what have you done to it?'

'It is only wine from the Emperor's kegs.' Jack took a sip, enjoying the warm liquid as it caressed his throat. 'You should drink it all, you'll need every drop.'

Ouster slowly slurped at the scarlet liquid.

'Enjoy it while you can'. Jack raised his head as the Lord poured more into his mouth. 'The information I seek is important, and my plans for you are even more so. I need you fully aware of my requirements, and I need you to submit to them.'

There was a knock on the door. 'Yes – one moment!'

'You may know your way around Negura Jack, but you'll never see me submit to your bastard deeds whilst I walk on my own soil.' Ouster proclaimed defiantly. 'What could I know about Joanas that would possibly assist your cause?'

'It's a small thing to demand, considering the power I possess, but here's the point. I don't know the Western Kingdoms as well as you, and to be honest there are times I don't even know my own home anymore.'

'Couldn't you get that information from any one of the soldiers you slaughtered?'

'I could, but I asked myself. Has any one of those prisoners fought the armies of the Dragon Bloods? Has any one of them led an army against the Dragon Bloods? Has any one of them killed a Dragon Blood?'

'That was a different time. You of all the Morre should understand that.'

'But Joanas' needs are different now, aren't they? Joanas is under new management now, isn't it?'

'Not while the west still stands. Hurry up with my torture. You're boring me with this nostalgia.'

'There's nothing nostalgic in the killing of Dragon Bloods', Jack said, turning his attention to the door, 'You may bring them in now.'

A jittery Hobsythe waddled in. He was starved to the point where his bones defined his shape, and his scales were covered in rashes from the oily chains Grigor used to direct him inside.

'Very good Grigor. Put him in the corner over there, that's a good lad.'

The goblin walked the Hobsythe into the corner behind Jack's chair. He chained him to an iron wall bracket and bowed to his master, awaiting further instruction.

'That's all. Go sit in your chair and await my counsel.'

Jack turned to the Hobsythe to stroke him. The beast was very reserved at first, cowering as the hand reached out for him, but he eventually had no choice but to be touched. Soon enough, like any animal starved of affection, the creature came to enjoy the attention.

'This one is called Rector. Besides his somewhat basic appearance, Rector here knows both Joanarian and the Dragon Tongue.' Jack changed to the Dragon Tongue. 'Don't you Rector?'

Rector nodded fanatically after Jack halted his caresses.

'Yes', he said. 'Yes, I do.'

'That's a good boy.' Jack smiled and patted the beast's scalp. 'Isn't he interesting Ouster?'

'I still don't see how that would make a difference in my torture'. Ouster's defiance demonstrated his heart's fearlessness. 'Have him tear my flesh apart! I will not tell you anything that could jeopardise my people or my agreements with the Morre.'

'Rector isn't for you', Jack said, taking a final sip of his wine as he turned towards the door, 'He's for them.'

Jack picked up Ouster's dread as he heard the little whimpers in the hall. He turned to Ouster as the girls made their entrance. His gaze had turned from a stiff fortification of denial to a frown filled with dread and horror.

Jack made great efforts to remember them by their names and ages. Louisa, with her blonde curls and curious little heart, was only four. Tammy, with her Navurian dress covered in silver beads, was thirteen. Ella, with her frizzled hair and exciting adolescence, was seventeen.

'Girls!' Ouster began to break into panic. 'You bastard! You sly, evil, cruel bastard!'

Jack covered Louisa's ears as her father cursed.

'Now, now sir Ouster, they're here to see you, aren't you girls?'

Louisa was unsure of the situation; she seemed more interested in the feeling of Jack's hands than her father breaking into a fit of rage. The elder two, however, were in tears and, as Jack read their thoughts, he realised that they had a very accurate grasp on what was planned for them. *Smart, young creatures.*

Ella whimpered at her father as he looked at them, his heart stricken with wrath.

'It's alright, Ella', he assured her, his face growing redder by the moment. 'Let them go, Jack. They have done nothing to you. They haven't even seen their first century yet.'

If Jack were alone with Ouster at that moment, he would have sucked the Hatred straight out of him in a fit of ecstasy. But instead he lowered himself to Louisa's level and, softly touching her shoulder, addressed her directly.

'Daddy seems a bit angry at the moment. Would you be so kind as to stay with me while your big sisters comfort him?'

Louisa gave a calm, slow nod and looked at Ouster

with a child's innocent pity. She opened her arms and Jack, as if she were his own daughter, scooped her up.

'Tammy, Ella, do your father the honour of saying goodbye.'

Both ran to Ouster. They wailed, knowing if they tried to free him they'd all suffer. This beautiful display of woe and love hit Ouster hard, and he began to sob.

'What do you want?' he cried, holding on to his daughters as their tear-swept faces looked up at Jack. 'Please? I will do anything if you just don't hurt them, please!'

Jack looked into Ouster's eyes, tasting the desperation. He looked out into the Knight's room, where Grigor was dancing upon the chair of Montfort and waving the scimitar above his head like a jester.

'Come take the child, Grigor.' Jack called out to him. Grigor obliged, placing the scimitar in the chair and scurrying into the room with open arms. Jack kissed the child on the forehead and carefully passed her to him.

'Take very good care of her now. Keep her away from that sword of yours.'

'Yes master', Grigor said, looking at Louisa as she waved goodbye, 'Grigor will take special care of her.'

'Very good', Jack said, closing the door behind Grigor and returning his eyes to Ouster.

'I understand you'd do anything for them Ouster, and I believe you. I believe you because I can see myself sitting there, facing the possibility that my daughters are going to be hurt.'

But they were hurt, he thought bitterly, as Ouster shook his head and held his precious daughters closer to his chest, *and they're dead for it.*

'It's just my partner, Sirius, who is marching for the west, doesn't believe us', he continued menacingly. "Don't accept any of his words until you have mutilated them', he said. And that's why I am only going to start with one. Ella, come to me.'

'No!' Ouster braced Ella as she sobbed in his grasp. 'She's only seen seventeen years damn you!'

'As was my eldest!' Jack bellowed, making the joists shake and the girls wail with fright, 'Now I say again. Ella, come to me, now!'

Instead of waiting for her to comply, Jack opened his hand and willed the energy to pull her into his arms. She came to him, screaming, limbs flailing, and her head latched into his claw.

'Shall I show you what they did to my eldest, Ouster?' Jack asked, studying Ella's golden-brown locks of hair and fair skin. 'Shall I show you how she died?'

Ouster shook his head, and tightened his hold on Tammy. With a loud crack, Jack bashed Ella's head into the side of the table, causing her body to flop to the floor.

'Ella!' Ouster screamed. 'This isn't necessary. I'll swear on the ghosts of the Knight's Republic - Please!'

Jack watched as Ella slowly writhed on the floor. Her hair parted to reveal the stream of blood oozing from the fresh scratch on her forehead.

'Sasha was only eighteen when she was taken from me', he said, turning to Rector, 'You were there, weren't you Rector?'

Rector nodded.

'You remember what they did first, don't you? How would you like to do it now?'

The Hobsythe nodded again and began to dance energetically like an excited dog. Jack patted him on the head before reaching down to the chain ring and releasing the beast upon Ella. Rector leapt onto her faster than a rabbit and began to tear at her ragged clothes as she slowly began to regain consciousness.

'She's only seventeen!'

'Yes, I got that the first time', Jack yelled, bashing his fist onto the desk. 'I said the same thing to them. 'She's only eighteen. Please – stop you bastards.' Yet they continued, and do you know why?'

Ouster shook his head.

'Because your bastard brother let his men do the same thing to their children. With my bitch of a father standing by and doing nothing!' Jack smashed his hand against the desk, causing a fresh crack to form. 'Nothing!'

Jack heard no fucking going on. He rounded on Rector, who had frozen, and was staring up at him.

'Did I tell you to stop?'

The beast didn't take long to regain his rhythm. Jack listened to Ouster's sobbing with a hard heart as he remembered both his father and Cain. How they had laughed at the news of hundreds of innocent Hobsythe children raped and slaughtered. *Bastards – the both of them.*

Rector soon slowed to a crawl and relaxed with a satisfied grunt and lapping of his tongue. Jack poured some wine, and tipped it down his gullet.

'Well executed Rector. Well executed indeed.' He turned back to Ouster. 'Shall we remind you what they did next, Jonathan?'

'Please stop this! I told you I'd tell you anything. Please don't hurt my baby anymore!'

'You need to know how serious I am', Jack smashed his fist against the table once more. 'You must know what will happen if you deceive me. You must understand it by seeing it!'

Jack looked at Rector as he sat patiently on his victim, looking down at her with the dried lips of a hungry lion.

'That's right Rector – feed.'

Ouster began to howl as Ella's flesh was ripped and torn from her bones. Rector showed no quarter, he had pinned her and was ravenous for meat. Jack's mind was filled with the putrid memory of Sasha's torture at the hands of the Kinas scum. But it then went further, where he recalled the most innocent of those poor creatures, piled up and burnt by the human mobs. Jack could easily imagine Kinas and his ilk watching every moment in the shadows, understanding their lust for vengeance with every deed. Admittedly however, the devouring wasn't inspired by the humans, but at that point it might as well have been.

Rector barely looked any different to how he had that night. He had feasted just as lovingly on Jack's children as he was on Ella, greedily, scratching and shovelling flesh into his mouth with bloodied claws.

Jack turned back to Ouster and held his stare until Ella's last, painful breath escaped her mouth. Tammy's sobbing filled the room and Rector's munching, no louder than her cries, soothed Jack's lust for revenge.

'Now you understand what's at stake here. I will gladly do the same to Tammy and Louisa, too. Am I clear in my message now, Ouster? Or do you need further convincing?'

Ouster clung to Tammy and nodded slowly.

Jack proceeded to grab Rector's neck and pull him onto the table in a claw-filled struggle. He grabbed both sides of the creature's jaw and, with a mighty roar, ripped apart the Hobsythe's head. He tossed away the top half and held down the body, which squirmed and gurgled on the table until it was completely dead.

'Ella!' Ouster cried. 'My baby!'

He embraced Tammy with a sense of urgency.

'Please don't hurt any more of my children. I'm sorry for what happened to your family. I admit my fault, and I will do as you desire as long as Tammy and Louisa are spared your vengeance.'

Jack slid the body off the table, kicking it to the side so he could sit.

'I appreciate your honesty Jonathan, I really do. But you must understand, this wasn't about vengeance. I still have the surviving Hobsythe locked away in my dungeon, and I have plans for Kinas' soul.'

Jack smiled as he kicked his feet back onto the table.

'I am just glad that we could come to an agreement before you made me endure another memory.' He assessed

Ouster's calming breaths and the small whines of Tammy. 'Now, about the part you played in the War of Sanctity?'

'The only difference that would help you would be when my brother and I made our last stand with the Necromancer.'

'That is the part that interests me. Between the three of you, you killed forty Morre. That's a remarkable feat, don't you think?'

'We were on our last hopes, we thought we were going to die. What matter is that?'

'It matters because no human has ever achieved something like that, before or after. Even with the skills of the best warrior, the three of you couldn't take forty humans, let alone Morre in such an enclosed space. With your brother slain by Kinas Kirk, and the Necromancer – well we all know what happened there, you're the only living human left to tell the tale. Usually I would steal the secret from their souls, but it's never easy when it happened so many years ago.'

'You're going down a path I am not sure I can follow, Jack. Your father might have been a brown-nosed coward, but he still cared about you. What would he think of this path you are taking?'

Fuck him. The bastard sealed his fate, and his right to my affairs.

'I am asking the questions, you are giving the answers. Personally, I don't think you're taking this seriously enough.'

'No, no I am Sir, please!'

Jack opened his hand, forcing Tammy out of her father's arms and up towards the ceiling. He turned his hand slowly to the right and her arms, legs and head began to twist in time with his movements.

'How did you kill them?' Jack bellowed, halting Tammy before she could touch the ceiling. Her neck was near to breaking, and her limbs stretched almost to the point of tearing. 'Tell me the difference between your attacks. Did the Necromancer show you a weakness?'

Jack could tell the child was in agony, yet her body did not falter and her hair hid most of her face from Ouster's view.

'It's been sixty years, give me a chance to think!'

With the flex of his little finger, Jack whipped Tammy's arm against the wood ceiling with a loud snap. She bellowed out in pain, writhing against his hold.

'Please don't hurt her anymore damn you!' Ouster cried.

'Tell me then. You can't have beheaded them all.'

'I don't know. Stop this, please!'

Jack, with a scowl and a snarl, clenched his fist and twisted his hand quickly to the right. Tammy let out another scream as a loud crack came from her right leg. She was sobbing, and Ouster was becoming more desperate.

'It had something to do with the children!'

Jack's mind lit up quicker than a fire doused in gunpowder. By the stories he'd been told, the Necromancer slaughtered all the captured slave children, and hung them from Forecourt Cathedral's ceiling. He felt foolish not to remember it now. It was there in plain view amongst the other memories.

'Tell me more.' he said, swishing his hand up and down and forcing Tammy to crash repeatedly into the ceiling. 'It couldn't have just been the children. Killing a Dragon Morre is like trying to skin a pig with a stick. You knew something else, and you used it against them.'

'No I didn't, I swear. They just didn't seem willing to fight the Necromancer; they were more interested in the children. It was almost as though it was their own children hanging from the ceilings-'

'What did you say?' Jack interrupted, releasing Tammy and dropping her onto the floor atop Ouster's feet.

'Tammy-'

'Focus, Commander Ouster', Jack ordered, pulling her

up onto the desk. 'The Morre and the children; you said they acted like they were their own. What did you mean by that?'

'Exactly like I said it', Ouster answered, trying to reach out for Tammy from his pinned position. 'They seemed distraught by the sight of them, some were even moaning names or going into a frenzy.'

'Indeed.' *The Necromancer must have induced a charm; made them see their loved ones hanging from the rafters.* Jack slowly caressed Tammy's bruised cheek, allowing Ouster to watch the bright pinks and purples on her face recede.

'Please don't hurt her anymore Jack.'

'It'll do for now. Just shut up and watch.'

Jack moved his hand down to her mangled arm and twisted leg, squeezing the flesh as he channelled the spirit energy into her broken bones. Ouster's face lit up as the limbs repaired themselves and aligned properly with her body.

'I am not a complete monster, Ouster. I still reward those that deliver what I want.'

'What about Ella?' Jack released the flesh to reveal Tammy as she was before. 'Can't you bring her back?'

'I'm afraid not.' Jack looked down at Ella's mutilated corpse. 'She lies with the rest of my cache of souls, waiting to serve me as I desire.'

'Please don't cause her any more pain. Please. I will swear loyalty to you until my death, and beyond if needed. I will surrender myself only if you don't hurt them anymore.'

'This seems like a fair deal, Ouster. However, when Louisa and Tammy come of age for their flowering, they will be forced to make a choice.'

'What choice will that be?'

'Either be raped daily by my subjects, or surrender to me.'

'So long as they live and have that choice fairly, I shall not raise a word or finger against you my Lord.'

Jack's smile could have touched both of his ears if he let it, but the cold of his body made it too much of an effort for what it was worth. He already knew their choice; they would surrender to him, as he would be kinder to them. This was what he could promise to Ouster, and indeed to them.

'I'm glad we could come to an agreement. Would you care for some more wine?'

Letters of Joanas

'Good morning everyone', said the Captain of the Guard. 'Thank you for coming on such short notice. Please be seated - we will address all the main attendees in good time.'

Drake's back felt uncomfortable against the pressure of his armour. The heat was causing his face to itch, and the eyes of the large crowd were peering at him as if he were a fool. But he could not remove his helmet.

'How long will this meeting take?' he asked Jefferson.

'Most of the morning', he replied. 'Why?'

'It's too hot in here.'

'You should have thought about that before deciding to wear your bloody armour.' Jefferson said, raising his eyebrows. 'Even Weir decided to keep his off today on account of the heat. I suggest you at least take your helmet off.'

'But I can't.'

'Why not? What fool wears metal today?'

'I don't want to be recognised here.'

He longed to tell Laura the truth but could not stand the thought of losing her trust.

'Then sit down.' Jefferson growled irritably. 'There's plenty of room to stick out your boots. So long as it stops you whining; some of us want to hear what they're saying.'

Drake obeyed Jefferson's instruction with a grunt. Several men glared at him as he sat, but he ignored them. He pulled off his damp headband, wiped his face with his handkerchief and turned his attention towards the Captain, who had just finished his speech.

The Captain proceeded to introduce Tiana Rivera. Drake craned his neck to catch a glimpse of Laura as her mother took to the stage, but his view was blocked. So, he slumped back into his chair and, as the High Lady began her address, he allowed his concentration to slip once more. *Father's meetings were never as boring as this, and Mother's maiden gatherings were full of excitement,* he thought bitterly, as her voice droned through the hall.

He had fond memories of those meetings, the energy of the attendance and the respect and power he held in the court. Girls admired him then; he would often flirt with them and sometimes even take them back to his room. There would be no such luck here obviously, but then, with Laura hot on his mind, would he want that anyway?

Weir was talking by the time Drake returned his attention to the present. He was discussing the plans that were already in motion and explaining the reasoning behind his actions.

'Regardless if the humans are willing or not', he said, 'the Morre in Joanas Sorrow agree that we must take action. We can't abandon the Joanarians, and we can't keep hearing silence from Jack and Stanley Penance.'

'What of the King?' asked Tiana. 'Has he not commanded the Prince to remain here until his order permits a movement?'

'My lady, it's clear that communications are being held back', Weir reminded her. 'If the previous messages we have received show any logic, the Throne is probably back in the timeline where Doncaster is due to be named Emperor. Even with our new messenger making flight towards Centra as we speak, it will take her two further days, maybe more, to reach Morkor. That's two days too many of bloodshed and loss of life. By the Torre, you of all the Morre understand the importance Joanas has over Alcadia's affairs, and why waiting for orders in light of what we have heard is against our duties as Dragon-Morre?'

Tiana did not respond. Weir turned to address the crowd.

'And what does Joanas-Sorrow have to say about the matter now that the exotic fruits, pelts, fish, ale, and timbers have stopped coming from Joanas?'

There was no reply, or even a standing. The lack of

chatter from the audience indicated they were unfamiliar with the state of affairs.

'Regardless of their crimes against humanity, and against the Hobsythe, the Joanarians deserve our help. We cannot let the Western Kingdoms fall, and we can't turn our backs on the Penance family. That settles my thoughts on the motion. Captain, thank you for your audience.'

Drake watched Weir as he sat down, his face cold with the solemnity of his address, and began to converse with Gromwell and Bartarian. The hall was filled with questions, and many men stood to try and get their voices heard.

'They're acting as if they were oblivious', observed Jefferson. 'What kind of regime is this to allow such an outcry?'

'They must be angry about the imports', Drake replied. 'I think they were under the impression the disrupted trade routes were only temporary, and would be reinstated in due time.'

'I actually meant the way they are lashing out against them.' Jefferson pointed to one muddied and swaying man as he delivered some profanities towards the attending. 'Look at this one.'

'What is he doing?' Drake tried to get a better view, but the crowds blocked him from doing so. 'Jefferson?'

Jefferson studied the commotion as the voices grew louder and more impatient. The crowd's anger was drowning out the Captain of the Guard, who was attempting to regain order. Drake heard a smash – one of the water pots must have been thrown. He felt Jefferson grab his arm.

'We need to get out of here.'

Swords were drawn. All Drake could see was a crowd of helms merging together. He was scared for Laura but, as he tried to ascertain her whereabouts, he caught Gromwell's waving hands at the front.

'Tony', he shouted, 'Get Drake out of here!'

Drake knew what was happening. His father made him drill it every six days whenever he was in Morkor. They'd have the court squeeze together and make him or one of his attending guards push through the group as it pushed back. By memory Lord Aldwin led the escape best, but he'd never tried it with Jefferson. Regardless of how many times he had been through it, his heart was beating as fast as ever. The tide of angry men began to claw at one another.

'Edward', shouted Jefferson. 'Where will we meet?'

Gromwell's head was just visible above the silver helms as they pushed for the southern exit.

'I don't know', he answered. 'Just get the Prince to safety first.'

'What do we do?' Drake asked.

'Get your hand off your sword', ordered Jefferson, slapping his fingers away from the hilt. He raised his hands and addressed the crowd. 'We don't want any trouble here. Let us out and you won't be harmed. We're not the problem.'

The crowd continued to stare at them. Then Drake caught the eye of a woman whose face was clinging to her bones, one eye clouded with a corruption.

'Save Joanas', she said with a whimper.

The crowd repeated her words. 'Save Joanas.'

Then again in a pitch as if addressing one another. 'Save Joanas.'

They continued to repeat it, their voices filling the hall with a trembling echo.

'Save Joanas!'

They turned their heads to the northern doors, and began to push towards it.

'Save Joanas! Save Joanas!'

Jefferson tugged at Drake's gauntlet.

'Come on Drake', he said. 'Before they take us with them.'

He pulled the Prince towards the southern door,

pushing and shoving the chanting crowd as it flowed towards them.

'Save Joanas!'

They were greeted by Gromwell, Weir and Bartarian at the door when Drake caught sight of Laura. He tried to run to her, but Gromwell stopped him half way and held him firmly on the spot.

'Hold there for a moment, lad', he whispered. 'There is time to say goodbye when we are safe.'

'But I might not get another chance!'

'Your secret is safe. She thinks as your lie commands. But this is no place for the truth. We need to establish a safe zone, where we have more control over your confession.'

Drake tried to wriggle free again, yet his attempt was met with a new pair of hands that spun him around to face Jefferson.

'Calm yourself boy', he said. 'Look at her; she believes the Prince is still inside. So shut up and listen to the city.'

Drake looked, seeing Laura calmly exchanging words with the humans. He caught brief glances in his direction; that was not the face of betrayal or discovering the truth. He nodded to Jefferson, and closed his eyes.

As instructed by Gromwell and the combat teachers over the years, he began to pull every thread of thought into what he was hearing. Previously, his attempts to listen to Morkor had been drowned out by the sounds of the river, but when he tuned his hearing to Joanas-Sorrow, he began to hear everything. He began to hear the uprising.

'Save Joanas!' came the call, more aggressive than ever.

Drake felt Gromwell's grasp loosen.

'What do you hear lad?' he asked. The loudness of his voice made him flinch.

The smash of a crate broke his concentration and hundreds of boots and slippers rushed past.

'Save Joanas! Save Joanas!' The crowd was rampaging. 'Save Joanas! Save the Ale!'

Damn that bloody Ale.

Another voice joined the commotion.

'Stand down! You will be fired upon if you do not stand down!' Its tone held conviction, as if it came from authority.

'Save Joanas!' The crowd replied.

'The guards are retaliating', Drake told Gromwell. 'What do we do?'

Gromwell retracted his hand.

'Wait a moment', he said. 'What else can you hear?'

Drake tried to listen for something else, but the energy of the confrontation overwhelmed him. 'I can't hear anything else.'

'Turn your head.' Gromwell put a hand on Drake's face and pulled it forcefully to one side. 'Do you hear it now?'

'Yes.'

'Good. Now listen.'

'-get the Dragon-Bloods to their port', the Captain of the Guard was saying. 'Tiana, how many will you need as an escort?'

'You still haven't answered my question, Donaldson', replied Tiana, her voice stern.

'It doesn't concern you', said Donaldson. 'Just get your people behind the walls and keep your heads down. You can take three of my men. There – that answers my question. The rest of you are to come with me. We will quell this uprising the way Cain should have quelled the Hobsythe.'

'But you can't use experimental technology on them!'

'I can do whatever the Mother blesses me with. We're vastly outnumbered, the city is rampaging. I will not be the one explaining to your King why I let his son die under my command!'

Drake lost his focus and snapped his eyes wide open. Donaldson's cheeks, fortunately, were red facing down against Tiana's calm serenity. *Bless the Torre. They don't know who I am either.*

Jefferson took a step back into the hall, surveying the emptiness left in the wake of the rebellion.

'Commander Gromwell', Tiana said, braking from the argument. 'Is the Prince safe?'

'Yes milady', Edward said with a bow. 'Commander Bartarian thought it best to keep him inside and away from view until we start moving. He'll be quite safe – Whatever you decide.'

'Good. But you best be on your way', Tiana ordered, before turning back to Donaldson. 'As for you, you great oaf-'

A series of bangs came from the north. All eyes turned to the source of the noise.

'I suggest you move now too Lady Riveria!' Gromwell shouted. 'I'm afraid anyone who doesn't join us now will only have to fend for themselves.'

'How do we do this?' asked Jefferson from behind. 'Do we split up?'

Gromwell walked out into the open road, all eyes on him as the sounds of the riot lashed out into the sky. He peered down the west road, clearly deep in thought.

'What's on your mind, Gromwell?' Drake asked, joining him. He looked down the road himself, seeing nothing but a river of cobble before him.

'We need to run against the walls', Gromwell replied. 'We can't be part of this, and we can't be put into a situation where we'll have to defend ourselves against these lunatics.'

'I heard that!' Donaldson shouted.

Gromwell grimaced away a retort, before addressing them all. 'We should split into two groups, less numbers mean less noise. Bartarian, take Laura and Tiana East. The rest of us will take the Prince west.'

Laura's eyes were glazed with a concern Drake recognised from his mother. She would always look at him that way the night before he set off on any prolonged voyage or training. If Drake shared such a look, it would have been because he was worried for their future.

'May the Torre bless your journey my Prince', Tiana called with a bow towards Jefferson as Bartarian shepherded her away. 'We must speak soon - Send us summons when you return home!'

'Thomas-' Laura called out, before being led away by her mother. Drake tried to watch her leave, but it wasn't long before he was jerked back to his senses and forced to focus on the task in hand.

'I could get used to being Royalty you know', Jefferson mocked with a sly smile. 'Where's your bow Edward?'

'Shut up!' Edward snapped, before heading off, wasting little time with stealth.

Drake followed with Jefferson at his back. *Walter's Wrath,* a snake-hilted rapier smithed in Dunfife, was in Gromwell's hand as he led them to the walls. The sword meant everything to the Morre, but its sharpness meant Drake had to be extra vigilant of a stray cobble.

Together, the three Morre rushed through the early noon streets. They looked to the wall spanning before them, which began to stretch higher above the rooftops like a snake stretching into the clouds.

The commotion in the central district grew louder as they moved closer. The bangs and screams of many different attacks carried across the rooftops, scaring the crows and gulls into clouds of shrieking black and white. 'Save Joanas!' Drake would occasionally hear.

'Move quicker', Gromwell shouted. 'Through here.'

They were soon sprinting, for the unrest was becoming visible in the distance. With each glance, Drake would see the scrapping hands of men. Towering above them were long, metal shafts. In the blink of an eye, they were level with shoulders and belching smoke. A set of cracks shot through the air. Drake dared not ask what those weapons were, or what they were doing to the rioters. If anything, they looked like small cannons, but the idea of them making such a weapon any smaller was preposterous.

The wall was beginning to curve inward, yet the towers marking the gate to the port couldn't be seen through the smoke and rooftops. It would have been easier on the main road, where the gate and towers could be seen the moment one left the keep. This path was mysterious, and Drake was beginning to feel a sense of fear crawl through his mind. After a sprint which seemed to last forever, the towers sleeked into the sky and the walls began to straighten.

The run to the gate seemed to last longer than the entire journey through the streets. Drake's heart was pounding and his back and head were already covered in sweat. As he dabbed the wetness from his forehead with his handkerchief, studying the unrest of the crowds of Dragon Morre behind the gate, he realised he had forgotten something.

'Gromwell', he said, panting from the fumes of his body, 'My helmet!'

Gromwell stopped between the two guards as they held the rails of the iron gating. 'I'm not going back for it', he said. 'We can get another one.'

'Another one won't fit. Too many Morre will know me - I can't let her find out like this, there's still a chance to make things right!' Drake tried to gauge the distance from the gate to the city hall. 'I can't see anyone on the road; I could make it.'

Drake turned to run back, but Gromwell's grip held him in place.

'You're an idiot and a fool! She has probably already put the two stories together', Gromwell said. 'I will not let you go back there for some stupid girl.'

Drake tried to swing free from Gromwell's grasp.

'She's not just some girl Edward', he implored. 'Please?'

'No.' Gromwell insisted. 'I cannot put you in any more danger.'

As Gromwell looked on, Drake couldn't help but think about his age, and how much longer he had left. The process should not have started so early for him, yet there it sat, as if staring at him.

'I have to get my helmet', he cried, as he pushed his way past Gromwell with all the effort he could muster. He felt his mentor's hands claw at his arms as he escaped, followed by curses as he ran.

A flash erupted from the keep. Drake couldn't see it very well but, in the silence, he felt his breastplate pull against him. He fought it as best he could, but the force overcame him and he could do nothing more but curse and face his captor. As he turned to the rear an explosion rang through his ears, its turbulence lifting him off his feet. He could just make out Gromwell reaching for him as he hit the ground.

Drake was unsure if he blacked out, or just closed his eyes as his head hit the floor. His ears were ringing and, when he opened his eyes, he found two pairs of boots stood in front of him. Two strong hands pulled him up, which he soon recognised as Jefferson's. To his left. Bartarian, with a scrunched face, was pulling a motionless Gromwell to his feet. Drake's heart sank. *Is he dead?*

Jefferson wrapped his arm around Drake and began to drag him to the gate. Drake looked at Gromwell – his eyes were closed and his mouth was wobbling with each of Bartarian's mighty steps. There was no trace of life.

They were taken inside the gate, where it was closed and sealed with iron bars. Laura, Tiana and a group of Morre were waiting for them, but Drake no longer cared about his lie or his secret identity. He cared about Edward.

Bartarian placed Gromwell onto the floor, calling out for help as Drake scrambled over to his body.

'Gromwell', he screamed, shaking his body as the ringing subsided. 'Edward… Master – say something!'

He neither moved nor replied. Drake wanted to go back and slap himself around the face for his stupidity, but it was too late.

'Out of the way', ordered Bartarian, 'Get off him you

Royal Tit!'

Drake was thrown to one side, Bartarian and Weir taking his place, searching Gromwell's body desperately for a sign of life.

'He's not breathing', Weir said after a short time. 'What did you do Drake?'

Bartarian, quicker than an owl that had spotted prey, was lurching over Drake. Pulling him to his knees by his breastplate. Giving him the coldest stare he could imagine.

'This is your fault', he growled, slapping Drake across the cheek and forcing him to the floor in a pool of tears, 'Your stupidity has killed him.'

Bartarian kicked Drake's rear, He squealed as the pain ripped through his spine.

'Get up and face judgment like a real Morre.'

Drake watched the crowd of Morre gather around him as he rubbed his struck cheek. There was no hiding from this. With a sob, he scrambled to his feet and faced Bartarian, tears still running down his face.

'You're an idiot!' Bartarian shouted, slapping Drake again. 'You're a fool.' He slapped him on the opposite cheek. 'You're not worthy of your father's name. You're not worthy of the crown. You are not worthy of anything but the shit in your arse!'

Drake did not cower, nor did he stumble. He merely stared at Bartarian as the memories of his mentor flushed his scolded skin.

The pig of a Morre readied another slap, this time arching his hand back, but the sting of the hit never came. He looked up at Bartarian. A sword was pushing against his gauntlet, and at its hilt was Weir.

'That's enough Bartarian', he ordered. 'Slap him again and I will bleed you where you stand.'

'Are you insane?' Bartarian screamed. 'He killed Edward!'

'It was an accident', Weir insisted, holding his stance as the tip of his sword moved to the base of the Morre's neck. 'Nothing more. Disgracing the Prince will not bring him back.'

'Karl, please', Jefferson said from behind Drake, 'Weir is right. It was Edward's decision to run after the idiot.'

Bartarian frowned, allowing his eyes to wander the pavement for a moment. Jefferson's expression was fearful and pleading. Weir, on the other hand, was trembling with fury.

'Release me then', he croaked.

'Stay calm, and walk away, Karl', Weir said, as he retracted his sword. 'We're not solving anything here. Not like this.'

Bartarian looked at all of them, Drake last. His eyes were still flaring with the heat of his temper, yet his hand collapsed to his side as Weir holstered his sword. With a grunt he walked away, pushing through the crowds towards the line of ships with their masts towering above the onlookers' heads.

Drake ran over to Gromwell, and threw himself across his body.

'I'm sorry Gromwell', he cried. 'I should have never left your side. Please don't leave me alone. Come back – please.'

'You… you're suffocating me-'

Drake shot up as Gromwell let out a long gasp for air and a cough. Jefferson, Weir and the group ran to him in a mass of relieved cries. Drake helped him sit up, and embraced him tightly.

'What happened?' Gromwell asked, 'Tony – Weir – Why are we at the port? Have we missed the boats?'

'You blundering fool!' Jefferson cried, getting on one knee beside him as he helped him to his feet, 'We thought you were away into the Passing.'

'I'm fine', Gromwell said, standing. 'I just needed some time to think. Get me to the Vengeance. I haven't quite finished my rest.'

Drake stayed on his knees as he watched Gromwell

leave with Jefferson, relieved he was okay, but now concerned as to whether he would ever speak to him again. Weir stood by his side, looking down at him with a pair of folded arms and a look granted by the mistress of disappointment.

'He'll come around', he said, 'Give him some time.'

'I don't think I would forgive myself after doing something so stupid.'

'But Gromwell isn't you, is he? Battarian was half right. You are a fool. But it was honourable accepting his wrath like that. I think you may find things easier for you now amongst the soldiers. They like seeing an ungrateful fool slapped, but they like it even more if he takes his punishment with honour.'

'Would the sailors think the same?' Drake whined.

'Of course they would', Weir let out a sigh as he looked up at the town, slowly being consumed by the shadow of an immense smoke cloud. 'We'll need to settle this turn of events with the humans first before we sail. The Riverias will need some help.'

Shit. I forgot about Laura.

Drake scanned the departing crowd for Laura. He stood and began to walk to the main dock, feeling Weir's presence behind him as he scanned the crowds.

'Who are you looking for, Drake?'

'Laura Rivera', Drake replied, stopping at the crossing between two piers. 'I need to talk to her before it's too late.'

Weir tapped him on the shoulder and pointed him towards the end of the north jetty where a maiden was sitting on the stone pillars, back arched and eyes peering into the waters. Drake focused his sight, and ensured it was Laura before he ran to her. He called out her name. She looked up, showing the tear-stained cheeks of a sadness that froze his heart. *She must know. After all that she must know.*

'Laura?' He asked, walking calmly towards her. 'Is

everything alright?'

'Leave me be.'

'What's wrong?' Drake asked, stopping a few paces from her, 'What's happened?'

'Nothing', she said, wiping her eyes with a silk handkerchief embroidered with the golden wings of the sparrow. 'I asked you to leave me alone.'

'Laura, please? I need to-'

'I'm just not in the mood right now', she said. 'Please go away.'

'Can't we talk?'

'Enough', she growled, throwing the handkerchief at him as she stormed past. 'Just stay away from me!'

Drake watched as she flew past Weir towards the west docks. Her footing and her hastened escape told Drake it was serious, and probing would not help the situation. For all he knew, it could have indeed been him. Weir, curious with the exchange, walked over to him.

'She seemed angry', he said, keeping his arms folded as he stared ahead into the waters. 'What did you say to her?'

'Nothing', Drake said, showing Weir the handkerchief, 'She told me to leave her alone, and threw this at me.'

'Curious', Weir said, studying the embroidery on the handkerchief, 'She threw her tears at you – It seems you have broken her heart.'

A Mother's Love

It wasn't the first time a man and his family had begged for asylum during the Hobsythe Uprising, and Emelye knew that it wouldn't be the last. She had seen many faces with many expressions, all begging the court they listen to their stories of terror. Without the leadership of Jack Penance's word, Joanas was breaking and, like the dozens of others before him, Nassir was doing all that he could to protect his Clan.

'But why come to Centra?' Sepherance asked, stroking the stocky brown curls of his beard. 'Navuro is just as powerful as Centra, and it is entering a technological revolution. Surely it would be more fitting to keep your family there?'

Emelye turned to look at Nassir, who had his back to the Dragon Council and was kneeling on a rolled quilt of Joanarian silk. He resembled a starved worm; his leathers stuck to his bones and snagged what little flesh he had.

'My family has no place in Navuro, your Highness', he said, his brow gleaming with sweat. 'I love my sons too much to allow them to work the railroads and they have no skills beyond trading in the cities. We had nothing of value to trade for our lives in Navuro.'

'What of Draberia and Titeria then?' Sepherance asked. 'You must have made stops for provisions there, Draberia especially. Draberia would have-'

'I beg your pardon, my Lord, but we came here directly.'

The Council lit up in a myriad of distinctive chatter. The Sea of Sorrow was a very cruel mistress for the northerly travellers, and any smart man would dare not cross her waters beyond the Joanarian straight. It was clear to Emelye that Nassir was desperate, but she could not quite tell whether he was stupid, very lucky, or just a good liar.

Sepherance stood and bashed the tail of his silver

sceptre against the clawed foot of his throne. The metal clangs restored the silence as if he had roared a curse in the Dragon Tongue, and Nassir stopped pulling at his garments.

A moan of the rafters drew Emelye's eye, and she became aware of the distant sound of cathedral bells. However, she didn't drift with the tune for too long, for she soon noticed that the eyes of the court were fixed upon them both.

'You came via the Sea of Sorrow?' Sepherance asked, wetting his tongue against the silence.

'Yes, your highness', Nassir said, 'Seventeen ships left the port of Westerlock for Centra. My ship was the only one that made it here.'

'A lucky escape', Sepherance said, sitting forward. 'Is it not breeding season for the Sea Worms, Lord Thomas?'

Lord Thomas stepped forward. He was an elder Morre who had seen his fair share of travelling, yet today he held a smile humbler than the children of Dunfife and bowed like no lowlier servant.

'No, my King. But the weaker stragglers have been known to overstay their welcome after the spawning.'

'Thank you, Lord Thomas', Sepherance said, allowing the Morre to step back into the Council, 'Nassir, were you attacked by a straggler?'

'We were', Nassir said, 'But that is not what doomed most of them.'

The hurricanes, Emelye realised. *It must have been the hurricanes.*

'Sorrow was cruel to the survivors', Nassir continued. 'After we survived the worm, a storm came for the rest of us.'

'Then you owe the Torre your lives', Sepherance said, sitting back with a look of acceptance. 'What do you think of Nassir's plea, my Queen?'

Emelye smiled at him, and touched his hand as she turned to address Nassir.

'Your family, Master Nassir', she said. 'Do you envision them all as traders?'

'Yes, your Majesty', Nassir answered, bringing his hands together. 'My sons are very interested in the deals we do in the Draberian routes, and they have always loved coming to Centra to taste the wines, nectars and the juicy breast of the Gaul elk.'

'So, you bring goods to Centra and sell our exports?'

'Before the uprising', Nassir replied, 'the merchants always looked forward to handling Centurian goods. They were always very fine, your Majesty.'

'By our news, the Eastern ports were hit the hardest during the first wave of the uprising', she informed him. 'And Lord Montfort with the last. Is this correct?'

'We're from the Western shores, your Highness', Nassir said, keeping his eyes on her. 'We have not heard from the Eastern traders since the beginning, nor received any news about Lord Montfort.'

'The *Western* Shores?' She asked, catching a questioning glance from Sepherance. 'By the Torre and the Mother, the uprising is not *that* out of control, is it?'

'By all accounts it is, your Grace.' Nassir stuttered. 'Two Emperors slain, and the last unified army destroyed. Then we heard your armies were on the move, sails and rudders set for Joanas. With respect, my father fought your armies. He talked only of their strength, and the destruction in their path-'

'That's enough', Sepherance barked. 'We get the point, even if your father exaggerated. Forgive us for doubting you, but it all seems a bit far-fetched. *Especially* the part about my armies on the move. Tell me then, how did you come to learn of this information?'

'The Prince. His messenger-'

'What messenger?' interrupted Sepherance, standing up as a wave of chatter flooded the court. 'The last message from Drake stated that they were landed in Joanas-Sorrow, and it held nothing of concern or worry. By my understanding, you were lied to.'

'Please listen. Your understanding is mistaken my Great King', said Nassir, bowing and quivering. 'The bird came to me with the truth. Of how your messengers are working with our enemy. An enemy worse than the Hobsythe.'

'How dare you! These are lies. You have not spoken a word of truth. Tell me now, or else I will have you sent away.'

Emelye could see that Nassir was genuinely fearful; he dared not make eye contact with Sepherance and was hiding his face as if the Torre themselves had demanded it. She stood and placed her hand on Sepherance's shoulder.

'May I have a moment with you?' she asked.

'What is it, my Queen?' Sepherance enquired, as they both sat down.

'Look at him', she said quietly. 'He cowers under your gaze and averts his eyes when you shout at him.'

'That's because he is a weakling', Sepherance replied. 'All of them are. They are deceiving peddlers at best, making up stories about their plights. Ask the Council how many of the other beggars helped Centra. Ask them if they think the humans are worthy of being here. Then you'll understand.'

'You've always been sceptical of them, Sepherance', she whispered angrily. 'This entire Council has, but there is something about this whole situation that makes sense. The stories and the refugees, Navuro's silence-'

'My dear Emelye', said Sepherance, 'Should we listen to what this messenger has to say then? What am I to do with Nassir and his family?'

'Address the matter with the Council. As fickle the matter of asylum is, you can't keep letting humans through our gates without investigating the real problem.'

'But Drake is-'

'You've told Drake to sit on his hands until your command', she said. 'Please Sepherance. Let's listen to the message before we take a serious motion.'

Sepherance smiled and nodded before turning to the court.

'Where is this messenger?' he asked.

Nassir closed his eyes and pointed to the upper court's balustrade. There perched a falcon, looking back down at them with a pair of curious beady eyes.

'Greetings my friend. Welcome to my court', Sepherance called, watching as the bird flicked its feathers. 'We need your message. Nassir needs your message. Would you be so kind as to share it with us?'

The bird turned its head and studied Sepherance as he took a step forward and reached out his left hand.

'You may make perch on my gauntlet if you'd wish?'

The creature held its hesitant stare, before flexing its claws and opening its wings. It let out a small squeak, and then leapt off the railing. Emelye watched as it glided down over the heads of the Council, taking note of its familiar colours and grace as it landed on Sepherance's gauntlet.

Sepherance took a moment to study the creature's form. It appeared the two of them were judging each other with their calculating stares and silence. Emelye was unsure of what Sepherance intended, because he was granting her more time on his gauntlet than usual. *He had never taken so well to a strange bird before.*

'Nassir', Sepherance said, keeping his eyes on the bird as he stroked his beard. 'Where did you say you found this creature?'

Nassir was muttering a Joanarian hymn into the golden dragon of the carpet. At Sepherance's address he fell silent and slowly raised his head.

'She landed on our ship during the second night of awaiting the tides', he said. 'Many of the others were in doubts, hoping it was all rumours. But this beautiful bird, Mother bless her, confirmed everything.'

Judging by the Council's reaction, and Sepherance's look of realisation, something was amiss. The bird's ears were scanning every word that clattered around the hall.

'What is it, my King?'

'She is one of ours', said Sepherance.

'But what is the significance of that?' she asked. 'We have messengers fly out to all corners of Alcadia and to the Dragon Lords.'

Sepherance smiled at her and shook his head.

'This is the one I used specifically with Stanley Penance.' He turned to the falcon and stroked the base of her neck with the tip of his metal fingers. 'I thought we had lost you, and I think I remember your name. Krista, was it?'

The bird tweeted and clicked her left claw against his gauntlet, as if correcting him. Emelye knew of the bird language only in familiarity, recognising some of the gestures from the countless bird messenger addresses in court and royal functions.

'Ah yes: Kristen, that's it. If you would be so kind Kristen, I'd like to know about Master Nassir. How did he and his family treat you, and do his words speak truth?'

The bird's return was a structured paragraph. It came through as if a long, instrumental song.

'Very good', Sepherance replied, smiling towards Nassir. 'You have been redeemed. He speaks the truth! Now, tell me – what of this message, is it really from Drake?'

Kristen scanned the room before beginning her passage. It seemed to go on far longer than the first, and used more syllables Emelye might have recognised if she had studied the bird language in more depth.

But there was one word she knew towards the end, repeated at the tip of Kristen's speech as if spoken in urgency. The word was Drake. She knew it down to the syllable, the scratch and click of the beak. She would know his name in any language.

Sepherance cast his eyes down to the floor. Emelye expected him to frown, but he did not. Instead his eyes returned to her, poised and just as alert as they were when they had gazed into the sheen of the marble.

'Very enlightening, thank you. Were you able to find any trace of Stanley's family?' he asked, as the whispers passed around the room.

Kristen answered him, without a chirp towards the court.

'No- I thought as much. My final question; is it as bad as he says it is?'

The whispers were being exchanged faster now. They spoke of the Commanders, their decision to sail to Joanas, and of Drake. But Kristen's final words forced the Council into a silent shock. Sepherance, although now holding a troubled stare, simply smiled and nodded.

'That'll be all', he said, 'Thank you, Kristen.'

Kristen was quick to leave Sepherance behind, locked in a vacant stare. By the time she disappeared into the rafters, his carrier arm was by his side and he was scratching at his forehead. Like a crow that had lost a good meal, Sepherance slowly trundled back to his throne and dropped into the arms of the Dragon with a slow thud.

'What's wrong, Sepherance? What did she say?' Emelye asked.

Sepherance rubbed his head, took in an extra huff of the court's air, and looked at Emelye with the eyes of a Morre broken by news.

'We've been betrayed by a silent enemy. Unseen, like a snake hidden in plain sight.'

'How can there be someone other than Kinas Kirk involved in the uprising?' Emelye asked.

'The Commanders suspected it', he explained with a flutter to his words. 'The First Fleet suspected it as well. They've sailed for Joanas because of it.'

The court's silence held the air. Sepherance's tongue paused, and Emelye watched as he scanned the crowd.

'You heard the message. Every one of you. No Snuggle-Tail would dare lie, or hide a lie at that. Summon the Imperial Army and ready the King's Armada. We sail with all intentions to reinforce the First Army, and bring the Commanders to boot. Besides, they'll need all the help they can get.'

Sepherance stood, leaving his sceptre so he could address Nassir. 'Nassir, where has your family made port?'

'They remain in the City of Citadel my Lord', Nassir replied. 'What would you have us do?'

'I will have a messenger sent to Lord Destrin', Sepherance said. 'Until Centra resolves the conflict, you and your family will remain there. If Lords Destrin or Thomas will the work of your hands, or the hands of your sons, it would be in your best interests to oblige them.'

'Thank you, Sire', Nassir said, falling to his knees and raising his arm. 'I am in eternal debt to you.'

'Leave that with your person. I can't have you owing the Crown deeds. You are our guests, and you will be treated as such.'

Nassir smiled, and Sepherance returned to the foot of his throne.

'Now leave us, all of you. The Queen and I must discuss this turn of events. We shall convene on the morrow after the messengers have flown.'

With lowered heads and humbled smiles, the court headed towards the main door and streamed out into the streets of Morkor. Emelye was always impressed with the way they made their leave. She waved to the guards to close the great panels of Dunferian Pine behind the last Councillor.

Sepherance spent the next few moments breathing heavily, supporting his head against his palm with a look of despair.

'What are we to do with the Commanders, my Queen?'

Emelye offered her left hand to console him.

'The rules are clear, an example should be made of them', she said, reminiscing the words of duty penned in the ink of the Torre. 'Exile them, perhaps?'

Sepherance sighed the temper away from his face, kissed her hand and stood.

'You don't just exile the First Army's Commanders, my Queen', he said, bringing his hands together behind his back as he gazed up into the rafters. 'Lord Gromwell sacrificed his son for the freedoms of the Fugulian people and our victory in the East. What am I supposed to tell the Free Countries when they receive the father of a legend of Sanctity on their shores? Let's not forget the debt we owe for his service to Drake- he took him in as his student without complaint or demand. There is much left to be desired in Drake, yes, but he is a far greater Morre than he would have been without Gromwell. With the right push-'

'Sepherance, please', Emelye objected. 'Don't hide from the discussion with your hopes and regrets for Drake again.'

Sepherance turned to her. His eyes had widened and his lips were pursed. He kept his arms locked, and his chest stiff whilst she gazed upon his glistening brow. Although the subject was sensitive and the mood sharp, she could not help but relate his stance to a dog, listening to his keeper as if the world had come to a standstill.

'Edward is also my greatest champion', he said, lowering his eyes. 'The entire army would follow him rather than discredit his name. As for Jefferson, his exploits and rumoured history grant him enough respect in this Council to start a ruse. As for Bartarian-'

'That brute is a different beast entirely', Emelye concluded. 'He considers the court a pack of unworthy charlatans – Drake especially. I still say it was by Bartarian's influence that those Morre spoke ill of Drake in the eyes of the Torre.'

'That influence would not only be Drake's undoing. We'd lose Carpathia the moment the word landed in its streets, and on the following day we'd have a mob at our front gates.'

'We'd need to dream up something dire to make them

understand, then.'

'We'd need something honest.' Sepherance let out a snort, as he flashed his chuckling frown at her. 'What a terrible decision we have before us, my love.'

'Not that terrible if you consider how influential Captain Weir is in this moment. He is also from Carpathia, isn't he?'

'I don't think it would be enough to sway the entire city.'

'It might if he was acting under the banner of Drake?' Her ideas were beginning to take shape in her mind, yet she exercised caution where her own influence grew. She respected Sepherance, and ensured enough of his power was granted to him through his own efforts and thoughts.

'You're right', he began. 'It sounded as if he was following Drake's banner, yes. This might work to our advantage. But it would mean we'd need to make an example of Drake.'

'Drake's always had a disdain towards matters of honour or Royal Station. I think you know as well as I what that would mean, especially considering how excited he was when he learned he was going to Joanas-Sorrow.'

'He never mentioned such excitement to me. It's almost as if we weren't on the same page as we were before his hundredth year. What has changed in him, what am I doing wrong?'

Emelye leant a little closer to him, shaking her head as she remembered the times when Drake would look upon his father with the eyes of a puppy.

'Drake is growing up to be a fine Morre, Sepherance', she assured him. 'How was your relationship with your father when you were such an age?'

Sepherance huffed, studying the head of the Dragon.

'He'd give us his orders from behind a table full of books, sipping on his nectar. Most of the time he didn't even look at me.'

'Maybe that is the problem', she advised. 'You're not

your father. It's all good and well encouraging him to lead an army, giving him orders and punishing him as if he were one of your Commanders. What he really needs is some compassion; a little fatherly talk.'

'And perhaps some discipline.'

Emelye smiled at him. 'Only when required.'

'I can't flog the boy or lock him in the dungeons, Emelye. He'd lose all control of the soldiery, and his Kingship would be as good as dead.'

Emelye's mind was weaving together another idea as if it were one of her family tapestries.

'Aren't you leading most of the Centurian Army to Joanas?'

'Of course!'

'Perhaps we could name him protectorate?'

It was an interesting concept, forcing the title upon him. He liked to avoid any kind of court summons or affair, preferring instead to ride his horse or mingle with the crowds. Emelye thought that if the weight of the country were to fall upon Drake's shoulders, he may take it as a message to take responsibility for his family name and be the leader he was born to be.

Sepherance seemed interested, for his gaze had come closer.

'But what about you? How do we run him as protectorate if you are still here?'

'We could stage a call to reserve. A drill if it would please you?'

Sepherance shook his head.

'The court wouldn't allow it. I think we should use it as punishment, and make it clear with the Commanders. With that in mind, we also bring the Dance of the Skylarks forward.'

Emelye stopped her train of thought on the dance. She knew he would be upset, and she knew Drake would hate them for it.

'That may be too rash, Sepherance.'

'Nonsense! If duty is his punishment, then it must come forward in every term. I will not have him make a mockery of our most crucial law whilst holding court.'

'But that is a human law, not ours.'

'It's human only in the aggregate of the Dragon Keeper order.'

Sepherance would not reason, and she knew it.

'He'd destroy more than the peace between us and Joanas if he were to wed a maiden of the lesser clans. This must be done. It must be complete before the fool falls for someone.'

Emelye's head lowered against the pounding tone of her husband's voice, and merely nodded.

'As you wish, Great Father.'

'Stop that. You know I hate it when you do that.'

Emelye's eyes shot back up.

'Then at least speak to him before you forsake his bedding.'

Sepherance's hand was raised, clenched and pointing at her.

'Fine then. I will speak to him before I bring the dance forward. But it is still coming forward.' Sepherance blew out a long sigh. 'My father would burn the light back onto his candle to know, Emelye. Death on the Peaks of the Forgotten Kingdoms, for what?'

'Maybe he would be marrying the Morre he loved-'

'Stop it', he barked. 'You know it is not that simple.'

'It's simple enough for Drake.'

Sepherance slumped back into his throne, making every effort not to meet her gaze. There was no way hers would be the words to break the silence.

'Was there ever someone, Emelye?'

'Of course not, you old fool', she said, humouring him. 'Maybe he will fall for one of the girls we selected? If we let him meet them before we could-'

'No', he groaned, getting back up onto his feet. 'For my entire family line, there was never any courting of a

Prospective Skylark. Not with Grandmother, Mother, and not even you. It is a sacred passage of rights, not some…some sleaze's ball!'

'All right', Emelye huffed, standing and storming towards her drawing room. 'Message received.'

'Emelye, wait-'

'Enough for now, Sepherance', she barked. 'I need a moment to myself.'

And with that, she slammed the door on him.

By the Torre, Sepherance, she stewed. *Of all the times to be stubborn for the good of Centra, he's your only child.*

'Your majesty?' called a handmaiden from the shadows of the lamplight.

'Yes, Raisa?'

'A messenger awaits your leave outside. I believe you have already seen her, so I took the message in case you didn't wish to again.'

Raisa was always a good girl. Her mother had to go into early retirement, and she had quickly taken her place. She had a good attitude, and a close understanding of a Queen's routine, just like the woman before her. It was a relief, and the thought of it was already eating away her anger.

'Thank you', she said with a smile. 'I'll read it immediately. Please thank the messenger for me.'

With a deep curtsey, the girl produced a tiny scroll from her sleeve. It must have been important; no one would waste good ink for such a small message.

'Who was it from?' Emelye enquired, just before Raisa slipped away.

'Tiana Rivera, your Majesty', she replied. 'By request of Captain Weir.'

That only meant trouble. Sitting down, she unrolled the paper and took in the first words, knowing them to be the harbingers of her worst fear. Halfway in, a tear had materialised, and by then the fear for her son was grave enough.

‘Oh Drake’, she sighed sadly. ‘You young fool.’

For the Pleasure

The darkness of the Joanarian night covered the landscape, with small wisps of fire signalling the only source of light for miles. If Jack wanted to, he could close his eyes and see what the millions of souls outside were doing, especially those animating the Fallen. But he chose not to this particular night. He had taken the life of a man's daughter and mentally fractured another. The whole ordeal had him deep in thought, and his mind was taking him places where the rot could not follow. It dragged him deep into the memory of his killing, allowing the flagon he held to slip in his grasp.

He recalled the terrible wails of his daughters as, one after the other, they were raped and eaten alive. The screams of Ella haunted him. If he tried to let go, or clear his train of thought, the sickening laugh of Kinas would storm into his mind and restart the process. He tried to support his head with the flagon and then, realising this was foolish, dropped his arm back down to his side and let the other try to support his misery.

'Jack', whispered an unwelcome voice that tickled his senses.

He looked around, trying to locate the source of the voice. After several swirls and stares, he concluded that it was just teasing him. He closed his eyes and opened his mouth to take a sip of the nectar.

'Jack', the voice called again, this time booming.

Jack dropped the flagon, causing it to clang against the stone floor. This had happened before, many times, but he couldn't explain why. The thoughts and memories of that horrible torture moved him so much, that when *the voice* talked to him, he would break down into a crying mess. His thoughts went from one side of the turning to the other, like the battering of a thousand human skulls against the hull of a boat in a storm. From feeling bereaved and sickened at the loss of his family, to curdling hatred towards his father.

'What am I doing?' he wailed. 'All of these people. Their families and their homes – What am I doing?'

He stopped sobbing and looked to the grand window, its steel frame tucked neatly inside the stone, rusted and ready to break. With enough of a run up, he could knock the entire frame from its support and plunge into the depths of the city below.

'What are you doing, Jack? We know you won't do it. There is so much to be done.'

'Shut up', ordered Jack. 'You know nothing about me!'

'We know you enough.'

Jack turned from the window and gauged the needed distance in his head. He began to pace towards it, denial running through his mind.

'You don't control me.'

'The plan controls you now.'

'You don't run my life.'

'You don't have a life any more, Jack.'

He turned and faced the window, where the blackness of the shadow covered his naked form. Its invitation was now a door, well-oiled and unlocked. He called it a *door to freedom* on the last day. Smiling at it, he prepared his footing to break out into a run.

'I have a life – I'll get it back. I'll get it back!'

He sprinted towards the window. His heart did not thump and his lungs did not reel. His muscles simply obeyed, and never fatigued. He screamed at the window, willing it to break. It did not. Worse – the roaring Torre-like spectre he'd seen before appeared in front his eyes, filling his mind with its voice.

Just as before, he panicked, slipped and lost his footing during the final pace before salvation. However, this time his head smashed through the glass pane, and his right arm broke through the one next to its destroyed sister. He blacked out for a few seconds before awakening to his failure.

'No', he wailed as he hung from the window.

After releasing his self-pity, he settled himself. His thoughts were blank as he watched the little droplets of blood flow over his knuckles and leap into the darkness below.

'Why won't you let me die?' he bellowed as the tide of red rain began to slow. 'Why?'

'Because of the plan we agreed, Jack.' The voice did not comfort him, nor did it make him quiver in fear. It was just there, speaking. 'It was your will.'

'These horrors are beyond me', he cried. 'I can't follow the plan like this. I will find a way to escape whatever this is, I promise you that.'

'You need to be fed, Jack.'

Jack closed his eyes as he remembered what was to happen next. Just as before, a strange feeling crept over him as if he were being doused in a pool of liquid fire. If he opened his eyes, the liquid would seep into their sockets and blind him with the rage he did not want.

He had to keep them closed this time. He had to remain aware of what he was doing to the world, and he had to keep his conscience if he were to escape. But the doom was washing over him, and the liquid was drawing closer. He felt his body being pulled up, and the liquid covering his wounds as it re-assembled his flesh. It tickled his eyelids. *No. Fuck you. Fuck the plan. Fuck them all.*

'I will not open my eyes!' he asserted, as the coldness of the rock stroked his feet.

'We will open them for you.'

Jack shook his head and gritted his teeth in defiance. 'No!'

The Hatred stroked his neck as it moved up to his chin, and as he screamed out his last free breath. It forced his eyes to open and behold its presence. The black mist in the form of a Torre sparked into his very soul, its bright, white eyes crushing it as its silk-like tentacles covered his pupils in hate. It was there his hatred towards his father exploded tenfold, and he fell into a timeless blackout.

***

In the darkness and dreams of the thousand hurting tongues, Jack roused from his black throne, still naked and with a new scar running down his right arm. He looked at the broken window as if it were just another crack in his history, and cursed it in the Dragon Tongue.

'Grigor!' Jack shouted at the top of his voice.

He waited for a moment, and listened as the mud-goblin's waddling paces filled the hall. When he arrived, he was presented by a much larger belly than he had expected. Jack looked at him in disgust and turned his eyes back on the window.

'You're such a disgusting pig. Was it another soldier?'

'Yes, Master', said Grigor with a whimper.

'What happens when we run out of soldiers to turn?' asked Jack, scowling at the mud-goblin. 'Will you start snacking on the turned men, then?'

'If Master wishes it.'

'I won't', said Jack, pointing his finger at the beast. 'I need them for the fight against the Dragon King. Can you not feast on the other mud goblins?'

'They taste like soil, Master', said Grigor.

'You need the minerals', said Jack as he turned back to the window. 'Man-flesh just makes you obese.'

Jack slapped the creature's stomach. 'Summon one of the girls for me.'

'Is there any preference of choice, my Master?'

'Bring me the one you'd like to eat the most.'

Although barely audible, Jack heard a snort from Grigor's nose. He smiled in self-gratification, and began to ponder which girl would come strolling into the throne room as he sat down. There were many creatures of beauty down there. He'd be greeted by fear but, with a slight tickle of his influence, whoever it was would honour him with their pleasure.

Yet he knew he should have felt something there, eating away at him. He was sure it was the thought of his wife, but it was blocked by the Hatred. Any memory of her could only come to him like the screams of his daughters could –when the hate was wearing down and running out. He'd have to do it all over again if he were to feel the warmth of her memory.

As he wallowed, the pitter-patter of bare feet filled the room. He turned to behold the smooth skin of a woman with hair just as dark as the Hatred's mist. She was young, pert and far beyond her flowering judging from the way her form was shaped. She humbly shielded her breasts with her bony arms.

'Cold, dear?' he asked her, as he picked up his robe.

'No', she whimpered, not daring to look at him. These were the ones he loved the most; the ones that were scared and barely touched. He tossed the robe back onto the throne, and took slow steps towards her.

Ever since the turning, his body's needs had become ravenous. His emotions were dulled, as well as his pain, but his other senses were more receptive, and his lust was like that of a boy who had just discovered his adulthood. Fucking everything that moved, or even himself if he were ever caught bored and alone.

Excited and warm, with his throat dry and skin tingling, Jack reached out for the girl. The touch of his fingertips caused her to reel and whine. He caught a good picture of her face, burning it into the back of his mind. She looked limp with fear and her face was wet with tears, but she still looked tasty. *Very, very tasty.*

'I can make it easier for you', said Jack in the Joanarian tongue, as he reached out for her again. 'You do not have to suffer this.'

'No', she begged. 'Please leave me alone.'

This time she allowed him to touch her, and although she trembled, her fear steadied and her breathing slowed.

As he slowly brushed his fingers against her arm, he began to read her as he did with so many others.

It was a familiar story now. A farmer's family caught in the takeover, dragged to the Capital and forced to watch as each family member was subdued and tortured. All except for her were killed, and she only survived because Jack's minions knew that she would turn his eye. He cared not for her name, but only for the effect she may have on him. Her mind was battered and broken, and would not wilfully entice her to serve him. In these situations, he would focus his power on her mind and create a haze over it, making her think that she was safe and with a former lover. A former lover he was about to find.

His hands cupped her head, forcing her to look up at him with glazed eyes and a quivering lip. As soon as the connection was made, he began to read her memories. It was a happy, albeit slightly sheltered life she had led, yet it had its surprises. Jack soon learned of the son of a merchant who had settled in the city. They just happened to pass by her father's farm one day, forced to seek shelter from a storm.

As he read her and began to guide her thoughts, he could sense her becoming ever more ecstatic. Their first meeting was only light conversation, sharing memories and bonds like children would do, but as the years passed and they grew closer to adulthood, they began to lust for one another.

They were awkward encounters at first. Many nights of sneaking out took place, and it thrilled Jack to feel their young love blossom. After a few sexual encounters, he had her fondest memories in his grasp, and the sessions were now extremely passionate and would sometimes last the whole night.

The coming encounter was everything he could have hoped for. He shrouded her mind in the dream, took his role as he did for many others before her, and released her head. No longer were her eyes curdled with fear, for they were now in her father's barn after a long and lonely weekend away from one another.

Her eyes were sparkling with the tenderness of her arousal. She placed her hands on his chest, pushed her head upwards and began to kiss him. With the choreography of the dream playing in his mind, he played along as if he were enslaved to his own trickery. She led the dance by taking him in her grasp, stroking and rubbing him as she imagined him inside of her.

She moved her head downwards, and took him inside her mouth. Jack closed his eyes and clenched his fists as he felt the warmth engulf him. He throbbed with every caress of her lips, enjoying the wetness now covering him. As the heightening sense of excitement grew deep within him, she pulled him down and laid him on the floor.

Needy and now fumbling in her excitement, she hovered over him and opened her legs to calmly pull him inside of her. As soon as he was in, she began to ride him. He could not help but kiss her breasts as he felt each tickling rush run up his spine. With each thrust she would whine and he would moan, enjoying the sounds of each other's excitement as they kept moving together in the dream. Moving together in the lie.

She soon yelled out in ecstasy, rubbing the tenderness of her body as she climaxed. Jack continued as his pleasure quickly brought him to the edge. He wailed out in happiness, and she slowed to a stop before releasing him. His lifeless seed dripping from her, both breathed a sigh of relief as the sweat rolled down their bodies.

She opened her eyes and looked at him, her head leaning backwards and arms spread wide, still taking in breaths of satisfaction.

'David?' she asked as she began to tremble.

'No, my dear', said Jack as he pushed her to the side. 'I am not David.'

She brought her hand to her mouth, and began to sob in her realisation. Jack ignored her, walked over to his office and put on his leathers for formal appearances with his minions. The wailing was a comfort for his ears, considering he could no longer grieve for his wife.

'There is no remorse for the Fallen, child. Be grateful that I *only* enjoyed your warmth.'

Although continuing to cry, she had stopped wailing. Pulling on his shirt, he returned to the throne room to look at her. She had found a large piece of glass that could pass as a dagger. When her eyes found him, he merely gave her a questioning stare, taunting her with his fearless look.

'I'll stab you!' she warned as she rushed towards him.

He held his stare as she approached. When she reached him, she did not hesitate in plunging the blade straight into his heart. It felt like a scratch followed by a cold pressure, the power of the Hatred blocking any pain.

She pushed the glass in deeper. He pushed back, allowing the shard to penetrate further. Blood seeped through her grasp and down his shirt. He grabbed both of her wrists and forced her hands away from him.

'This is my favourite shirt!' he exclaimed as he raised her hands above her head. 'I can't have you tearing up and bloodying my favourite shirt!'

He looked down at the precious garment, seething with rage. It was torn through and the hole was saturated with blood.

'Do you have any idea who made this for me?' he shouted, releasing one of her wrists and slapping her face so hard that she fell to the floor.

'You tricked me', she cried, clutching her bright pink cheek. 'You're a monster!'

Jack reached for the shard and began to pull. Although the pain was worsening, he gritted his teeth against it and gave a mere flinch as it came away from his flesh. With a quick inspection of his new scar, he threw the shard at the girl.

'Yes, I am a monster, my dear', he said, storming towards her and grabbing her by the chin. 'But we all are, every one of us. We are capable of such terrible atrocities, and expect no punishment for it.'

Still holding her chin, he picked up the shard and placed the bloodied end against her cheek.

'I have already paid for my crimes, and I expect the rest of you to do the same. Such a terrible shame it is, though. If only you hadn't ruined my favourite shirt. We could have fucked until the end of time.'

Jack felt the girl's control drift from her body as he slowly claimed it. He wiped the blood from her brow, kissed it, and allowed her to take the shard.

'Goodbye, my sweet. Rest with your sins and tell your family you have done well.'

Her wails rumbled against her locked jaw as her hand guided the shard upwards until it pieced and ripped through her throat. Blood poured from the cut as if it were nectar from a bottle and pooled at her knees as she fell to the floor in a heap. Once she had stopped moving, Jack looked down at her lifeless body and shook his head. *A great fuck,* he mused to himself, *but with no hope for life.*

'Feed this one to your mud brothers, Grigor', he ordered, raising his finger. 'Remember – not for you. You need your minerals. You fat, idiotic, mud-boned freak.'

He hesitated for a moment. *Was I too rash?* However one look at the mud-goblin, slouching there feeling sorry for himself, told him the answer to that particular question. *No.*

He gathered his thoughts and used them to channel his emotions into a ball of rage. Closing his eyes and holding his breath, he soon found himself in the frozen world of the Grey.

In the Grey he could not fatigue, nor could he concern himself with provisions. His body's functions were as frozen as the millions of slaves in his birthing Empire. Here, he could take every one of their lives in an instant, but that was the extent of his power. Outside of that zone, steadily covering all Joanas, he was as weak as Thias and

Drake. *But that will change soon*, he assured himself.

With a breathless sigh and a disgusted look at Grigor's frozen form, he began the journey to the City of the Forgotten Kingdoms. Unfortunately for now, he had to go on foot, but time and energy held no quarter here. This existence was known as *The Afterlife Time has Forgotten,* and it was here he first met the Hatred.

Upon arrival to the city, he found that Sirius and Ouster had already ploughed through the Western Country with his armies. The fires and the chains of defeat littered the farmlands and blackened the townships. The path to the Forgotten Kingdoms began at the base of the great southern peaks, once guarded over by a magnificent gate. Now, however, a shadow of its former self lay in a pile on the side of the track. The iron of the gate was forged by the Firth-Wrights when they came to Joanas, seeking a haven from the terrors of the Dragon-Lorre. *Nothing but myths and fantasies. They must have come here because of the famines.*

The path snaked through the pale-tipped peaks with little care for the horses or carts that traversed it. The hamlets on the lower region were unfamiliar to Jack, with pale foundation stones and bricks that were fired during the current century. Not even Sirius or Ouster were able to taint their freshness, despite smashing them to rubble. But, higher into the mountains, the towns grew older, with their walls made from the very crags that towered above them. The people in these towns held out against the fires that tried to break them over the countless Ages of the Joanarian Wars, but their experience could not save them. The scorched ghosts of their houses and businesses were a reminder of just how temporary they really were.

As he advanced towards the remains of the Black Forest, he was greeted by a cindering mass grave which surrounded the Capital of the Forgotten Kingdoms. Although small in comparison to Alcadia's other cities, its walls were twice the size of Negura's, making the grave appear huge. Her tallest building rivalled Jack's citadel, with a majesty surrounding its stonework as if every piece of masonry were carved by the artisans of the Torre. As his eyes took in its beauty, he noticed a column of tar-black smoke rising from the building's centre. *Has it been taken already?*

His minions were looming, all focused on the main gate in their tight formation. As Jack passed through each gap, it became apparent that a fire had started in the heart of the city. Walking through the ranks was like sniffing in the highs of the Centurian tick-leaf; the souls of the inhabitants filled his mind with promises of his destruction. It was these thoughts that excited him the most.

However, this excitement came at a price. The thoughts also reminded him of the Hatred, and what they may do if he didn't co-operate with his end of the bargain. He stopped for a moment and considered whether it really would be as bad as he feared. *It may not matter for me, but what of my daughters? What of Emma? What of my brothers and sister?*

It wasn't fear that came over him. It felt more like remorse, or a concern that would make a normal Morre tremble. He could feel his mind digging deeper into the pit of despair, but the blockade the Hatred had on him was powerful. Worse, he could feel a new, somewhat disturbing sensation deep within his consciousness.

He continued to search for Sirius and Ouster among the crowds, but could not distinguish them from the thousands of Fallen. Each figure was opaque with the brightness of their souls burning through their armour. If he even tried to listen to their thoughts, he'd be overwhelmed by the constant battering of the souls against their consciousness. However, he knew Sirius would look different to all the others, for his existence was based upon a constant connection with the Hatred.

It didn't take him long. In any area where there had

been a killing, Sirius could usually be found feasting on the lingering spirits. In the Black, where time had control, he looked like a sea monster plucking fleeing specks from the air. When Jack found him, he was almost as tall as the towers of the city, reaching into the bowels of the clouds. Of course, he was frozen with the rest of his minions, but that didn't stop him making sense of how long they had been there. He paced around the walls to where the creature's bust began and leapt back into existence. Upon arrival, he noticed the screams and the men's faces filled with horror, which they attempted to hide upon noticing his stare.

'Don't hide your feelings, my friends', he shouted over the wails. 'Your feelings are what keep you alive, and what keep you aware.'

'But there are women and children in there', replied a man to his left.

Jack looked at him. He was a thin, sickly shadow of a man, apparently beginning to realize the errors of his choices.

'I know', he said, taking a step towards him. 'Would you rather them suffer the torture of those in Negura?'

'No, my Lord', the man replied. 'It's just hard to ignore.'

Jack compared the outspoken to the man on his right. He was broader, taller and stronger. He then compared him to the one on the left, who was an even greater man than the first. He looked beyond and behind him, they too seemed far more capable than this one who spoke to him.

'You're an interesting lamp amongst lifeless beasts. Who are you?'

'I am Thomas', he replied, showing no fear at all. 'Thomas of the Elkwood.'

Jack's taste for fear was as strong as the Hatred's thirst. He could smell the terror radiating from the broader men, but it was absent from the man he addressed. Only a man with no family, or no hope, could be so fearless before him.

'What purpose do you have amongst these ranks, so close to the front?'

The man looked at him with saddened eyes.

'They said I was expendable', he said. 'That I should be put with the rest of the useless bodies.'

Jack gestured for him to step forward. He obliged.

'Come with me. I may have some use for you.'

Use indeed, what were those fools thinking?

'Sirius, Ouster', he called. 'Why is this man in the forward ranks?'

Sirius' face, absent of any life except for the jewels of his eyes, looked at Thomas as if he were any other, before turning back to the city.

'A weakling has no place amongst the Knights, my Lord', he said, with the thousand voices of the Hateful echoing in Jack's mind. 'Do you not agree?'

'The man is absent of any fear', said Jack. 'Have you actually looked at him? Have you smelt him?'

He turned to Ouster, who seemed just as absent as Sirius.

'What about you Ouster? You're no stranger to another man's fear. Can you not see it?'

Ouster's eyes studied and compiled Thomas' complexion as if he were a mud goblin.

'I follow only your will, Master', he replied, staring at the ground. 'That will was extended from Sirius, my Lord.'

'He's exactly what we are looking for you imbeciles', erupted Jack. 'We can't disrupt the Dragon Prince's attack, let alone the Dragon King's attack, if we are sending our best assassins to die like unwanted cattle!'

His minions became more alert and approachable following the scolding, particularly Ouster, who looked curious.

'Disrupt, my Lord?' he asked.

'Yes', said Jack. 'You didn't think I was going to kill the King and all of his Morre, did you?'

'What about the Prince?'

'He's not a threat', replied Jack. 'If he becomes a problem, he will be easily dispatched.'

Letters of the Musket

'Behind you', called the voice again.

The Fallen growled as its piercing eyes caught Drake's gaze, and he jolted awake, opening his eyes to a dark room and the calming slosh of waves. His dreams of late had him worrying about silly things, almost as if he were a child. But, as he listened and breathed in the air, his only concern was the slow rock of the ship.

He stood up and reached for his little oil lamp, which he used to locate his dressing gown. Throwing it on and tying it tightly, he made for the cabin door and, with a creek, he was away into the lower decks, heading for the stairwell at the rear of the ship.

When he reached the threshold of the stairs, he stopped and listened for any recognisable voices. Thankfully he heard no Western accent, only the common King's tongue and the occasional Northerner. No sooner had he decided it was safe to proceed, than he was startled by the sensation of a rough hand squeezing his shoulder.

'Off for a midnight snack?', asked Gromwell sarcastically.

'Sorry –I wanted to see if we were near land', Drake replied, studying his mentor for signs of sickness. 'Are you okay? I haven't seen you since we left.'

'I'm fine. Fighting back a headache of all things'.

He sat down on the lower steps. 'Is it true you stood up to Bartarian?'.

'Not so much stood up as took his beating', Drake replied, taking a seat next to him. 'In front of everybody, no less. Since then I have seen him around, but he has kept to his own business. Jefferson hasn't stopped pestering me about the whole ordeal though.'

'Ah, good old Jefferson. And what of Laura?'

Drake pulled the handkerchief from his top pocket and handed it over wordlessly.

'Oh dear', he sighed. 'Now we're in trouble.'

'I know. Why did I have to lie to her, Edward?'

'Because you're an idiot', the old master huffed, tossing the kerchief back at him. 'I was actually talking about you keeping the bloody thing. Do you have any idea how to handle something like this?'

'What else am I supposed to do with it?'

'Didn't your mother teach you anything about a lady's tears?' Gromwell groaned as Drake stood up. 'What are your feelings?'

'I-I don't know-'

'Liar. You want her, I can tell by the way you're holding the thing', he snapped. 'You should have set fire to it! By rights I should have thrown it overboard for you. At least that way her tears wouldn't fall alone.'

'It's just a handkerchief, Edward', Drake insisted. 'All this talk of tradition is making me seasick.'

'Fool. Tradition and laws might save you, you know. Besides, Walter said the same thing.'

'I thought you said he never married?'

'He fell for someone.' Gromwell let out a pained sigh as he closed his eyes. 'Before Forecourt, on the fields of Nukuoro after our landing, he met some girl during the main encounter. He described her as the 'classic Astorian huntress'. You know, well built, stronger than a Morre-man, very masculine, and with those brunette locks every young fool fancies.'

'She sounds like a good match for him. What happened?'

'She was in the First Division.'

The First Division was on the front line in the Battle of Forecourt, where the Lorre's venom fire rained down the hardest. Those Morre suffered the worst casualties, with Walter and Drake being stationed in the Third. But even from that position, the screams of the Morre were loud enough to drown out everything.

'Are you saying Walter's death was attributed to this Morre's death?'

'I'm just saying - It may have been the catalyst.' Gromwell sighed away the memory. 'No sane Morre would go running into the enemy's final stand like that, its…'

'Hey', Weir called from above. 'Who goes there? Show yourselves!'

Gromwell started, his head turning to look up at him. Drake could just make out Weir's face looking back down, but he knew he wasn't alone. Cautiously, he stepped back into the shadow of the galley.

'Where's the other one?' Weir's companion barked from above. Drake recognised the voice as Captain Gerald's, but he remained hidden away until Gromwell beckoned him forward.

'Prince Drake', Weir greeted him with a smile. 'How long have you two been down there?'

'Long enough', said Gromwell, his tone shifting from cautious to demanding. 'What in the name of the Torre are both of you doing here? Isn't your next command meeting just before landing?'

Gerald had no care for Edward's questions. His eyes were firmly fixed on Drake, making him feel uneasy.

'My concerns have been, and always will be, for the Centurian Navy', Weir insisted. 'If that means allowing my colleagues to come aboard without authority then so be it!'

It was clear to Drake that he'd missed something important. Weir was stern and fair with his words, but Gromwell's scowl grew deeper with every passing syllable. As he pondered what he might have missed, his eyes wandered back towards Gerald's scowling face.

'Is there a problem, Captain?'

Gerald looked briefly down at his sword as it dangled from his grasp, weaving slowly from side to side. Upon looking up his gaze was as piercing as before, and he gave an insubordinate spit to the side.

'How dare you Captain!' Weir barked at this display of defiance. 'What by the Torre has gotten into you?'

He managed to come between them both before any blow was exchanged. Despite his own rage, he could feel Gerald pushing against him as if a desperate weasel.

'Royal pups don't belong with the First Fleet', Gerald barked. 'You're unworthy of the respect it holds in Alcadia!'

'Enough - lower your tone', Weir hissed back, his eyes still on Drake. 'Every flagship has carried the crown. You know this'

'Every flagship carries the King!' Gerald replied, still struggling against him. 'Not some half-crown!'

'He's beginning to anger even me now', said Gromwell, his stare locked on the ill-tempered Captain. 'Shut him up before he rouses the sailors.'

'Keep talking fire, you filthy chamber slave', growled Gerald. 'Your family name is scratched on his ass.'

'Enough of this!' Weir shouted, shoving the bastard back. 'This is extraordinary behaviour Gerald, even for you. You will answer me, or I will throw you in the brig.'

Gerald froze, his eyes squarely on his fellow Captain. For a moment, he looked ready to stab him, but it was fleeting, and in its place came confusion. He retreated.

'In the name of the Torre, speak damn it!'

'Forgive me', Gerald stuttered. 'I don't know. I think ill of the Prince if I were to tell the truth but – but not to you. Not like this.'

Gromwell had squared up to the Captain. 'Then what in the name of the Torre was that?'

'I don't know', Gerald answered, his voice trailing off to a squeak. 'I don't know – I swear. I only meant to ask your business, but then-'

His eyes found Drake and immediately turned on him once again. The empathy drained from his face as if he had been possessed.

'You're rotten filth boy! Unworthy of your title!'

He lunged for the Prince, ignoring Weir's clawing hands. Luckily for him, Gromwell caught the insolent dog, but was struggling against the barrage of fists and curses.

'Shut him up!' Drake cried, wincing as the two Commanders struggled to restrain him.

'You will die!' Gerald snarled. 'The hounds will feast on your eyes and the crows will send your skin to the unseen enemy! Remember my words! Don't take them as folly!'

He broke free again, this time hurtling straight towards Drake. In turn the Prince thrust his writing arm back, fist held level with his shoulder for a strike.

With a crack, Gerald tripped and fell onto the deck with a loud grunt. His lifeless face was less than a pace from his foot, making Drake's anger drain against the shock. Whether it was intuition, or the eerily familiar sound of Gerald's demise, something made the Prince look back up, in time to catch a glimpse of the figure lowering the same weapons he saw in Joanas. A *musket.*

Weir and Gromwell rushed to Gerald's side, but Drake could not take his eyes off the mysterious stranger. He could not make him out or identify him; only the smoothness of his head was a notable feature.

'Is he dead?' Gromwell asked.

'No', Weir replied as he began to unbutton the Captain's jacket. 'But he's hurt bad enough. Check for any wounds, quickly! The affected always have an injury.'

'Edward?', Drake asked.

'Not now lad', Gromwell replied, distracted.

'What about the shooter?'

'What shooter?'

'He's on the command deck.'

Gromwell glanced at the empty deck briefly before turning back to Drake.

'There's no one there'

'But there was', Drake insisted. 'I saw him! Didn't you hear the shot?'

'We only heard Gerald', said Weir, ripping open Gerald's shirt to reveal an open wound. 'There's no shooter. There's no technology of the sort on board. What are you talking about?'

'Check his back', said Drake.

With a slow and cautious nod, they flipped Gerald onto his front. His shirt was saturated with blood.

'Oh shit', Weir gasped. 'Someone call the doctor!'

The bell in the crow's nest rang three times, and the ship's crew began to stir. Drake tried to piece together the whereabouts of the stranger and the musket, but his efforts were in vain. Without so much as a thought for anyone else, he made his way to the stairs leading up to the command deck.

In the corner of his eye he saw a Morre, still in his nightgown, running towards the commotion with a leather bag. He cared little for who it was, or even what the crew were doing as he began to climb. To his surprise, when he reached the command deck, he could not find a trace of either the stranger or the musket.

The voices he could hear below were calm, yet authoritative. The doctor would ask a question, and either Weir, Gromwell or a crew member would answer. Drake remained hidden out of view and stared absent-mindedly at an expressionless helmsman he could not identify. *By now they must think I am crazy*, he mused. *I had best not bring another Morre into the judgement.*

His eyes caught the gaze of the helmsman. Aside from the questioning glance, Drake was sure the Morre also motioned towards something on the deck. Turning to look for himself, he caught one of the moon's rays escape the clouds and fall upon the varnished panelling. As they shone, they revealed a strange texture, almost like a fine spray of dirt. Drake thought nothing of it until he turned back to the helmsman, who was now rubbing his fingers together under his nose, seeming to make extra effort to ensure his sniffing was heard.

Drake took this as another sign. He kneeled and stroked the panels, feeling the dust cling to his skin as he did so. Showing his fingers to the moonlight, he beheld an ash-like substance covering them. Carefully, he smelt his fingers. Aside from the smell of sea salt and varnish, a whiff of metal and soot flooded his senses. He recognised this substance. Though he couldn't quite recall the name, he knew he must have heard it countless times on the many ships he'd been aboard during the War.

'What is it?'

Jefferson was standing on the other side of the dust, looking at him with the eyes of a curious cat. Drake barely had time to respond before he grabbed the substance-covered hand and smelt it himself.

'It's gunpowder.'

'The deck has a sprinkle of it', Drake explained. 'Someone was standing here with one of those muskets from Joanas-Sorrow. He shot Gerald.'

Jefferson looked at him with an expression of disbelief.

'Were you focused?' he asked, releasing Drake's arm.

'I think so', Drake replied, watching as the group of Morre below began to disperse around the ship. 'I was about to punch him.'

'The shooter?'

'No', Drake snapped. 'Gerald. He was coming right for me.'

Gromwell, Weir and Bartarian appeared behind Jefferson. Drake peered nervously at Bartarian, who looked irritated and displeased to be awake.

'What did you do now, boy?' he snarled.

'He didn't do anything', said Jefferson, calmly. 'A musket was fired here. There's a sprinkle of gunpowder, and there's no cannons on this deck.'

He pointed to where Gerald had been struck down.

'Muskets aren't very accurate either. According to the guards in Joanas-Sorrow, it takes a lot of training to achieve a shot like this. They haven't even mastered it themselves yet.'

'The Prince's secret meetings could have catered for that', Bartarian said. 'Or do you have an accomplice on board? You are getting tired of us old Morre mocking your right to the crown, eh boy?'

'Shut up Bartarian!' Gromwell snapped. 'I may grow tired of your illness towards Drake myself if you insist on keeping it up.'

Bartarian clicked his teeth irritably.

'Fine then', he said, heading for the stairs. 'I best mind my own damn business.'

'You'd do well to do so, Sir', Gromwell said. 'He's our future King.'

'I pray exile comes of me first', Bartarian muttered. 'Future King indeed.'

He continued to mumble angrily as he walked away, unsettling Drake's nerves even further. It did not help that the group kept silent as they waited for his voice to trail off, yet there may have been a purpose to it.

Drake could not hold his silence for any longer. 'Does he have to travel with us?'

'Not for much longer', said Weir, with a cursing tone. 'You'd all do well to silence that one or send him home. I would've had him bound to the main mast and whipped for such insolence by now.'

'Bartarian has been with the army for far longer than we have', Jefferson replied. 'We can't just send him home. Half of the army will follow him, and the other half will blame Drake for his dishonour.'

'He's disrupting the integrity of my ship with his malcontent', Weir snapped. 'You must keep him quiet in my presence, and in the presence of my men. I thought you understood that better than anyone. The war isn't in Centra, or on my ship, it's out there.'

'If you really meant that, then you should tell Jefferson and Drake what you told me', Gromwell piped up. 'Go on – tell them about the corruption.'

Drake and Jefferson turned to Weir, who continued to hold his stance like a true legend. He kept his tone calm and his eyes forward as he began to explain.

'Very well. One of our sailors jumped ship last night', he said. 'He spoke like Gerald did; but instead of wishing to attack Drake he was trying to flee from him. According to his commanding officer, he wasn't one to fear anything, let alone dishonour himself by taking flight. They say he must have been 'corrupted' to do such a thing.'

'Where is he now?' Jefferson asked.

'At the bottom of the sea, probably', answered Weir. 'He was too busy cursing Drake's crown than steering his longboat.'

Drake felt uneasy. He was no stranger to a Morre's death, but a death that may have been partly his fault had his mind in a frenzy. He felt Gromwell's hand on his shoulder and this calmed him, though only slightly.

'But why call it the corruption?' Jefferson asked. 'Morre are just as privy to fear as men, if not more so. Could he have just lost his mind?'

'Maybe. But these episodes have started since we came in sight of Joanas', said Weir. 'Gerald is the third Morre to have gone such a way.'

'What of the first?' Gromwell asked.

'The first is confirmed dead', Weir replied. 'The Maiden of Gaul-Hon reported the occurrence earlier this day. According to the Captain he almost took three others with him before he was subdued.'

'How many know of this?' Jefferson asked.

'Only the Commanders', said Weir.

Jefferson motioned towards the helmsman Drake saw earlier. 'What about him?'

'He keeps the secrets of the Commanders', Weir explained. 'I was counting on the Admiral to release information to the crews at some point. Hopefully knowing what is going on will ease their spirits, especially since we are in sight of Joanas.'

'Be sure he makes it quick', said Gromwell. 'I'd rather not witness a panic or have Drake the centre-point of tonight.'

He made to leave, but Jefferson stopped him. 'Do you think Bartarian has it, Gromwell?'

Gromwell's mood was already damp with the sea air, and his face had dropped with the exchange, yet Drake could tell when he was telling the truth.

'No', he said, as he turned back towards the stairs. 'He is just a traditional old fool.'

'I should return to my quarters too', Jefferson said with a nod, before making his leave. 'This is an unholy hour for me.'

'Sleep well, Jefferson', said Weir, watching him depart before returning his attention to Drake. 'And how do you feel, my Prince?'

'A little shaken', Drake replied. 'Will Gerald be alright?'

'Gerald hasn't reached that stage in his life yet', said Weir as he walked to the banister overlooking the side with Joanas' shadow. 'He wouldn't let some bullet wound kill him that easily.'

'Do you really believe that?' Drake asked. 'The Legends of the Morre, I mean?'

'When you were in the War', the Living Legend said, keeping his head held high. 'How many Morre died in front of you?'

Drake traced his memories back to the time of marching- the first time his body and mind were truly tested. The first time he heard Morre wail out in pain and felt the unsettling flood of horror as the Necromancer's horde rushed towards the Centurian Legions. But all of that paled in comparison to the Lorre, and the power of its venom fire.

Everyone knew when the Lorre had come, its roar trumpeting across the battlefield, causing both sides to look up in terror. It swooped over his thoughts as it did the skies, filling his head with the curdling screams of both men and Morre, and the unmistakable smell of cooking flesh. Then there was the ash, dancing around the aftermath like the seedlings of the Centurian dandelion. He dared still not wonder which pieces of ash were his friends.

'Too many to be right', Drake answered, his tone dragged down by the weight of his memory. 'I remember their screams. A couple of my friends were there, in the first lines. Father insisted I stay in the rear flanks with him, Edward and Walter.'

'Ah yes', Weir recalled. 'Walter Gromwell, the Last Legend of Sanctity - The Slayer in fact, if you believe the accounts.'

'He was a great Morre – a friend', Drake sighed, pushing away those painful memories of not just Edward's son, but of the others as well. 'They could be true. I thought he wasn't one to go running into a dangerous situation like that, but things change. What you think you know about some Morre may only be half the story.'

'True words those', Weir said, turning around to face Drake and lean against the rail. 'All it would take for a reasonable Morre to storm into the Lorre's den would be to see something- someone they care about in danger. The Necromancer had many talents, maybe he bewitched those poor Morre?'

Drake dared not share what Gromwell had only just confided earlier. He and Weir were still at the professional stage in their familiarity and telling the Legendary Captain about the Astorian now would do little for them both. To Drake's relief, the Captain merely sighed and continued.

'I think they're real', he said. 'I also think when we watch a Morre die, no matter who it is, we start to understand the reality of the legends. You'll understand our mortality is more damning than man's. Just because we possess the blood of the Torre doesn't mean we have more right to live. A single thread of doubt and the death consumes you.'

'It sounds too tragic to be a real effect', said Drake, trying to push back the ridiculous notion. 'It also sounds like you have seen some die?'

'Maybe I have', Weir said, 'The war had been going on

for far longer than when Centra sailed on Fugula and Titeria. It's just respectful to call it as such.'

Drake reflected on Weir's words for a moment. With a little more time he'd understand better, but the sound of the sea could only keep him alert and awake for so long.

'We should settle for the night soon', he said, with a yawn. 'Is there any point to make in this conversation?'

Weir nodded. 'If a Morre isn't careful, the same could happen to him. If, for example, the love he has found in Joanas-Sorrow is denied by the laws of Centra.'

Drake's face tensed.

'It will not matter', he said. 'When I am King, my first order of business will be to change that stupid law.'

'But you are not King yet, my Prince', Weir reminded him. 'As a King of Centra, entitlement is the first thing you must destroy. Just because you wear a crown, doesn't mean you can violate the laws which have kept Centra in Alcadia's affairs for a dozen Centuries.'

'But we are the most powerful nation on the planet', Drake protested. 'Why must we cave to the demands of men? Why is it so important I marry a pure-blood?'

After a few moments of looking back and forth at Drake, Weir gave him an answer. 'The crown follows and accepts it so that Centra's sons and daughters continue to have the right to marry the ones they love.'

Drake tried to object and point out the need to have that continuity in the crown, but Weir spoke again before he could summon the first word.

'It's unfortunate that you'd suffer the price', he said, 'but for what hope you may still have, the world is changing. If Navuro can build a railroad between two oceans in less than an age, then some ancient marital law can be forgotten and buried just the same. In the meantime, I suggest you focus on something more productive, and perhaps something you can control.'

'I will try', Drake said, noticing the crewmen descend for their shift change. 'Should we mark the night?'

'I think I have impeded on the officer's shifts for long enough.' Weir placed his hand on Drake's back. 'Come Drake, I'll take you to your room.'

'Will you tell the men at first light?' Drake asked as they walked down to the main deck.

'The First Officer will', said Weir. 'I need to speak to my colleagues – I'll probably start with the Maiden of Shauna. The other Captains should understand the threat before noon and would have briefed their crews by sundown.'

'Do you think what happened tonight will happen again?' Drake asked as they reached his door.

'I hope not', Weir said, reaching for the handle, 'The bullets are new trauma weapons that our doctors aren't fully aware of yet. For the sake of Gerald, I hope it is not too serious. But do not worry yourself too much over the happenings. We believe you and that will be our story.'

'Will you hunt the shooter?'

'Probably not', Weir replied. 'Stow-away assassins tend to jump ship after they have completed their deeds. There will be an investigation, but it'd be foolish to expect to find anything. It'd be like finding a swan in the desert.'

'Very well. Goodnight then, Captain Weir.'

'Donald would work just fine, Drake. See you on the morrow.'

Drake smiled as he shut the door. His eyes had settled well with the darkness, but he was too preoccupied with the events of the evening to sleep. Worse, as his mind continued to wander, the mistakes of Sanctity began to overpower his thoughts.

He let the memories stoke his mood like hot pokers, wrestling with them as if doing so would change them. He longed to turn back the clock and fix those mistakes before he made them. But, as the list of errors slowly brought a tear to his eye, he began to accept that his future was more important. Especially since he finally had an influential Commander treating him with respect.

The thought of this respect spreading across Centra had his imagination bubbling. Images of a court of friends wishing to assist him in his Kingship filled his thoughts. He imagined overturning the traditions expected by man, and with that a wave of new thoughts about Laura soon began to take over.

Without a single regard for what Weir had advised him earlier, he began to think about her in ways a young Morre would be expected to think. Horny and very much captivated by memories of their meetings, he could not help but relieve himself against the silence of his room. His only thought was *I'm such a pathetic idiot.*

A Mother's Duty

'Sit, my Queen', Tristan said, pulling out a chair for his sister as she walked into the room. 'Tell me, what is troubling you?'

Emelye took her time to settle. She squeezed her coat tightly to ensure her feelings were not magnified by the chill of the halls. *A gift from Drake for my last birthday*, she pondered. *It makes the matter even more ironic.*

'It's about Drake', she began, as Tristan passed her a cup of tea. 'I received a letter before we came here. I was hoping you would guide me, as you always have.'

'You're too kind with your words. Whenever Charles and I talked it was always he who had the solutions.' Tristan took a sip of his own tea. 'But never mind. What is this message and what has it to do with Drake?'

'It's from Tiana Rivera.' Emelye pulled the rolled-up parchment from her sleeve and handed it to her brother. 'Read it first and tell me your thoughts.'

Tristan took the parchment and began to read, muttering under his breath as he did so. He stopped where she knew he would; at the very line that had brought her here in the first place.

'You know what this means, don't you?' she continued. 'All that talk on the table yesterday evening-'

'But it is our most sacred law.'

'I don't care!' Emelye cried, clutching at her cup. 'He's our only son, and I can't lose him to heartbreak. Not like Muriel.'

'With all due respect, dear sister, Muriel committed suicide.'

'How do you know Drake would not do the same?'

'How would you know he would? How do you know this infatuation will kill him? If, indeed, he even feels the same?'

Tristen bit at Emelye's silence with a loud slurp of his tea. 'It's no secret that Drake holds little respect in the greater court, but have you considered his time in the mountains? He's stronger than we think Emelye. Far stronger.'

He came back half-dead, and very different, Emelye recalled silently. For at least a year, she'd thought she had lost him.

'Whatever his purpose was up there, he never told anyone. He didn't even tell Lord Gromwell. My point is, Tristan, I want that barbaric law abolished!'

'Be reasonable here.' Tristan's tone was warm and quiet. 'Navuro is the only country that seems ready to address that side of their marriage laws, let alone abolish it entirely. You may get support from Draberia thanks to Tiana's involvement in this, but that's all it would be, support.'

'There must be a way. Don't the Dragon Keepers have any say in this age?'

'The important thing to remember is that a Keeper is just that – a Keeper. They are there for guidance and advice only. To suggest something like that would see them thrown out. Or worse. They'd call us barbaric.'

'But that is a very backwards viewpoint to hold over the entire system. Surely you'd understand that whilst Chantelle sleeps in your bed?'

Tristen froze, his cup poised in mid-air.

'I'll let you have that one, since you are my favourite sister.' He gave her an icy glare and slammed his cup down on to the table. 'Besides, that was different.'

'By the Torre, Tristan, have some sense! It was just the same.'

'This whole conversation will do us no good. Either find another solution or let me rest.'

'I don't know if there is any other solution.' Emelye sighed. 'Sepherance's will is set in stone and Tiana seems certain that Laura will break.'

'Why are our children such fools, Emelye?'

'It is not foolish to fall for your destined soul.'

'Then why haven't we?'

An interesting question, she pondered as she played absent-mindedly with the buttons of her coat. *I never got the chance I suppose.*

'I don't know what it feels like', she answered eventually. 'Between the two of us, I don't think Sepherance was the one I was destined for.'

'Nor Chantelle I, if I could be so truthful with you.' Emelye was taken aback by this, for he had always seemed so happy with his wife. 'I genuinely believe she was matched with Charles.'

'Then why her?'

'Because you don't dare deny your brother's will!' Tristan barked. 'Before I even understood it, we were sharing a bed making our daughter. It's so strange.'

'So, is that how it really happened? I didn't realise caring for someone meant sleeping with them, Tristan.'

'Neither did I at the time.' Tristan sighed. 'And after all these years, I still don't understand why he chose me. Perhaps he believed it?'

'Then you must understand why this is important for Tiana and I. Think of something for me. My mind is blank with worry.'

'Looking back', Tristan began as he rubbed his stubble, 'before we chose one another as Skylarks, we had to ask the Dragon Council's permission to be wed.'

Emelye let her eyes ask the questions; she knew Tristen would understand.

'Well I couldn't just marry a widow.'

'So you do understand.'

'It isn't as simple as that', Tristan said with a raised hand, 'Even if we got the Council's blessing for their marriage, the human Kingdoms would still be up in arms.'

'Then we ask for the Kingdoms' blessings.'

'Again, not so easy.' Tristan sat back in his chair. 'The human Kingdoms' blessings are based on a compromise, or mutual understanding. When Sanitaria inherited the throne, the human Kingdoms thought his wife to be an ill-gotten whore unworthy of the title of Queen. The council denies it to this very day, but Charles and I always felt this was the reason no Keepers existed in Joanas or the colonies until she was buried.'

'Until the War of Sanctity.'

'Of course. But that was the compromise', Tristen sighed. 'So what would Drake's compromise be?'

'I'm still clueless', Emelye answered, trying to pry through her worries, 'What was your compromise to the Council?'

'Chantelle and I were not to have any more children.'

Guilt stricken, Emelye cast her mind back to her numerous conversations with Chantelle over the years and the countless times she had questioned her about having another child.

'Forgive me. I thought-'

'It's all right', Tristen reached over the table and grabbed Emelye's hand. 'Stella was the only child I ever needed, and it has been a pleasure to raise Charles's children.'

'I should not have disturbed you with this. If only I'd known. I'm so sorry.'

'Enough. Look at me.' Tristan ordered sternly. 'At the very least, I can send out a messenger to Draberia. Perhaps there is a way around this that the humans would consider. But there is one thing I am going to need from you.'

'Anything. What?'

'Get Sepherance to postpone the dance of the Skylarks until we have the Kingdoms' blessings.'

Emelye knew how hard that would be, for they had already talked about the issue. 'That is going to be very difficult, Tristan.'

'It is for the sake of the Keepers, and their responses.' Tristan stood up, holding his cup against the table top. 'There's no guarantee that we will have enough before then. Any extra time is a bonus, for Drake's sake.'

'Thank you', Emelye said, grabbing Tristan's coat, 'I

will repay you for this. I don't know how but I will.'

'Take thought on it, little sister. We'll discuss it when it is delivered.'

Tristen kissed Emelye on the cheek, just as he did back in their childhood days, and took his presence into the darkness, leaving Emelye alone with her thoughts.

Torre bless me, she thought as she brought her hands to her head. *Save him for me.*

***

The night was cruel on Emelye, though the bedchamber's fire was warm. Her fears worked against her, dreaming up the chaos their suggestion could cause. She thought of Sepherance, and how he'd condemn her or even exile her for going behind his back. She only slept for a short time; far too short to ease the tension of the world, and thus felt irritable when the suns came up to greet her. The journey was swift, and without error, and they reached Citadel by suns down.

They entered the large valley via the only highway in the south; that which rolled down the steep hills at the edge of the forests of Gaul and Soule. Halfway down the valley the forest grew sparse and bore into a vast, clean carpet of grass and violet. In the centre, at the base of the loch of Pitied Souls, stood the lone city of Citadel. The loch's gentle curve to the west allowed it to catch the shimmer of the dawning suns, and the few summerwood trees that dared stand by the shoreline were plump with the rich nutrients of the silts.

This time of the year just after nature's flowering was the prettiest in Emelye's eyes, for she thought the vibrant colours in the sunsets were too spectacular to be regarded as beautiful. The Church of the Torre sat waiting for her in the centre of the city and, as with every visit, she ascended the stairs in the tower to bask in the evening views. As she watched the suns disappear, she decided that it was here she would tell Sepherance, and it was here she would beg for their son's future.

As she basked in the natural spectacle of the view, she could not help but recall her last visit here several years ago, when Sepherance sailed for Joanas during peacetime. Back then there was merely a single Imperial Ship amongst the litter of masts and folded sails. Now however, the King's Imperial Navy filled the port with their clutter and blotted out the noise of the forests with the wails of the ordered sea folk.

Remembering her beloved who stood several paces behind her, she turned to address him, ensuring the letter from Tiana Rivera remained well hidden.

'Do you not think he is capable?' she asked.

'You know how I feel about the matter', Sepherance replied, with a shuffle of his boots. 'He's not ready to lead, and he's not ready to take responsibility for the costs of his decisions.'

'Yet you would leave the care of Centra to him?', Emelye asked, her voice trembling with the thought of her son's upset. 'Destroying his hopes and dreams in the process?'

'We've talked about this, Emelye', Sepherance raised his voice. 'How many more times must I settle the matter? He must uphold the duties of the King before he takes the Crown!'

Emelye looked at him as tears filled her eyes.

'He's our only child Sepherance', she retorted. 'He is beyond the age we were when we wed. He may have already met his match.'

Sepherance became agitated, pacing back and forth in his frustration.

'Compromise destroyed my father, as it did my sister', he reminded her. 'Compromise here will destroy us too.'

Emelye could no longer contain her secret. She slowly pulled out the letter, opened it and presented it to him.

'What is this?'

'Just read it', she said, watching as Sepherance's face stiffened in disgust, 'Please!'

He took it from her hand with a look that stabbed at her.

'You were never one to keep secrets from me.'

'This is different', she said, holding back any further tears. 'Please just read it.'

With a sigh and a nod, he began to read. He had not even read half the passage, before his eyes rose to question her.

'So this is where all of this is coming from? This is why you are so driven about the Dance of the Skylarks?'

'It's too late Sepherance. If you force them apart now, they are both as good as dead. You have to delay it, please.'

Sepherance returned his gaze to the letter, and read it again, this time more slowly.

'She's a Dragon Keeper?' Sepherance asked, refusing to look up at her.

'Yes. Rumour has it that she is a very fine Dragon Keeper.'

'Yet she is born of a human father?'

'Her father was honoured by the Morre, the first in Centuries!'

'Yet that still makes her a half-blood. You know what will be said in the free countries.' He guided his displeasure to the ledge. 'Every Dragon Keeper will be returned dead. Or in chains.'

'I do not think so. They'll listen to reason, they are listening to reason now.'

'But you don't know that! You have not seen what they did to the Morre on the eve of Sanctity. You don't know how they'll react to this – to find out that we have succumbed to some barbaric tradition!'

'Forcing your son's bed is a barbaric tradition!'

'It matters not what we think Emelye. Everything our ancestors have bled for will be overturned, their memories nothing but ash-'

'Your legacy will become ash if you do not allow their love.' Emelye shot back at him. 'You know I cannot bear you more children.'

She began to sob. Having watched her own sister in-law take her life at the hands of the same damning, she knew it wasn't myth or over-reaction. It was real, and she couldn't allow Drake to meet the same fate

'Alcadia and country before all', Sepherance said, reminding her of the Dragon Keeper pact. 'Until death takes our souls. Do you remember that pact, Emelye?'

'The dead drafted that pact Sepherance, and it has been far too long ago for anyone to really remember why.'

Sepherance shook his head and threw the paper at her.

'I cannot take this blasphemy any further', he said solemnly as he pulled open the hatch to the stairs, 'I will not allow my son to destroy the values of Alcadia. By the Torre, do we even know if he has fallen for her?'

Emelye shook her head with a slow retreat of effort.

'So you don't know if this is just another of his exploits?' He was right, and she knew it. 'I've had enough of this-'

'Sepherance please – I cannot risk losing him!'

'Enough - I have settled it.' Sepherance barked. 'I am tired of making excuses for that boy. It's high time we put our foot down and did away with this fleeting fantasy he has over his duty. Lord Gromwell will suffer my wrath for this!'

He clanked to the bottom of the stairs and pushed open the two aging oak doors to reveal the amassed troops and sailors, with his personal Commanders formed in his path. He barged past them. Emelye followed, but came to a halt as he turned to face her

'Leave her!' Sepherance spat, glaring at her. 'Get ready for deployment – we sail immediately.'

***

Now that Sepherance was gone, Emelye composed herself, closed her eyes and tried to empty her mind of its concerns. After a few minutes alone with her thoughts, she heard faint footsteps behind her and a familiar voice whispering her name. Tristan.

'Did you hear it?' she asked him tearfully. 'Did you hear what he said?'

'I heard enough to understand, my sister', Tristan replied. 'He makes a point, except where he believes you're doing this to avoid re-living the past. I don't think I have ever seen him like that.'

He paused for a second. 'Have you thought of your return favour yet?'

'You must want something Tristan. Tell me what it is?'

'That would disturb the surprise', Tristan said, clearly pretending to not care. 'But there is one small favour that comes to mind.'

'Speak it.'

'It seems rather silly-'

'By the Torre Tristan, say it!'

Emelye's eyes were fixed on Tristan. Like Sepherance, she very well understood his face, and could almost tell what he was thinking. It had to be something close to him, or something that mattered very much to him.

'Chantelle and I wish to have another child.'

Emelye turned towards the rear of the fleet as it circled within the lock. 'What is wrong with the children under Charles' marriage?'

'They are growing up to be fine Morre, but they are not our children. David is due to take a place on the Council after Colette, meaning Charles' seat is secure. We – I mean I- have no real heir, Emelye. And, if the legends are true, that means that I would die in the afterlife.'

'Nonsense! My son's life is at stake here. It is hardly a solution the Council would see as worthy of accepting.'

'But as King, it is a solution Drake can empower.'

And there it was; Tristan's real solution. *The clever fool.*

'What makes you think Drake will take the crown so soon?'

'I am not one for encouraging bleak futures, Emelye.' Tristan's face darkened. 'But Sepherance is no more immortal than you or me. The moment Drake takes part in the Dance of the Skylarks, he begins his duties for the crown. You know as well as I that this is a very quick process, and the Council will begin pressuring Sepherance to pass on the crown the moment Drake is married.'

'To Laura, yes.' Emelye was not about to allow Tristan to forget his side of the bargain if she was to encourage the favour. 'How far are you with contacting the Keepers?'

'The first batch of messengers are away. You'll know the moment there is anything.'

'I just hope it won't be too late.' Emelye said, gazing into the loch. 'I will pray they return good, timely news.'

For the Secret

Jack studied Thomas intently as he strode over the piles of charcoal-black twigs and bramble. The way this scrawny creature sifted through the torched pine forest was as methodical and silent as any assassin he had ever seen.

'What should I call you?' Thomas asked as he approached. 'Calling you Master feels insignificant.'

'Call me what you will', Jack replied, as he turned to face the looming mountain on the horizon. 'My chain of command is deeper than titles or names.'

It was more peaceful in the Grey. The lack of shrieking and the roars of the distant fires were music to his ears, however he thrived best in the silence of a frozen world. Better yet, his thoughts remained secret here.

'My army's power comes from the deepest pit of resentment, Mister Elkwood. Any being that can muster it, let alone control it, holds a respectable place in my command to call me whatever they wish.'

'Does that make the Hatred the ruler of all, then?'

Jack approached the felled trunk of an elder tree, its upper mass broken and cindered to the point where it had caved into a pile of ash. It reminded him of the first time he encountered the Hatred in the void of his demons, the forest and his grave deteriorating as if alight with an invisible, odourless flame.

'It's anything but my ruler', Jack explained. 'The Morre are never meant to stay on in this world after they perish. We're supposed to join our families in the Rest and be reborn anew in a world less hurtful than this. But I didn't. The terrors of my life were still roaming free, even to this day; thus, I am forced to live on. Just as I was forced to wander through this plane for an eternity before they found me.'

He knew he should fight back those dark memories, but instead he welcomed them. Every time he came too close to the darkness, and every time he battled for his chance to move on. He failed every time, watching those sweet endings drift away as if they were just wishes and dreams.

'Do you have any idea what's it like listening to the malcontent of millions? All at once, for forever?'

Elkwood merely shook his head.

Of course not, Jack thought with resentment. *You still have your life.*

He closed his eyes and let the Power of the Hatred creep into his thoughts.

'We can renew you', they whispered with a hiss.

But I can't renew what is already lost, Jack thought, as he felt their presence slither across his body.

'We can avenge you.'

I have nothing to avenge.

'We can free you.'

My freedom is already forfeit.

'We can free them.'

Them?

With a tiny, peddling thought about his family, Jack remembered the first time he opened his eyes since his awakening. His first sight was the Hatred, presented as a powerful spectre. The spirit was as clear as the ash beneath his feet, with its ghostly tentacles slithering across the open space, stroking the air around him.

'Together, we can save your family.'

I couldn't save my family. Why am I here? I am supposed to be with them. With the Torre.

'The Torre cannot help you, and they cannot help them. Only we can, Jack.'

I'm an abomination; it's not supposed to end like this.

'Together we can fix it, Jack.'

I don't know where or how to start.

That was when they showed him. As if Jack had touched one of the Fallen, with a flash of visions flooding his mind. They made him relive the sights and sounds of his daughter's torture, and the breaking of his body that came straight afterwards. They made him feel the helplessness again, that locked feeling of grief as he looked up at his crucified wife. Flesh torn and face brutalised, dead from the heavy bleeding.

'She was lucky', The Hatred interrupted. 'But they will not be.'

And then, the glory of his future was shown to him. Ripping across the jungle, pushing those lizard cunts on like feeble children, slapping the fear of their lives into them. Capturing them all and doing onto them a thousand times what they did to his family. It was wonderful, if not beautiful. And then, when he had his fill of vengeance, the Hatred turned his attention on humanity.

'Penance?' Elkwood's voice tore through Jack's memories. 'Penance, is everything alright?'

Jack turned to face Elkwood, his eyes as curious as they were when he delved into the memories of his turn.

'Everything is just fine, my friend', he said, smiling through his clenched teeth. 'Do you feel it yet?'

'No. I only feel cold. Are we meant to still breathe here?'

'Only if it crosses your mind', Jack said. 'Here, the physical needs of the body are frozen in time, and the soul is the only power. It is so tuned to the physical world, you think your blood is still pumping. I believe you just need more practice, Mr Elkwood. Thankfully the Sea of Souls isn't going anywhere here.'

Elkwood seemed disappointed in Jack's comment, and his expression reminded Jack of his son after a long days' worth of enjoyment. He could tell Elkwood learnt more during this day than he ever had before, and it was that same sigh, and that same heartbroken glare Aland gave when it was time to retire. *That weight. That terrible, painful weight.*

But that was where the empathy ended. Instead of dread pulling at the strings of his heart as he clutched his daughter's muddied ponytail, only the power of the Hatred prevailed. He knew there should have been something there, but the horrors made him delve deeper into his dreams of dominion.

'Should we return then?' Elkwood asked, staring at the column of smoke to the south. 'There are secrets to unearth back in the city.'

'You're right', Jack replied, 'Do you remember how to focus? How to jump back into existence?'

Thomas smiled and closed his eyes. With a soothing grace and a slight whimper, his body froze, leaving Jack to delve in the emptiness of the timeless world around him. The Hatred could not touch him here. His state was that which he left in the physical realm; never changing no matter how hard he pushed. He'd play with the idea of working up a stress, or a storm of anger, but when he entered the existence all his effort drained back into silence.

Instead of trying again or moving beyond the base of the mountain to overlook the world below, he held on to the moment and focused purely on the frozen form of his apprentice. He was as human as any other, but so curiously detached from his emotions that his presence seemed to dull the surroundings. Before Sirius bathed in the Sea of Souls, he was like Thomas in so many ways. But, unlike Thomas, he had the fear, at least before Jack and the Hatred consumed every part of its presence. Thomas must have had the fear inside of that bony body somewhere, even if it was difficult to detect. *What a very curious creature,* Jack mused.

With a quick stroke of Thomas' cheek, Jack closed his eyes and took in his surroundings, feeling the emptiness as they came back to life. His mind elevated against the rush of thoughts, and he ripped back into existence with the putrid taste of death filling his mouth. He opened his eyes and found Thomas on his knees, gagging away that same aftertaste.

'Still not used to the jump home?', Jack asked.

'I will be in time', Thomas said with a spit.

He struggled back up onto his feet, maintaining a strong control that reminded Jack of an old friend's first time. Thomas had handled the transition so much better; the friend had released the evening's meal upon the grass whilst cursing the lies his mother told him. Jack was pleased that Thomas was stronger and more adaptable than him.

'Be quick to reclaim your feet', Jack ordered, turning to face the huge column of smoke rising from the city, 'Listen to my voice and focus on my back. It'll help distract your stomach.'

'Were you ever affected like this, Penance? I can't speak for a Dragon Blood, but surely it would have been just as harsh?'

'It was worse', Jack replied. 'So much so, that most of our training was focused on preparing for it.'

'Was there many of you?'

'What do you mean?'

'You said 'our'

'Yes', Jack reminisced with a smile. 'There were three of us.'

'Who were they? Did they feel it too?'

'The other Morre in our company suffered it the worst', Jack said, locking the memory into his thoughts. 'The human I trained with seemed oddly familiar with it, but he still suffered. The night of our first return was a long and troubling one.'

'Who were they then?'

'Does it matter?' Jack was impressed with the speed of Thomas' recovery, watching him as he walked effortlessly in a stable line. 'I took the man's head before the jungles of Negura, and the Dragon Blood will soon join him.'

'The other Morre is the Prince, isn't it?'

Jack stopped and presented a face he hoped he'd never use since his turn.

'It is the Prince', he replied with a cold whisper, 'but,

rumour has it, he remembers nothing of the training. This is where you will have the advantage, and this is where you will strike.'

'But he may still know how to focus?'

'Pathetic folly.' Jack's temper was quelled very well, but its influence showed in Thomas' eyes staring back at him. 'I don't care how you do it. Use a dagger to cut off his head for all I care. As long as it is done, we'll face less resistance during the later phase of our plans. Our training is the rarest, and most dangerous kind, Thomas. We were either left spiritually dead, or wishing to be dead so much, that we soon forgot about all of it. Remember that when you kill him, remember that when he begs for his life.'

'Were you left spiritually dead, Penance?'

You wouldn't understand the dark places I visited after my training, he thought bitterly, placing his hand against the warm stone of the city wall and taking in the smell of freshly-cooked flesh.

'That's enough for the moment', he said. 'Sirius and Ouster's work sing through these walls.'

The souls of the dead were stirring within the courtyard, their wails filled with the names of their loved ones. The fulfilment of Jack's plan was sound, but he could not help feeling the secret floating between the souls of the fallen, like a white lie cockily dancing in the distance. Whatever it was, he was sure it would be something he would find very useful to his cause.

'Stay here and keep practicing, Thomas', Jack ordered as he took a step back, 'Do not listen to what goes on inside. Remain in the forest until I summon you.'

'But what about all that talk of being spiritually dead after the training?'

'That's why you must learn more of this without me.' With this, Jack jumped into the Grey. 'Learn or die, man of the Elkwood.'

Jack found the only open gatehouse guarded by a pair of the meanest-looking mud goblins one could ask for. He passed them and found his way into a group of many more of them, who were piling up the dead within the courtyard. He trundled through the fire, feeling nothing but the tickle of the lifeless flames in their dull and unimportant dance. There he was greeted by Sirius, with a precious few survivors bound in chains in a circle around him.

Jack looked at each of them in turn. All were burnt and afraid. He could see how much was taken from them, with their tears leaving streaks in the soot on their faces. Such sorrow could only come from the pits of their woe, and the insufferable weights of their failures. The secret of the city grew bright in their hearts, tantalising Jack's lust for it like the smell of a virgin's innocence. It glowed especially bright for one old figure, doused in loose, fire-torn robes. Jack returned to the existence without a blink or a struggle and walked straight into the sounds of wailing and sobbing.

'You', Jack said, pointing his finger at the man. 'Your heart is stronger than the others. There is a secret about this place, and you know something about it.'

Sirius looked at Jack with a pair of curious eyes.

'My minions have clearly missed it', he continued. 'Tell me - what are they not seeing?'

The old man seemed frail but proud of his position. He was also immune to Jack's promises of torture and illusion. The only thing that gave away the man's weakness was the way he looked at the small circle of survivors.

'This is a peaceful state, and we are a peaceful people', he said with a dry tongue. 'Our houses were made from the stones of the mountains. Our walls were erected to keep out the demons, not lock away secrets.'

The Hobsythe in company let out a set of cackles, forcing Jack's hand to quell their noise.

'Demons do not force the hammer of the Knight's Republic', he said, turning from the old man to face Sirius. 'Everyone here understands that it takes a valuable trade, or relic, for a city like this to remain standing against an era of wars.'

'We weren't spared the Necromancer's war. We lost ten times as many sons as the Morre, and the scars of our lands remain', said the old man. 'The forests that you burnt down did well to hide those scars. Did you see them? Did you see what he did to the land? I promise you – they'll grow back. They'll grow back just as they did after the Necromancer was long gone.'

Not if I burn the life from the soil.

Jack looked at the old man whilst considering his response, still holding posture like a defiant Lord. He knew the secret had to be something special, something that only the elders knew. But what was it?

Jack studied the man's body, looking for clues and even scars. The palms of his hands were wrinkled and grey with the soot of the fire, and his clothes were even darker with the ash of the dead. There was something on his neck, yes. It looked like a star, or at least it looked like one at that distance without focus. Jack knew when he found it, for the old fool pulled his garments up to cover it.

'This is your last chance, old man. Tell me your city's secret, and I'll spare the last of your people', Jack said with a snarl.

The old man looked sadly at the circle of prisoners. Their hair and eyebrows were burnt clean from their faces, and their skin was riddled with blisters and rashes.

'Our people are gone, you fool. We'd be better off-'

'Dead? I suggest you reconsider that; there's more to death than you may realise. Either tell me what your secret is, or I will take it from your soul.'

The elder's defiance was clearer than the sun on a cloudless day. He faced forward, on his knees, with his chin up and his eyes fixed to an indistinguishable point in front of him. 'If that is how you see it, then there is nothing left to discuss.'

Jack was standing in front of the old man by the time he had finished talking. He lowered his head so that his lips were close enough for him to whisper his next words straight into the man's left ear.

'Before the Era of the Darkness', Jack began, 'there was a great battle. A violent debate if you will.'

'The parties of this debate believed in their cause so strongly, that they were very close to tearing the very fabric of reality apart. The only reason they didn't was because if they succeeded, one party would conquer them all.'

'It would interest you to know that this party is working for me. They've already shown me things you cannot possibly hope to comprehend. Things that the Necromancer only dreamed of having. Unlike him, I have the power to steal your soul from your body, harvest every secret I desire from it, and use it to power my armies. You'll be forced to endure the wrath I wreck upon the free peoples of Alcadia. Does this still sound like the death you and your people are expecting, old man?'

Jack retracted his head from the old man's ear, slowly letting in the screams and wails of his people's souls into his mind. He watched as the man's bravery began to melt, recognising each voice, gently caving in against the weight of his horror. It was a brief demonstration, for he soon closed his eyes and straightened his composure in defiance.

'I said there is nothing left to discuss', he said. 'Do as you will.'

Jack stood and looked at the elder's survivors. Some were fidgeting, others were sobbing, whilst a few held the same brave face as he did. 'At least tell me your name.'

'You have no right knowing my name.'

'As you so wish', Jack said, filling his lungs with the taste of the dead. 'Don't say I didn't try, old man.'

Jack closed his eyes and allowed the hate and despair of a thousand gencrations to flow through him. They made his body quiver as the energy they fed him multiplied. He reached out, feeling the Sea of Souls wail to him as he drew his fingers close to the stream. As he felt the power peak and his blood boil with the rage of the Fallen, he clutched the stream with an immense roar.

The Power of the Hatred ripped through him faster than the beats of the man's heart, energising him with a blinding white fire. His vision was filled by the shadows of the mortals around him, their souls glistening like the stars of the night sky. The power oozed from his body, its tentacles slithering towards each survivor as their screams stoked his thirst. Their terror tantalised it into a ripping frenzy, taking them one by one. It surrounded the Elder, allowing only the sounds of the reaping to reach him whilst he slowly began to drain. His fear gave Jack access to his thoughts, and to the great secret which shimmered through his panic. Jack stroked it, like a precious gift, letting the Elder fall apart with his fear.

By the time he had consumed every survivor's soul, the power had grown and surrounded every part of the Elder, and his fright was now a succulent meal. It wasted very little time forming itself into an image of the Torre and sinking its claws deep into the old man's body. Suddenly, and with a mighty roar, it ripped the tiny soul from the mortal's desperate grasp.

Jack released the stream and opened his eyes. The Elder's body had frozen with its arms out and mouth wide open. After a moment he fell backwards, and his muscles flopped into a lifeless jelly.

Jack stood over the corpse, which reminded him of a shrieking ghost. He carried this image with him back to the Grey, to be greeted by the soulless landscape and soon the Hatred.

'Your plan proceeds well, Jack.' they said, with a slow slither across his mind.

By the time the Morre get here, I'll have them cut off

'What about your deviation? We don't recall discussing this, *secret* with you.'

I only have just discovered this secret's existence. I was not about to waste time or energy consulting it with you.

The Hatred drew close, with barely a blink.

'Time is no factor for us. We have plenty of energy to share. The closer your people come to us, the more we infect their minds.'

I didn't realise that this was a consultation now. Are we not a partnership?

'We honour no such codes. We have no such rules. Do you not think our gifts fair?'

I must protect my interests. It's all good for you, you need not care for such things.

'Don't assume anything of us Jack. We also can make deviations to our plans. After all, our directive is not bound to a single timeline, like yours.'

Not for very long.

'Yes, but not yet. Go. Find your secret. But do not deviate again. We do not grant this one pass out of kindness.'

Jack watched the Hatred make their leave. Sometimes it would erupt into a ball of white fire, or just crackle into a mist of fine black powder. This time however, they chose to dissipate like a settling mist. There was a point when they had truly left; he knew after so many conversations. He never drew comfort in the hopes of snatching a last word or besting their remarks. He was still a single entity after all, and they were many.

Irrespective of whether they had left or not, he began to search through the taken souls, keeping his eyes closed and his hand hovering over the collective spirits as he read them. He felt every one's emotions and curses, dreads and memories. There must have been a thousand different words for him, but none as colourful as *Dragon Slayer.* Such a strong-hearted curse could only have come from the depths of a very clever being, one who knew of the legends of the Morre that led the first – and last crusade against the Lorre. Such a powerful name. Such a wonderful swear. *Jack the Dragon Slayer.*

He found the Elder, dipping between families of the Fallen as they bickered about the lies of the next life. He was distraught but back to his old fighting spirit, so it took an effort to overcome him and bring him into his capture. Jack remembered the first time he captured a soul; a little girl ripped into the Grey by something terrible. She was just as stubborn, but her young memories were easily entranced.

The Elder wrestled with Jack's lock but, like the others caught before him, the fighting did no good. Jack analysed him like a science project. He soon found what he wanted and fed upon every morsel of energy that it had to offer, before discarding the soul back into the pool of the captured. Sure that he had the secret, he returned to the Bright.

'Do you have it then, Jack?' asked Sirius from his left.

'Whatever it is, we'll find it at the cathedral', Jack replied, looking towards the ruins. 'Come Sirius and Ouster, be my shadows.'

'Is the fire's touch a concern?' Sirius asked.

'Of course not', Jack said. 'I suspect whatever it is, there is merely a key or map. You should be concerned about the secret itself. If the fire has touched that, then the Torre will be unable to save you.'

Jack jumped into his energy and plucked the Elder's memory of the secret from it. It was so clear, he could make out the city before the fire, and the people living there without a care or concern. He took his time, carefully watching for anything extraordinary as the Elder spoke to the merchants of the market.

Jack soon felt himself following in the Elder's footsteps, matching every word and pace, sometimes even replying to the merchants who greeted him as if they were there. Between every stride and sentence, the elder gave the cathedral a glance. The secret seemed to burn at him, whilst a rampage of thoughts kept his mind on Centra and the Morre. *Why Centra and the Morre?*

The culture was off for a city following the legends of the Morre. Its cathedral was nothing like those Jack saw in

Collas-Firtheria, and its people spoke of the Mother rather than the Torre. But there was no mistake in Jack's understanding of the Elder's thinking – *by the Torre* this and *by the Torre* that.

He was soon upon the rubble of the cathedral, still considering what the Elder's thoughts might mean for the secret. Scurrying over the piles of stones and ash, he approached a bricked-up fireplace. The wall supporting it seemed untouched by the destruction; holding the dull stone-grey colour seen all over the colder Alcadian townships and cities. The bricks hiding the fireplace were loose, brittle and scratched by the destruction. There was something special about this fireplace; it seeded fond thoughts of the Legends behind the Morre. The secret's path was with that fireplace, or not at all.

Jack reached out for a brick clinging on to its brother, and with a light scrape it fell into the darkness. He began to pull at the bricks; some crumbled while others held their strength in groups. He discarded each piece of masonry to one side, hoping with each movement that the path might show. A dozen attempts later, he reached for one that looked no different than the others.

The memory of the Elder overseeing a bricklayer leapt before his eyes. It seemed innocent and unrelated, yet the man's thoughts were now crowded by worry. It was a worry over the legends, and Alcadia. Jack studied the brick intently, trying to understand why this one was different by comparing it to the bricks in the Elder's memory.

'Have you found it?' Sirius asked.

'No', Jack said, turning back to him. 'I thought I had it. The Elder was unusually worried about the legends of the Morre and this fireplace. There's no other explanation for it – but why this fireplace?'

'What's that on the back of those?' Ouster asked, pointing to the pile of rubble at Jack's feet. 'Etched into the coarse sides?'

Ouster gestured towards a group of three and a half

bricks, their smooth faces laying atop their brothers. The markings were embossed in such a way that indicated they were designed before the bricks entered the kiln. As Jack inspected them, it began to come together- the bricks had a map on the back of them. In his excitement, he reached over the remainder of the wall and looked at the inside. There the remaining half stood, glaring back at him as if it were the most beautiful thing he had ever seen.

'Well done, Ouster', Jack said, pulling his head from the recess. 'You have found it.'

'A map?' Sirius asked.

'Yes', Jack said. 'This is our way to the secret.'

He began searching the Elder's memory for a moment where he looked at the entire map. He scanned the whole wall's creation, trying to find something that would help him. But as he started again, he saw it, in the corner of the Elder's eye. One of his companions was surveying with him and dictating which brick should go next. It was enough and, as he watched the paper burn before the fresh wall, Jack let out a lasting laugh.

'And now we have it', he celebrated. 'Bless your excellent eye, Ouster.'

'So where is this secret?' Ouster asked.

'Below our feet', Jack answered. 'The map leads to the entrance and through the catacombs, no point trying to break through this rock. Be my shadows once more - come.'

Jack led them all back to the square where he took the Elder, and towards the great gate house. The souls of the passing began to sing to him as his paces slowed. They sung of their lives and the promises that were made to the people of *Joanaria.* Each soul could hold a tune better than any musician that attended the Court of the Knight's Republic. They weren't just singing about Joanas or the Knight's Republic, either. They were singing about the Promised Land.

Jack had to stop and listen to their singing. He knew he

couldn't touch or influence them; their energy was too powerful, and they were heading to a place that had called for them the moment they left their bodies. But he knew such power wasn't fully out of his control, he just needed to find the key to harness it. He understood the Hatred's need for power, but he secretly wished for it in the hopes of being taken and set free. But, like the legends of the Promised Land and Joanaria returning to her former glory, it was a fool's hope best left buried in the heart.

'Why have you stopped, Jack?' asked Sirius. 'Is the secret here?'

Jack ignored Sirius, and the feeling of expectation, and let the singing comfort him. It was a long time since he had listened to the legends of the Promised Land and the fables of what it was like to live in Joanaria before the fall of the once Great Kingdom. It was as if he still had his family and was living in a world far less cruel.

'Penance', Sirius called again, his voice echoing the scratch of the Hatred. 'Where is the secret?'

'This place is full of passing souls', Jack said, opening his eyes. 'Can you not hear them?'

'You know I cannot', said Sirius, 'I am curious to the significance of their existence. Are they not everywhere?'

'Not everywhere', Jack said. 'Not like this. Considering what we have done to this place, it makes little sense for any of them to be here.'

'Are they a threat, then?' Ouster asked.

Jack smiled and turned, looking at Ouster as he held the compliant face of the enslaved. He couldn't be sure if it was his emotions that made him look that way, but it saddened Jack to know it was more likely because he only obeyed. He would have to work on Ouster's will, if he was ever to help him beat the legions of Centra.

'They pose very little threat. Only their songs of Joanaria and the Promised Land concern me. Why sing about them now, after an era to sing about them? Why do they not sing about the great wars that tore Joanaria apart, or how the Promised Land was just some lie?'

'Mother used to sing such things to Cain and I when we were young', Ouster said, allowing a tiny smile to escape. 'It's just a thing parents did, our parents anyway.'

'It can't be that. It would take much more than a childhood rhyme to influence these souls to sing only about Joanaria and the Promised Land. It's perplexing to me. Maybe the secret will have a clue.'

Jack's eyes found the northern gatehouse, guarded by a pair of turrets smaller than those that guarded the corners of the city. The map was leading to the left turret, its trail ending at its' footing, with a patch of rough grass blocking the view of the foundation stones. His focus drained, leaving the emotions left over from the elder's memory. He turned to Ouster.

'Ouster, in your brother's time with the Knight's Republic', Jack began 'Did you ever review the engineering drawings of the fortifications?'

'During Cain's reign his focus was on the missions to assist Fugula in rebuilding their towns and cities.' Ouster replied. 'Rebuilding after the Necromancer was his key concern, and we were exposed to many plans'

'Did they not hide their secrets of the war in a similar fashion?'

'Yes, they did', Ouster said, with a trickle of realisation running across his face. 'In fact, the engineers came to Joanas'

He stepped towards the gatehouse, entranced by its turrets. Jack could feel his mind skimming through the memories of the rebuilding effort and, soon enough, he remembered it himself. The Necromancer burned through the states that opposed him. This must have been one of them. *The foolish Elder revealed it to us.*

Jack watched Ouster scan the stonework of both turrets for a moment, sometimes turning to the gatehouse for guidance. His mind was aglow with thoughts. Jack loved to watch them perform for him as he considered his answers like a wise and careful man. They all stopped when his eyes caught the murder holes at the top of the stone expanse, right below the extruding shingles of the coned roof.

'That one is newer', Ouster said, pointing to the western turret. 'In fact, it looks Fugulian.'

'How could you tell?' Sirius asked. 'It's identical to the East turret.'

'The murder holes', Ouster said, as he pointed to the top of the turret. 'They're too high. The East turret's holes are lower, where the archer's rest. Murder holes closer to the roof is a trademark of the Fugulian engineers.'

Jack compared the two murder holes himself and agreed with Ouster's observation. 'Very good, Ouster', he said. 'That's definitely where we will find the entrance.'

Letters of an Assassin

'Can you see anything?' Bartarian asked as a dozen Hobsythe screamed across the parapets of Halos Fortress. 'Is there anything we can use?'

Jefferson shook his head and peered into the clearing, holding his body flat against the dirt whilst the rest of the Morre held against the treeline. Drake's view was blocked by Bartarian's head, yet he could make out the sand-blasted keep against the blazing sun.

'What are we waiting for again?' he whispered to Gromwell, who had his back to him. 'It's just a quick dash across the plain and we're at the walls.'

'You're forgetting the dead-ground, Drake', Gromwell answered, turning towards the clearing. 'And the traps and whatever stash of weaponry they might have. Let the Fleet make a breach for us first, so they focus their forces there.'

Drake looked towards the keep, which stretched out over the parapets. The stonework of the castle was a warm yellow, with the occasional wooden hoarding casting shadows on the walls. Occasionally he'd spot bobbing Hobsythe heads, all looking in the direction of the beach where the fleet had formed up offshore.

'It'll be a shame to destroy something so neat and clean.'

'That is part of the problem', Gromwell said. 'It's too intact. It doesn't make any sense.'

'Shut up!' Bartarian shouted. 'Both of you!'

Jefferson spotted something. His head froze and his body flexed like a hunting cat.

'What's wrong?' Bartarian asked.

'Up there', Jefferson said. 'On the primary tower.'

Drake tried to find the tower, his eyes scanning over Bartarian's head and the view he had of the keep. Bracing himself from the horizon's glare, he made out a dark protrusion from one of the windows.

To his shock, six cannons blasted from the fortress.

Their balls zipped across the landscape with a belch of smoke spreading like a white blanket towards the sea. The fleet rang out in response, with a series of bells and calls as the water received all but two of the balls.

'How do they know how to use cannons?' a Morre sat beside Gromwell asked.

'They're not that stupid', Gromwell replied, 'but it'd be interesting to see how they would react next. Karl, Tony, shall we ready?'

'Not yet', Jefferson said, keeping his stance low and his eyes on the fortress, 'Give it a moment.'

The fleet released a volley. It must have been several dozen rounds, slamming through the fortress, sending patches of stonework flying and Hobsythe screaming. Jefferson started and flailed a gesture towards the fortresses' westmost side.

'Riders!' Jefferson exclaimed, scrambling to the undergrowth as swords were drawn. 'Human!'

Drake watched as the rear flanks vanished behind the bushes. Every other Morre concealed themselves behind bramble or rock and, once set, only the approach of the riders was heard.

A stampede of horses bolted past Drake and a cloud of loose leaves and dirt obscured his vision. On the command of a Morre towards the rear, they all whinnied and came to a dust-filled halt. Then, under the guise of the fleet's second volley, the riders were rushed and pulled from their mounts.

'Captain Hindrel – report!' Gromwell called as the troops settled.

'They were bound and gagged, my Lord', Hindrel answered, 'Either half dead or half drunk.'

Gromwell looked ahead at Jefferson and Bartarian, both of whom appeared confused. They weren't alone, Hobsythe these days weren't ones to free prisoners.

'Any messages?' Gromwell asked.

'None sir', Hindrel replied between snorts from the

horses. 'All clear.'

'Time to make a move', Gromwell said, turning to the front lines. 'On the third volley.'

'The fort hasn't fired a second one yet', Jefferson protested. 'Let me see if they took the bait!'

'Make it quick', Bartarian barked. 'The fleet's third volley is almost due.'

Jefferson peered out again. A moment later, the fleet's third volley boomed across the land and all the Morre watched the cannonballs crash into the Eastern wall. *He's not signalling,* Drake thought in frustration. *This is the perfect time to move! Come on Tony!*

'Tony', Gromwell called just as Drake was about to snap. 'Now or never – Stop stalling!'

'Very well.' he said with a nod and wave. The army raised their swords and, without as much as a snap of a twig, charged past the Commanders in a sea of silver and white. Behind them was the barer of the humbly-sized Centurian flag, keeping pace as if the pole weighed no more than a bow.

With that final Morre, Gromwell led the Prince and the Commanders to trail behind. Drake tried to focus on the clattering of his armour, and the flapping standard just ahead of him. It wasn't enough; the dread was settling in. He decided to favour the drills of his training instead. *Eyes up, feet apart. Eyes up, do not loose heart. Breathe steady, not hoarsely. Breathe steady, with sword at the ready.*

It was working, but the fortress was growing exponentially as they closed the distance. Drake focused on the parapets and barricades, concerned only with what diabolical contraptions may lie ahead. The gatehouse was shut and the southern wall intact, albeit with several cracks. Suddenly, he caught sight of movement on the parapets, and the army let out their cries of attack as they began to sprint the final distance.

A spear birthed from one of the slits of the walls and missed Drake by a foot. But, with only a shocked yelp and a slight disturbance in his rhythm, he continued the final stretch. He reached into the small space in his breastplate, feeling the lace of Laura's kerchief. *Torre bless me. I'm going to die.*

Bartarian, Jefferson and Gromwell reached the walls and looked up as if expecting oil at any moment. Drake was shocked to realise he had stopped, and any straggler was now facing a rain of spears and arrows.

'Wake up, you scrawny toad!' Bartarian cussed.

'Run, Drake!' Jefferson wailed

As Drake broke into a run, he was overtaken by another Morre. This was much to his luck since, not but a second later, the soldier was struck by a ballista bolt. Drake's first reaction was to try and help, however the voice of Gromwell brought him to a halt.

'Leave him', he ordered. 'It's not safe!'

'He's hurt', Drake said, watching as the Morre began to lose strength. 'We can't leave him out there!'

'Get over here now', Gromwell ordered, looking to the fleet as their distant sails crawled into view. 'The fourth volley is imminent.'

Drake reluctantly left the Morre and joined the Commanders, covering his head. *I'll be back for you*, he thought with determination. *Don't give up – I'm coming.*

The volley roared through Drake's ears, rattling his armour as several dozen cannon balls smashed against the Eastern wall. He had lost sight of the injured Morre and was beginning to panic. *Don't give up. Please don't give up.*

Jefferson rushed through the rising dust cloud with three others and made for the Eastern wall. Drake didn't know or care why. The dirt slowly settled and, as the clearing came into view, so did the Morre, neither moving nor making a sound.

I'm coming – I'll save you.

'Stop, boy!' Gromwell ordered, holding Drake back. 'The next bolt will be for you!'

'No, Gromwell!' Drake fought. 'I can't let him die! I

can't!'

'Wait, damn you!' Gromwell snapped. 'If he dies now, he will be remembered and glorified by the Dragon Council and our people. What more do you want?'

Drake didn't know why this Morre mattered so much to him. He knew of the traditions and recognitions, the stories and the legends. He had read and heard about hundreds of deaths on the fields of battle and felt neither remorse nor sorrow. Even on the field of Forecourt, with the wails of the burning Morre, he only felt horror. He had never felt sadness or loss on such a level.

'Dragon Morre – attack!' Jefferson called from the East.

The army rushed past Gromwell and Drake. Even against the sound of swords and the Hobsythe cussing, Drake only cared about the injured Morre.

'What's wrong with you?' Gromwell shouted as he pinned Drake back down. 'What has gotten to you? Years of drilling and practice for you to nearly kill yourself over some unlucky bastard?'

'Gromwell, please', Drake shouted as he tried to wriggle free. 'I need to be with her!'

Drake didn't care what happened, or why Gromwell released him, but he was suddenly free and running towards the Morre. Ignoring the calls of his name, and the pieces of Hobsythe being flung into the dirt, he reached him quickly and with ease. Hands wild with attempts to wake him, Drake burst into tears. He was not breathing, and already his skin felt unnaturally cold. He allowed himself to be led back to the fort, keeping his eyes on the Morre all the while.

'Listen to me', Gromwell shouted, shaking Drake vigorously. 'There's nothing you could do. Do you understand me? Nothing. He's gone. You can't save him – you couldn't have hoped to save him.'

'I should have-', Drake moaned. 'I should have dragged him to the wall. At least she had a chance!'

'Are you hearing yourself?' Gromwell grabbed Drake's breastplate. 'He was a male Drake, not a female. What's getting into you?'

Drake stopped his musing and sobbing and looked at Gromwell with a worried expression.

'Gromwell – I didn't say 'her' – did I?'

'What's going on with you?' Gromwell asked, panicked. 'What have you done?'

'I don't know', Drake replied. 'I can't have it, can I?'

Gromwell stood up and looked at the parapets, leaving Drake to listen to the clang of metal and squeals of Hobsythe.

'You can't have it', he said, 'I don't think there is empathy in the Corruption. Now shut up and follow me.'

Gromwell picked up Walter's Wrath, and clapped Drake's cleaver into his lap. Drake took it and stood, pushing the sadness out of his mind as he looked at the Morre. *What* is *happening to me?*

He followed Gromwell's steps, dodging the cleaved torsos and claws of the Hobsythe, holding his throat against the nausea that came from seeing so many entrails and so much blood. Several Morre had fanned out through the bailey and around the fort's outbuildings. Some were still engaged by a Hobsythe whilst others were overseeing the grim stories of the lizards' occupation. All that he could do to stop himself vomiting was focus, this time on his hearing.

Gromwell tracked the steps of Jefferson and Bartarian and soon found them in a group of six, hauling a large log against the keep's front door with several others surrounding the battering. He stopped at the drawbridge and investigated the moat.

'Whose idea do you think those were?' Jefferson asked, nodding to one of the ugly looking steel spikes protruding from the water.

'Humans – They're too permanent, even for the scale', Gromwell said, spitting. 'Some never learn.'

'But not all', Drake said, surprised he could remember such things despite the clashes of the ram. 'Navurians are different.'

'Maybe; there's still time to let their madness show.' The great doors were beginning to buckle and crack. 'Don't forget. Now's the time to prove yourself to the Morre, and Bartarian. Bartarian especially.'

Bartarian needs to prove himself to me first, Drake thought. But he nodded and stiffened his brow.

'I'm ready', he said. 'I'm fine, Gromwell.'

Gromwell smiled, awaiting the ram to break the door. It took several more hits but, as the door splintered and broke apart, so did the Hobsythe that braced it. The log was dropped, and the charge was called. The group rushed into the keep, with Gromwell, Jefferson and Drake close behind.

In the murky oil-lights of the great hall, every Morre had a mark, and was duelling with the ferocity of their might. Drake looked for a pair, or three on one, but all were taken in fair matches. Slowly loosing hope, he began to skulk and move to the walls that were not covered in battling bodies. Against the squeals and chants, Drake began to get lost in awe as he watched every Morre cut down their mark. Even Tony had one, which was a surprise and even more of a disappointment.

Unsure how long he stood and wallowed, he soon found a door to his right. Pushing it carefully open, he heard the rumble of footsteps and Hobsythe culls. Taking his chance, he pulled open the door and looked up the steps into the darkness above. He needed to do this, if not for Gromwell, for himself.

Calmly, he traversed the steps. The battle below began to dull into a constant drill of swords and rattles, and whisperers above took hold of his hearing. At the top stood a doorway, with the door held open. The exchange was now loud, clear, and Joanarian.

Drake paused at the last step, hidden in the shadows.

Not far from him a man was arguing with three Hobsythe, and dread quickly overcame him as he tried to make out what was being said.

Suddenly, they stopped talking. An eye caught him off guard. The owner snarled, and he fell immediately backwards into a strong pair of arms.

'You take 'light on your feet' far too seriously', said Jefferson. 'Come on boy, let's take them together.'

With a push and a smile, Drake lunged for the Hobsythe. Both he and Jefferson roared as they entered the room, making for the group. Excited and pumped, he slashed at the first enemy. It hit the beast's breastplate, sending him tumbling backwards, whilst Jefferson's mark only scored a scratch on his armour.

In the struggle, Drake cut open his mark's throat. The creature gurgled and dropped the blade as blood rushed down its neck. Together, Drake and Jefferson took hold of the remaining two, beating them after three hits and turning them into flailing, bloody messes. As the creatures flapped helplessly on the floor, the two Morre turned to the stranger, whose back still faced them.

'What do you think, Drake?' Jefferson asked, panting. 'He's more bone than man. Do you think he is a friend or a foe?'

'I'm certainly not your friend', said the man, turning to reveal a pair of eyes which protruded from a cut veil covering his face. The mood that oozed from him was as dreadful as the blood on Drake's armour. However, he was thinner than the trunk of a sickly tree, and this made him feel more confident.

Drake and Jefferson did not hesitate. But, to his horror, before his sword could even make contact, Drake was being thrown back violently against the wall. Jefferson soon followed with a wail; his own sword had been impaled between his armour plates and his hip. Worse, when Drake tried to scramble up, the man wasted no time in grabbing him and slowly lifting him into the air with his unusually strong grip.

'I know you', he said in his thick Joanarian accent, his eyes seeming to delve into the depths of Drake's soul. 'You're the Prince, and that means this is my lucky day.'

'What?' Drake asked, searching for a way out. 'Why?'

The assailant looked at the window behind him, and dread flooded through him as he came to understand the plan. Before he knew it, the assailant hauled him across the room and head first through the glass. There he fell, down towards the moat. Down towards the spikes. Down towards his doom.

He felt several of the spikes smash against the metal, piercing it as if it were just cloth. That left only his flesh and his bones. Had his lungs not given out, he would have screamed. Instead his sight dulled into blackness.

But it wasn't over. In the void, he felt his form. There was no pain, but a part of him seemed to scream, telling him his body was a broken and twisted mess.

The next thing he remembered was an arm dragging him across the ground. The pain took control of everything, and it was so severe he was already blacking out. He tried to make sense of what was happening between the bursts of consciousness and agony. Before fading into darkness once more, he felt a wooden plank against his back.

He woke again. This time he was moving, and a dull, white sheet was flapping above him. The agony remained, but it no longer controlled him. Even better, he was able to breathe, albeit with a gurgle to his wheezing.

'Where-where...', he croaked, a sharp click of pain shooting through him with each word.

'Hush, my Prince', Gromwell whispered, his eyes full of worry. 'Everything is going to be fine. Just be still.'

Drake knew the hiss, and the subsequent feeling of a hot poker without even thinking about it. It came fast, deep and aggressive, rippling up his back like a whip being slashed repeatedly against his skin. He wailed and struggled, causing even more pain to riot through his body.

'Shit! Be still damn it boy!' Bartarian roared, before Drake plunged back into the blackness.

What is this? Bartarian tending to my wounds? That's a first.

It went around in circles. He would regain consciousness, be comforted and held down, and then fade back to black when the poker touched him. It went on for what felt like several days. He felt the pain as his wounds were cauterised, and he muttered all sorts of muddled questions. In response, he was told to relax and focus on the future.

What future? Am I going to be alright? How many times have I been hurt?

The cauterising stopped, for now. He awoke not long after the final touch, this time beside the warmth and crackle of a fire, feeling stronger but still dazed. He could barely move his head and was struggling to keep his eyes open. He saw Bartarian, snoring away under a blanket, and Gromwell, sitting up and looking into the fire. He looked weary and afraid. *Afraid for me?* he wondered. *Not likely.*

Jefferson was by his feet, rocking back and forth. His fist before his mouth, looking as if he were chewing his knuckles. There was also someone else, someone new. He sat on the other side of the fire, just in view, and seemed familiar in a way Drake couldn't quite explain. He had the greying beard of an old man, but his head was clear of any hair and, if Drake focused harder, he'd have seen a set of scars running down it.

'Who is that?' Drake asked.

Everyone turned to him, eyes worried and scared.

'Hush Drake, you should be resting', soothed Gromwell, reaching for the blanket strewn over his body. 'Regain your strength, you idiot.'

He pulled the blanket up to his chin, whilst Jefferson threw a couple of logs into the fire. Drake could not help but watch the stranger – his eyes were still, catching the streaks of flame in their reflection. After a moment of staring, he caught the stranger peering at him. *As if I were something important to him.*

Drake had no recollection of the night. He rose to the song of birds and the chatter of the jungle against the hot breeze. The fire was still burning, although a half form of itself. Now he was alone with the stranger, his back was to him as he stoked the fire.

'Who are you?' he croaked.

The stranger turned and peered at him.

'Was it the fall, or the attack?' he asked, with a dry tone and an even drier look. 'I did not leave you like this. You have become so different. So- stupid.'

Drake began to black out, once again having to battle to keep his consciousness. Again he returned, this time he found the stranger standing, looking down at him through a raging fire he was feeding. Drake was sweating, searing from the heat, and yet the man seemed to encourage it.

'Don't waste your energy', the stranger said. 'Your body needs it. You've been badly hurt.'

'It's so hot.' Drake whined. 'Where's Gromwell? Where's Laura?'

'*Laura?*' The stranger looked perplexed. 'I have not seen any such as Laura here, boy.'

'Where is she?' He asked again, spotting his things in a neat pile just below his elevated bedding. Atop of it, neatly folded, sat her handkerchief. *I need it.*

'Weir!' The stranger wailed. Little time passed until the Morre was in the light, looking worried. 'It's time – Take his things.'

'No!' Drake wailed, flinging himself for the kerchief. 'Laura, no!'

The pain ripped through his body as he hit the dried dirt. His arms refused to move, and he soon discovered he was tightly bound in a white rope covered in strange writing.

'What is this?' He flailed, hopelessly watching Weir pick up his things. Taking her away from him. 'No. Weir, please!'

Weir gave him the look of an apology and nodded towards the stranger. With that, he turned and disappeared into the night.

'You're a fool, boy', the stranger said, producing a flask and bringing it to him. 'Drink.'

Drake refused to allow the rim to touch his lips. He wouldn't give up. This one took her, and he needed to get her back.

'Don't make me force you', the man said with a growl. 'You're delirious, and your injuries are still dangerous to you. If you do not drink, you will die. And so will she.'

Drake wanted to call him a liar but, as he investigated his eyes, he knew where he'd seen his face before. *My dreams. You – You're the elder.*

'Yes, Dragon Prince', the elder nodded, as the bitter liquid touched his tongue. 'Swallow hard; it's not Joanarian Ale.'

Between swallowing and choking up a laugh, Drake had to take another sip just to be sure. Each gurgled chuckle made his bones scream and his lungs vibrate in horror. It made him wonder if he'd ever be able to laugh again.

'Now rest, Dragon Blood. Tonight will be harder than anything you've ever experienced.'

Drake was soon overcome with a warm, fuzzy relief. Whatever the liquid was, it felt familiar and welcoming. Allowing himself to fall into the darkness, he welcomed every dream with open arms. Soon, the blackness of sleep gave way to dreams so vivid he almost lost himself.

They started with visions of his mother and father, standing behind a raging fire, scowling down at him. No clamouring or aligning to their whims would ever change those expressions. Then without warning, their faces changed to those of Gromwell and Jefferson. Both of them had the weight of his risks on their shoulders, Jefferson especially. Drake cowered away from their unsettling silence, and when he looked back, Bartarian stood towering above him.

'You're not worth anything except the shit in your arse!' he roared. Despite the familiarity of the attack, it still felt unnerving to Drake. But the next vision made what came before seem like an innocent daydream. It was Laura, and the very sight of her caused feelings of shame to swell deep within him.

'I'm sorry', he wanted to say, but his mouth remained shut.

With that attempt, her furious scowl turned into the veiled face of the assassin. The world turned crooked and Drake fell back down towards those ugly spikes. However, before he could hit them, the process restarted. He was back in the hands of the assassin, being tossed through the window, and falling towards the spikes.

'I know who you are', the assassin's voice taunted him between cackles. 'You are the Prince. Today is my lucky day.'

We all know who you are, son of Sepherance. That wasn't one of his thoughts, but it came with a creeping coldness at the tip of his nose. And it was spreading…

'Wake up, Drake', cried Laura's voice. 'Wake up!'

'Wake up!' Gromwell's voice joined in. 'Wake up Drake!'

Drake's eyes snapped open.

'Cold – I'm c-cold.' The chill had spread across his face and was beginning to crawl down his neck. *It's fucking freezing.*

'Hold on, Drake', Gromwell cried, scrambling up, 'Help! Shingdu! Get the fuck over here! Something's wrong!'

The stranger was there in a moment.

'This is it!' He scrambled around for a moment, and then grabbed a pale of water. 'Hold on, boy – Fight it!'

'Leave me alone with him.'

'No, not in this state!'

'He'll be dead if you don't! Trust me! By the Torre walk away, damn it!'

It felt like hours before the Morre left, and now the chill was in Drake's lungs. His breath stung as if every slither of air was ice. Shingdu grabbed his arm. In a brilliant flash, the smoke of the smouldered fire froze, and the darkness splashed over his body in a writhing silk-like mass of blackness.

Drake could do nothing but shriek. The darkness was engulfing him, and angry whispers were filling his head.

'Fight it!' Shingdu shouted. 'I'll help you. Think of something you are afraid to lose!'

What's worth fighting for? Mother? Father? Centra? Home? Think, quick Drake.

'Stronger, boy!' he shouted, 'Think hard and fast!'

Shingdu produced Laura's handkerchief from his pocket.

'Who does this belong to – hey?'

Laura. Instead of the usual warm, hopeful feelings, the blackness of his fate hit him tenfold. His insides now felt like they were freezing solid and was flushed with fear. He let out a cry as his thoughts became loud, endless chants.

'Don't quit on me Drake, come on!'

Something was approaching him from the sky. It was hard to make out at first, but as the pierce of the cold grew stronger, so did the view of the creature. Its eyes were as bright as the stars, and its form was as clear and horrifying as the demons in his dreams.

'No – It can't!' Drake squealed. 'It's coming for me!'

'Keep fighting then', Shingdu ordered, shaking him from the grip of the darkness. 'Remember your training, damn it!'

'My-my training?'

Another memory then hit him, almost as if the blackness was reviving a lost part of him. He recognised the stranger then; the missing teacher from his earliest years. *It can't be…*

'Master?'

'Yes Drake, that's it', Shingdu confirmed, smiling. 'Master Shingdu, do you remember?'

'M-Master Shingdu?'

Drake looked at the approaching creature, which had stopped in its tracks. Its jaws hung wide open and its eyes flashed a brilliant shimmer of white. Then it turned, like a curious dog, and continued its descent tenfold.

In a moment shorter than a blink, the being smacked Shingdu to the floor. No sooner had it discarded his Master, did it gaze hungrily at Drake. The fear flooded him; he felt his limbs freeze. Then, to Drake's horror, he was floating towards it.

'No!' Shingdu cried.

A bolt of lightning ripped through the air and struck the creature, causing it to snarl. Drake experienced the sensation of falling but did not land. He felt his body's senses return, despite the coldness still clinging onto him.

Enraged, the creature darted to the floor. Drake's eyes tried to trace it, but by the time he caught up to it, Shingdu was thrown onto his back with a wail.

The creature came close and levitated him again. Drake dared to look down – there his body lay. *Oh shit – Oh shit.*

'Get off him!' ordered Shingdu, as a crack of thunder smashed over the clouds. The creature was dazed, and Drake was beginning to feel better. The darkness around him turned into a grand hall of grey, and suddenly the world around him didn't seem quite so bleak. Laura – dear Laura – was but a fond memory now. There was no pain, or woe, just happiness.

'Look here. What by the Torre is he doing here?'

This was a familiar voice; a voice never to be forgotten. *Tommila.*

'I wouldn't know where to start', replied another, not unfamiliar voice. 'The poor fool has more holes than a sponge.'

Jamil.

'What do you think, Walter?'

Walter?

'He's seen better days, hasn't he?'

Drake wasn't sure what to think of this. The voice matched his best memory of the Morre, but he could not see him. He could not see any of them.

'What brings you here, Drake?'

'I don't know.'

'Of course you do. You fell for someone, didn't you?'

'Oh, leave off him, Walter', whispered a soft voice, feminine and almost innocent. *Aunt Muriel.* 'He took a bad tumble, that's all. Looks like they came for him too.'

Drake still couldn't see. He felt formless, but still aware of his existence as his memories danced around him. He'd see Walter, as tall as he was last time he saw him, shield on his back and a very fine Astorian in his arms. *A classic Astorian Huntress.*

Muriel was alone, but she seemed content that way. She fluttered her hands in the air just as she used to before her end. As for Tommila and Jamil- they were embracing one another like brother and sister, drinks in hand, reminiscent of good times together. *What a strange place this is. Stranger that I can't find Biggs anywhere here.*

There were a lot of other, unnamed presences about this eerie hall, and Drake had a strange feeling that their deaths were somehow connected. Some of the attending were dancing, others played street games, but none of them seemed to be fully aware of where they were. It occurred to Drake that this could be a gateway into the next life, where the souls taken by that strange myth hung. *That means I must be one of them.*

'Calm yourself, Drake', Walter comforted him. 'You don't belong here. In fact, you don't belong on this path at all. It seems you might get a second chance at this.'

But what if I don't want one?

It was too late- he was back in his body. The creature was nowhere to be seen, and there was only a tingling warmth running through him. Shingdu, on the other hand, had flopped to his side, and was taking in long breaths.

'That thing is tougher than I remembered', he wheezed, scrambling up to untie him. 'How are you feeling?'

Drake shook his arms and legs, breaking away from the stiffness of laying on something hard for what must have been days. He shook them until the rope flopped to the ground.

'Not bad', he said, pushing himself upright. 'Where are we?'

'The edge of the camp, outside Castle Halos.'

Drake turned to look at the fortress. The tents around it filled the clearing, lighting up the night enough to blot out the stars. They must have been several paces into the forest, because the tents ended several strides away, and there were trunks blocking the full view. Drake also found something as he looked at the scene, not far from Shingdu's feet, laying out in the open.

A musket. Drake quickly put the facts together and was beginning to understand perfectly how Shingdu did it.

'How long were you following me?' Drake asked him.

'Long enough to understand', Shingdu said as he pushed himself up, 'Long enough to know who you have become, and what you have forgotten.'

'I think most of it is back, but I still don't remember what happened to us.'

'When the Hatred touched you', Shingdu began, still catching his breath, 'they must have returned something. That's how they overcome an enemy. Take a piece of you one day and then, years later, come back to claim you. I've been tracking them ever since that night.'

'What about the place beyond? Where my aunt and friends were?'

'Are your friends and aunt dead, by any chance?'

Drake nodded as Shingdu picked up the musket and inspected its barrel. *It was him that night.*

'Then I wouldn't know. Perhaps you got very close to

death – enough so to be able to see them?'

'If you can't tell me about them, then tell me about the Hatred. Please?'

'That's not a very good idea. You are not free of your wounds. It would be better for you if you let your mind catch up and tell you what happened.'

'Did they take any of the others' memories?'

'They affected us all differently.' Shingdu hurled the musket over his shoulder. 'I'm still trying to figure out what they took from me.'

'I dream of that night.'

'I know you do. No doubt you will dream of it at least once more before you are fully healed. The sooner you reach that point, the better you will be.'

'But I need to know now!'

'You need your rest, Dragon Prince. Come – I will take you to the tent they have set up for you.'

Shingdu took Drake's arm and led him through the camp against peering eyes and grateful stares. They stopped at a tent no different from the others, small enough to be a little tight, but big enough to hold a standing horse if needed.

'Here we are.'

Drake was pleased to see his armour and sword sitting beside a freshly lit lamp. Next to them lay a rolled-up blanket upon a bed of straw. It didn't look like the most comfortable bed in Alcadia, but it would do. Shingdu set Drake down on his back and unrolled the blanket so that he could slide easily in without a scrape. He could feel the aches now, piercing his back like needles.

'Thank you', he said, as Shingdu padded a make-shift pillow out of one of his torn and bloodied garments. He finished by slipping Laura's kerchief under the pillow. 'Thank you for everything.'

Shingdu peered out of the tent, looking ready to go and fight the Hatred once more.

'Where will you go?'

'To tell the others you're all clear'. Shingdu let a wandering eye flow back into the tent. 'After that I intend to continue hunting the Hatred.'

'Are you sure that is something you should do alone?'

'I was never surer of anything else in my life. There is a darkness about this whole country, and the sooner it gets dispatched, the better the Morre will be to take it back.'

Shingdu was never one for stories – that much was clear. The man would rather teach through action than demonstration. That was his way, and that was exactly how Drake remembered him.

'It's goodbye then?' Drake asked with a frown.

'No – not yet. We will cross paths again, hopefully next time for better reasons. Until then Drake – Torre favour you.' He gave a bow and departed almost without a trace.

***

Drake had no dreams that night, a welcome turn of events after the last few days. When he woke up, the sound of the camp roared in his ears, dominated especially by the chatter around a nearby fire. He forced himself out of bed with a groan, his first instinct to reach for the kerchief.

'Drake!' Jefferson and Gromwell called out as they barged into his tent. Before he'd had time to question their presence, they were helping him to his feet.

'Good to be back, hey lad?' asked Jefferson. 'You seem a little hazed. What did that old fool do to you?'

'Nothing bad', Gromwell answered for him. 'Look at him. Healthy and wide awake. Just shocked.'

'I have never known shock make a Morre scream like a girl.'

What?

'I don't recall screaming like a girl', Drake retorted defensively. 'I'm feeling better though, so thanks for that.'

Jefferson and Gromwell took him by the arms and

helped him out of the tent, where they were met by the grand cheer of several dozen jubilant Morre. Drake recognised those that had followed him from Joanas Sorrow and those who, until recently, had not given a damn about him.

'Well, here he is. Good as new.' Gromwell gestured towards him and the crowd broke into a fresh cheer. 'What do you think lads? Is he ready to face off against the Hobsythe?'

'Aye!' they all cheered.

'I'll try my best', Drake said nervously, rubbing away a stitch of pain in his wrist. 'I feel a little sore and numb though, so give me a moment.'

They all laughed at that. Drake couldn't believe it – he was the centre of attention, with no jape or curse to speak of. 'What happened to me anyway?'

'You took a rather nasty fall into a moat of spikes.' Jefferson said as the crowd fell silent. 'We thought you were done. All of us.'

'We even had a pyre made ready for you!' piped up an enthusiastic Morre. 'Would you care to see it?'

'I'd be happy to light it.'

The crowd laughed again. Drake felt like a ring leader, and even wondered for a second if they were all drunk.

'That will have to wait', spoke the voice of an unnamed Morre. 'At ease and report!'

All eyes turned to the source of the call and beheld the golden-clad armour of Sepherance's High Guard. Drake's newfound dread grew tenfold as they made their way through the crowd towards him.

'We're already at ease, Lord Aldwin', Gromwell assured him. 'State your business with the Prince.'

'Our Business is with the Commanders of the First Army.'

'Well then, the Commander stands right here.'

Gromwell looked fondly at Drake, as did many of the others who surrounded him. *They respect me.*

Aldwin, however, did not look respectful. His greying stubble surrounded a frown that left cracks in its wake. Even his helm, resting on his hip, gave an ill mood; the adorning golden dragon seemed to be glaring at him. Then there were the Morre's officers, younger lads that mirrored Aldwin's mood. Some even had their hands resting on their sword hilts.

'Our business', Aldwin said with a glare, 'Which is the King's business, was to summon you.'

His father's High Guard seemed darker than Drake remembered, and it wasn't just because of the burn of the Joanarian sun.

'All of the Commanders - the Prince included.'

'But he's barely recovered.'

'He looks capable to me. Besides, it is the King's command. I suggest you do not keep him waiting further in light of the current affairs.'

Aldwin's eyes locked on Gromwell during the brief stillness that followed. He returned the stare, chin stiff and lips locked. Drake knew this look; it was the look he always gave him right before he scolded him, and this was the most passionate stare he had ever seen. But Gromwell soon turned to Drake and loosened his expression to one of question, or perhaps the new-found need for advice.

'We knew this was going to happen, Gromwell.' Drake said, finding it surprisingly easy to read the old Morre. 'Let's just go and answer his summons.'

'We didn't know there'd be a freak assassin waiting for us though', Gromwell said. 'It seems wrong to expect you to answer for your crimes so soon.'

'I think it's time to accept my duties, Edward', Drake said, with a sigh of resignation. 'Lead us to my father, Lord Aldwin.'

Drake only received a point in the general direction, and a rude shove by one of the younger officers. He knew from experience protesting made the whole situation worse, so ignorance was what he favoured, along with his mentor. Still, he couldn't help wondering…

'What happened to the assassin?'

'A strange thing, that one', Edward replied, saluting some passing officers that recognised him. 'We found Jefferson hurt, and your old fool without a scratch. Standing over its corpse.'

'That's impossible-'

'Shh!' Edward chided, nodding towards the onlookers.

Almost there, Drake thought with worry. *He brought everyone!*

***

Sepherance's pavilion looked like any tent from afar. But, close to the cloth itself, one could see the tiny thatch work of a golden thread. Drake always used to visit it when it was bundled in Castle Morkor's storerooms. Whenever he went to look at the artefacts of the previous ages, he had to run his fingers along the threads of the fabric at least once, as if it were something majestic waiting to be revealed. To him now though, it was just a covering, and the way in was an ominous gate to his future. Although the material innocently flapped against the wind, it seemed cruel and hard against Drake's woe.

'Lord Jefferson and the Prince are to wait here', Aldwin said as they approached. 'Come, Lord Gromwell. He wanted to speak to you in private first.'

The High Guard took Gromwell into the tent, leaving Jefferson and Drake together at the entrance. Jefferson leaned in close to the curtain to hear what they were talking about inside. Drake did the same, showing no concern for the two remaining guards as they stood still and emotionless.

'-and you look as troubled as ever, you old fool', Sepherance's voice sounded through the door. 'Has my son washed you clean of your wit and your spirit? Or are you turning him against me?'

Drake recognised the severity of his father's tone and shuddered.

'Inspiring him to lead my First Army, break my forefather's holy code, and steal the heart of the next Dragon Keeper of Draberia in defiance of our most sacred royal law. Is this not why you are troubled?'

'I am not troubled, my King.'

'Then explain yourself. What did any of you have to gain from this?'

'A chance to save Joanas, my King.'

'Fuck Joanas', Sepherance crowed, 'Joanas has always been obsessed with power and dominance. Look what it did to the Hobsythe. Look where it got Penance. Look where it got his whole family!'

'That's not necessarily true.'

'The details are folly – same tinder, same fire. Take the boy for instance. He encounters his first battle as Commander and almost dies! You can't tell me that wasn't Joanarian bloodlust.'

'It was an assassin. They took Tony down in two strokes. Tony, of all the Morre in Alcadia! Joanas may be warmongers, but they are not blade masters. Not like that.'

'It was the boy defending himself then?' Drake and Jefferson exchanged confused looks with the question. 'Tired of the old ways and the old fools, defending his honour at last?'

'By the Torre, it was an assassin!'

'Don't take that tone with me', the King growled. 'I wish to believe you, but there is no body. Only the boy, tossed out of a window. That Morre could have easily done it.'

'He had help. Said help took it.'

'Ah, this old human from the mountains', Sepherance was now employing a mocking tone. 'And what use did he have in helping Jefferson, hmm? What did he have to gain by taking the body?'

'Only the Torre would know. By the bloody Torre, he

saved Drake. That should be enough to grant some lenience to the man! He could be fucking it for all I care – He saved Drake.'

That allowed a tense, but brief silence between the two. Drake felt his heart pounding but was relieved to hear that Gromwell wasn't backing down. Jefferson looked just as relieved.

'Fine points, as always. I will take them into consideration.' The King said with a grunt. 'But what about the girl? How could you let him court another? Against my wishes. Against your duty!'

'He is not a boy anymore, my King. He is a fully matured Morre, well past the age you married the Queen. I cannot keep my eyes on his cock all of the time.'

'But this isn't lust, Edward. We'd be on better terms if it was only lust, but it clearly isn't. There is no end to the amount of privileges I must grant Tiana Rivera to keep her tongue quiet.'

'Drake's too, I suspect.'

'There it is.' Sepherance's tone had stilled, but he held it at a tension that could break swords. 'Emelye was worried he had fallen for her too. Do you think she is right?'

'I don't know my King, who is to say?'

'You, you clout. You had one task – only one task. Watch Drake, mind his cock. Mind what he does, shadow him if needed. Tell me the truth Gromwell, or hand me your tongue right now.'

'He has fallen, yes',

'Then by the bloody Torre she was right! This is a dark path we have wound up on Edward. What are we to do? How do we fix this? This is my family name, turning to ash right under my nose. Tell me, what would you do?'

'I would allow it.'

'That seems a little too damaging.'

'Then face the reality of losing your son, Sepherance. And loosing Rivera. There is no turning back from something like this. Do you not see the problem here? Is me standing and serving with no heir not enough to scare you?'

'I didn't say I was blind, Edward.'

'No, but you might as well be. Why have you not sided with Emelye about this? Or have you forgotten Drake is your final heir?'

At these words Drake flinched, and the guards leant towards the curtain themselves. They listened intently, like pups for their master.

'I'll let you have that one- for your son's memory. And my ignorance. You're as stubborn as Emelye when it comes to the boy. The damn fool.'

'Sepherance, we have no choice.'

'It isn't a matter of choice, Edward. The old Kingdoms are talking about him. Do you know what they say?'

'Educate me.'

'They say he is a fairy – a queer!' Sepherance's snarl had returned, as did Drake's dread. 'If I let him have his way they'd think the marriage a sham. A cover for his unnatural deeds.'

'That's the stupidest thing I have heard. It's no more unnatural than forcing your son's bed. So what if they talk? It's his life. For all I care he can bed whomever he likes, it's wrong to dictate someone's affairs like that.'

'Stop telling me what is and isn't right damn you!' Sepherance groaned. 'I would change the law if I could. But he's forced my hand, and the Council's hand. He must marry a pure. A noble. Or nothing at all.'

'If that is what you and the Council has decided, then be done with this stupidity. Get on with your trial.'

'Fine. But don't think this is over. We'll talk again, I promise you. Send for them.'

The four of them- Drake, Jefferson and the guards- took a step back as Gromwell's footsteps headed towards the entrance. His head appeared from the behind the crack of the cloth, looking scolded and drained.

'Your father the King, is ready to see you', Gromwell

said, his voice droning. 'Jefferson, check on Bartarian, and make sure he hasn't done something stupid with the High Guard.'

Jefferson strode away into the depths of the camp, leaving Drake's dread to grow. Gromwell's eyes were glazed with the tears held back by his anger.

'Come, Drake', he said, opening the crack in the curtain. 'We can't turn back from this. Answer to him.'

Drake's heart filled with regret. Regret that he didn't run to the forest, or take more time to consider his destiny. He had fleeting thoughts of jumping into the afterlife and running forever. But he would eventually have to stop, and then, he would no longer be running, he'd be hiding. *Don't be a coward – face him.*

Drake took a step forward and looked at Gromwell with what he thought might be the final gaze they ever shared.

'It's alright', Gromwell said calmly. 'I will be behind you.'

He gave a small smile, before trudging towards the parting wall of beads before him. He held his chin firm and his gaze high, soon seeing his father sitting upon the great wooden chair that was once his grandfather's throne. Sepherance looked upon Drake no different than he would a subject; cold until the warmth of his words filled the void.

'My son', Sepherance greeted. 'My heir – kneel before your King.'

Drake dared not hesitate and kneeled immediately a few paces from Sepherance's feet. He knew what was coming, for he had seen it play out dozens of times before.

'Is it true?' Sepherance asked, 'You came before my Commanders and tricked them into sailing against my orders?'

'Yes Father. My King.'

'And you made a mockery of one of our most sacred laws?'

'Yes, my King.'

'And you took the heart of the Keeper of Joanas Sorrow?'

'She took mine, my King.'

'Do not correct me, boy.'

Drake was unsure if the scold hurt him more, or if it were telling of Laura's effect on him.

'These are very serious crimes, the punishment for which would be exile. Do you deny any of these claims against your name?'

'I do not deny them, my King. I understand what is due, and the price I must pay.'

Gromwell tried one last time. 'Sepherance, please-'

'Enough, Edward!' the King barked. 'Never has an O'Neil been exiled, and never has a Prince. The Dragon Council insists that I make an example of you. But I do not feel exile is relevant in this case.'

Drake would be lying if he told himself he was relieved to hear this. He knew his father too well to believe he'd got off easy. He could see it coming; the real sentence, the real pain of his heart.

'-My King!' cried a voice from behind. 'My Lord!'

Bartarian stormed into the tent, barging past Drake and dropping to his knees. He seemed to have little care for the undergarments that he wore, or his humility.

'Great Father, I beg of you', he pleaded, 'this was all a rouse by the boy; all of it!'

'How dare you!' Gromwell snarled.

'Wait', Sepherance ordered. 'Lord Bartarian?'

'And Lord Jefferson, sire.'

Jefferson joined Bartarian's side and prostrated himself against Sepherance's carpet. 'Mind not Bartarian. It was my fault.'

'What?' Drake squealed.

'It's alright Drake, the charade is over. My King, it was all my idea.'

'Enough! All of you! I know the facts. I know the

conspiracies and crimes. Don't try to lead me astray.'

Sepherance, his face wretched with the outburst and the frown of a thousand tempers, stood up and began to pace.

'Stand up – the both of you.'

'My Great Father-'

'Silence!' the King roared, shocking the two Morre into obedience. 'My head is aghast with the thoughts of treason, and the bastardisation of our sacred laws. Now I have a conundrum here, my dear Morre. The Dragon Council tell me that Centra will not rest if I exile everyone here, yet they will not rest if I exile no one.'

'Father, please', said Drake. 'This is my doing. Exile me.'

'That's not what is good for Centra. And what is good for Centra is that I make you Prince Regent.'

No! Please, anything but that!

'My Great Father, Drake is not ready.'

'As for you, Gromwell', Sepherance snarled, 'you will be stripped of your right to Lordship, and your estate and title will be surrendered to the people. You will be appointed head advisor to Drake's command and will spend the remainder of your useful years as his personal guard.'

'My Great Father, please-'

'And you, Lord Jefferson', he continued, keeping the rhythm of his rage burning. 'You will remain with Lord Bartarian on *human* shores, never to return to Centra, and never to fight for Centra. For so long as there is a King on the Dragon Throne.'

'Great Father, no!' Bartarian's squeal was louder than the snarl of Sepherance's voice.

'You'll pay for this! Retched, impudent little swine!'

Bartarian toppled Drake onto his back, against the panic and lashings of the others, and gripped him tightly around the neck. Drake could feel the strain of his grip against his spine and, as time crept slowly forward, the shouting and the bashing began to fade.

It continued to wane against the writhing panic of Drake's soul, until he found himself alone, surrounded only by the frozen figures of his Commanders. Bartarian's grip remained, but it no longer pained him or took his breath. Drake looked for Shingdu, or anyone that could have been in this dimension, but his search was in vain. Soon however, his eyes fell upon a lone soul floating beside Sepherance's angered head.

It was striking as it hung there, twinkling at him like one of the stars in the night sky. Drake was still trying to piece together his memories, but he had conjured up enough knowledge to understand that this was a happy soul, or a soul ready to pass on. What deluded him, however, was why it remained here, of all the places within Alcadia?

The soul did not answer the question, and Drake was unsure if it was part of the frozen, or part of the moving. Locked in Bartarian's grip, Drake could do no more than wriggle. He convinced himself that what was done, was done, and if he was to perish like this, then so be it. He'd caused enough damage to their lives, yet he could not settle the thoughts that all of this wasn't entirely his fault.

As he battled the woes of his past, he quickly understood that this was all but a fleeting moment. He believed, for a time, that he would do greater good in the passing anyway, and maybe he would see Laura there. But the very mention of her name in the depths of his mind suddenly felt like a mistake, particularly against the dread that overcame him, and the vision of darkness engulfing the light.

'Be still, Great Father', whispered the soul, 'All will be fine.'

The voice froze Drakes' dread. It tickled his thoughts and drove the very mechanics behind his conscience to whisper in a soft voice, very much like Laura's sweet kiss. *I am not the Great Father. I will never be.*

'You will. Wait and see. All will be fine. Everything will be fine.'

Drake looked up at the soul, twinkling again as before, bringing his mind into a slow but well-placed realisation. *Should I be concerned for you?*

'Only if you do not like my singing.'

'Singing?'

'It's a Joanarian hymn. I know you don't understand Joanarian, so I translated it for you. Would you like to hear it?'

Will it help?

'Only if you let it.'

What harm could it do?

Come ye all whom fallen to life's bitter fate.
Open arms on an endless lake,
To the Promised Land,
Where the Children of Joanaria,
Rest their spirits make.

In trees of scolding blue
And blossom of spirits anew.
The hope and dreams of Kingdoms true
Against the spirits take.'

Drake let the singing soothe him, and the soul repeated the lines to him dozens of times. With each verse, he felt calmer and soon he was closing his eyes and wandering for what seemed like an eternity in the darkness. He was ready to face the coming; he was ready to die. With a great heave and a rush of calm, the Bright restored, and so did the grip.

'You're killing him!' Gromwell was shouting. 'Bartarian, stop this, please!'

Drake could feel the strain of his body as it begged his mouth for air. He resisted and allowed the memory of the souls' singing to fill his coming void. He would welcome them with open arms and sing with them as gleefully as a child.

But it was simply not meant to be. Bartarian's grip lost its place after a loud clang of Jefferson's sword. Drake didn't try to resume breathing immediately– he was too engaged with the brightness to want to come back so soon. But as he dwelled, so did a vision, and a very real scream.

It was a woman's scream – that much was certain. It seemed desperate, and full of energy, as if her life depended upon it. Drake dwelled on it for as long as he could and, for a moment, thought it was calling out for him. If he dwelled any longer, he was sure he would call back, or try to save this woman.

He escaped and allowed the soothing rush of air to fill his void. Opening his eyes, he found Jefferson standing over him, giving him a look as if to say the deed against Bartarian was a hard choice. Sepherance and two of his High Guards were pinning Bartarian to the floor, and Gromwell slid onto his knees by Drake's side.

'You baffle me with every passing day, Drake', he said, wiping Drake's brow against a torrent of sweat. 'You're a stubborn idiot.'

Drake rubbed the pain in his neck and sat up slowly. He looked at Jefferson with an eye for gratitude and a mind wrought with concern.

'Thank you, Tony.'

'Don't thank me just yet boy', Jefferson replied. 'I would have done the same thing, but the bastard got there before me.'

So what's stopping you from killing me right now? Drake dared not ask. Jefferson's sword took a long time to return to her scabbard, as if wishing to taste his blood.

'It would be foolish to do such a thing now.' Jefferson unlatched the scabbard and sword from his belt, threw them at Drake and fell back to his knees. 'Do as you intend, my King. Take me away from this cretin.'

Sepherance waved his hand towards Lord Aldwin and

both keepers guided Jefferson away. Four members of the High Guard struggled to bring the groggy Bartarian to his feet as he mused and wailed about Centra. But he was just as submissive as Jefferson now, and neither looked back. Lord Aldwin himself moved to a post in the shadows near the entrance, leaving Sepherance alone with Drake and Gromwell.

'Get up, Drake', Sepherance ordered, 'You were barely touched.'

'I wouldn't call a throat lock a mere touch, Father.'

'And I wouldn't call a tower toss into a spike pit as a survivable encounter. Yet here you are, as if it never happened.'

'You've suffered worse.'

'But not with the need for death in my heart.' Sepherance's bark was loud, cutting at the air like a two-handed sword. 'You leave on the morrow. If you have any wounds to tend to, I advise you address them during the night.'

'Great Father, please-'

'Enough, Gromwell.' Sepherance snapped. 'Get out of my sight, both of you. I hope you beg the Torre they help me fix this mess that you have created.'

For the Master

The arid East Joanarian summer blazed upon Jack's armies, and the road's dust was a fine mist in the wake of their march. He had pressed them hard. Their sweat and decaying flesh filled the air, worse so whilst they pillaged the five hapless hamlets they had passed. The humans who dwelled there were stupid to think of coming back to the East. Their houses were husks of their former selves, and the farms only seeded death. *If only it were to be so easy for the Morre,* he mused.

'Did you have to bring my daughters, my Lord?' Ouster asked, as they trundled past a shattered signpost. 'Surely they are less of a trouble back in Negura?'

'It is no longer called Negura, Master Ouster', Jack said, peering at the wagon to the rear of his guard. 'And how long did you think they would survive there without our presence? One of Grigor's friends would have eaten them both alive!'

Jack's eye caught the hint of a snicker, which was shut down quickly with a glare in the perpetrator's direction. *Foolish little mud idiot.* The whelp didn't even have time to screech before he was turned to a pile of dust and bones.

'It'd be better to have them here with me', Jack continued, watching Ouster from the corner of his eye. 'Than executing some foolish escape plan.'

Ouster's smile vanished. He knew what Jack meant; he always knew. However, he was still a wilful man, and wilful men have always tamed their thoughts very well to appear loyal. That is, until the moment they have a chance for redemption.

Ouster looked down the line to the black wagon, pulled by a pack of mares from the last farm they had ransacked. He had put so much effort into that wagon for the children. The plush, blood-red cushions and pine panelling were set and placed by the time they had arrived, and Ouster's only hope was they were not too hot inside.

Jack's other minions dared not look at him. His anger had set an invisible whip to their backs but, despite that, he knew the Morre could still crush them. Taking a gamble would be the only way to win, and so he continued to lay out plans in his head.

But the more Jack delved into his calculations, the more distanced he became from reality. Since the turn, his dreams and his memories would come to life if he strayed, yet each instance seemed too real to be a dream. The world would slow, and the trees would stretch out over him. He'd soon find himself alone, upon a strange horse, wearing strange clothes. Looking down a road he was sure he'd seen in his life before the turn. And it was happening now. It was too late to turn back.

This feeling was new, and he wasn't yet sure what to make of it. It was absent of sickness or the Hatred, and it seemed surprisingly happy. The horse was bulky and well-fed, trotting slowly along as if on a leisurely stroll with nothing on its back but the sun. Even the saddle had a strange glow to it, the leather glistening like the souls of hope that pushed against his dominion.

He found a maiden riding to his left, her head covered by a shimmering silk gown. Although her eyes were veiled, her smile was open and wide. It was Emma.

'Where are you taking me, my Lord?' she asked him, a few paces along the path. 'What do you have in store for me?'

Jack was a more humble and awkward Morre back then. When he thought of a night before a naked fire, he'd always grin to himself. He almost let that same grin escape now, but instead it came out as a shallow smile. He looked away, knowing her beauty ate at him like the Hatred at his soul.

'What would my Lady have me do?' Jack asked, staying true to the memory.

She looked at him with eyes made only for him, and a smile not unlike his own. All that kept them apart were the traditions of the south, and the formalities of the human weddings. Such thoughts were filth in their minds, so she regularly shook them away.

'I should not say such things, it isn't right in the eyes of the Torre.'

'Only for the human gods, Jack', interjected the Hatred.

Jack began to tremble. He could feel the Hatred with him, like a tittering boy hiding amongst the brambles. He could not see or feel them, but the voice scratching the back of his mind was true to the word of the beings.

'What are you doing, Jack? Are you deviating again?'

'Can I not have my memories?' Jack asked into the wind, causing Emma to look curiously at him. 'Emma, please, get out of here. It isn't safe.'

'What's wrong, my Lord?'

'You were warned about deviations, Jack', the Hatred continued.

'Just get out of here. Push the horse as hard as you can!'

Scared, Emma looked for the source of Jack's worry. Her horse snorted a disagreement.

'Faster than the wind I tell you. Do it now. Take flight to the castle – Anywhere! Anywhere but here.'

With a child-like nod, she grabbed her reigns and pushed the horse into a full gallop. She was away with the dust quicker than Jack could imagine, but the dust refused to settle. It floated and stirred, then began to turn black and intensify.

'These memories are pushing you away from the plan, Jack. There is no reason you should keep them.'

The black smog crept over the surrounding trees, causing them to melt into black clouds of their own. Soon they turned to follow Emma's tracks. *Shit.*

'Please don't. They are all I have. I am not deviating-please!'

'This *is* a deviation, Jack.' The Hatred's words chilled the air. 'Your attention is not on the directive.'

Emma let out a terrible wail from afar, and her horse gave a pained cry as the smog caught up with them both. Jack slapped the back of his own horse with a need greater than any rage he had ever felt. The Hatred tried to speak to him, to channel their energy into the depths of his soul, but his desperation blocked it out.

Emma's screams grew louder as the writhing outcrop of black drew closer. The Hatred transformed into the shadow of a Hobsythe and attacked her, tearing at her clothes. Jack's desperation grew tenfold, and he pushed his horse with all his might. But, by the time he reached her, the figure was forming up into something real, and Emma had fallen unconscious.

He leapt off his horse and crashed into the Hobsythe's back, bringing it down to the ground. Before it could react, he tossed it aggressively to one side and drew his sword. Then, suddenly, he felt a heavy blow to the head, and the world before him vanished. When he opened his eyes, he found himself bound by a rope which tightened around him the more he tried to struggle free. Helplessly, he watched as Kinas dragged away his bleeding, broken, yet still screaming wife.

Fighting desperately against his restraints, Jack felt his precious memories drift away. As he came to terms with his capture, he could only curse until the light of his memories was extinguished, and all that remained was the fire of his own hate.

'Tell us, Jack – what is your directive?'

Jack's cursed memories faded away, alongside the hate. He knew if he didn't act soon, he'd lose his chance.

'Penance!' Cried a voice from the other side.

He realised the army had stopped, and the call had come from one of the Fallen. As Jack searched his surroundings, he soon found the body of Elkwood, bound and nailed to a tree with an open gash upon his chest. A sign was bound to his feet, a warning in the Dragon Tongue scratched into its planks.

The Unseen Enemy of Joanas - your sword shall go no further.

Ouster stopped his horse at Jack's side, staring wide eyed at the fallen assassin. Jack began to read him, finding his mind alight with thoughts of his children. As he began to unravel the threads of concern in the man's mind, he began to sense the growing buds of treachery.

The fool was mumbling the sign's words, but Jack noticed he slipped up on one in particular.

'You mean Joanas, don't you?' he said. 'Why did you not say Joanas?'

'It says Joanaria, my Lord.'

'Does it?'

Jack studied the passage for a few seconds, considering the words in detail.

'It is Joanas', he confirmed. 'But why do you think that it was Joanaria?'

'A slip of the tongue my Lord, I beg your pardon.'

'Maybe he heard it too', suggested Sirius's voice from behind. 'Maybe he can hear the soul songs?'

Jack was disinterested in Sirius's suggestion, regardless of its merit. He was more concerned with Ouster, and Elkwood's death. The Prince had help. No one, not even a small army of Morre, could have overcome his assassin like this. And what of the training they shared- did he remember any of it? *No, the Hatred were sure of that*, he reasoned with himself. *They wouldn't have tasked me with Elkwood's mission otherwise.*

Jack searched the Sea of Souls for the Fallen. Not one in his vicinity attested to the means of Elkwood's demise, and time was far too short to attempt to read them all. Scowling, he asked Sirius if he'd heard what happened. The fool merely shook his head.

'Useless!' he sighed. 'Prey tell then – What are the songs they sing?'

'The Promise of Joanaria.'

'That is an interesting choice', Jack mused as he recalled the words. 'Why do you think the souls are singing it?'

'It isn't clear to me.' Sirius scowled at the air. 'But every passing Joanarian soul sings it as it enters the Rest.'

'That is strange. I was under the impression that there would be no souls here. What is so special about these?'

'I haven't got that far yet.'

'Maybe you should. It could mean the difference for our victory on the morrow. Our friend Ouster here doesn't want to be so easily cut down. Do you, Lord Ouster?'

Ouster shook his head like a limp rabbit.

'Have you danced with the Hatred again, my Lord?' he asked, straight from the void.

'Why do you ask?' Jack returned, with a snap of his tongue and a turn of his neck. 'Am I any different after I dance with them?'

'I meant no offence, my Lord', Ouster said, 'but you do seem colder after every dance. And this one is no different. I was hoping for a warning, like you promised before.'

'That doesn't sound like me at all.' Jack could not help but think the poor fool was delusional. 'Why would I make a promise like that?'

Ouster reached for his collar and tugged on the breastplate to reveal the back of his neck. Lashings covered his back in a hatching of strokes all the way to his buttocks.

'I made no such promise during that time.'

'Again, I meant no offense, my Lord', Ouster whimpered, as he pulled his breastplate back up, 'Perhaps we should press forward, and put this behind us?'

I make the decisions here, not you. Jack held the words back; it felt far too easy to get angry. Instead he merely stiffened his lip and nodded, offering Ouster to lead the procession and scowling at his back as he rode away.

'He is right, Jack', Sirius muttered. 'You do seem colder. I can see it in your stirrings.'

'Shut up!'

Jack whipped his reigns and bolted forward; his horse a

perfect extension of his rage. He rode until he was only a few paces from Elkwood's body, and then proceeded to study it in detail. *How did it get there*, he wondered, *and who propped it up for the Morre*? As the time went on and the army drew closer to the port of Halos-Salle, Jack's mind delved deeper into the possibilities, hoping he wouldn't need to enter the Afterlife to find out.

But the hope was a folly, and he knew what he had to do to be sure. He took in the smells of the sea for a moment and felt the stroke of the Hatred against his skin. They were not hurtful or exceptionally cruel in this instance; on the contrary they seemed bland and not worthy of his touch. The Dragon Morre was killing their dark spirit, yet there were still rebels and stragglers with very dark words to share with Jack as he searched for Elkwood.

He had him in his grasp very quickly. Elkwood's soul was loud and abrupt with its cursing, and Jack wasted no time returning it to its home. He blew the soul into the body, making it quiver into life. Against the stillness of the Grey, Elkwood looked around with lucid eyes. Dread drowned his blank expression.

'Penance-'

'What happened to you?' Jack asked, 'Did you kill the Prince?'

'I think so – I mean – I don't know.'

Elkwood's memories were burning against Jack's reading; displaying a fight in the Fortress of Halos. It was a fight he had not expected, especially from Drake.

'Still your thoughts, man', Jack ordered, struggling. 'I can't read you.'

'I can't find the thought!'

Jack forced his hand and stilled the soul. He could see the forest vomiting a horde of Dragon Morre and the walls of the fortress crumbling under their attacks. Screams and battle cries issued from both sides and the clangs of swords rang out from the courtyard

He followed the commotion up a vast flight of stairs, at the top of which he found the memory. Drake was there, accompanied by an unfamiliar companion. To begin with, both seemed inexperienced and frail but, as soon as Elkwood grabbed Drake and hurled him out of the window, the companion snapped. He became far more formidable, and suddenly transformed into a warrior well versed in the dance of the sword. So much so that the assassin had to put more energy into subduing him.

The fatal blow struck, swift, timeless and veiled by the shadows. It did not come from Drake's companion, however, but from the Grey. Elkwood searched desperately for the attacker as he bled out, and eventually his eyes fell upon an acquaintance Jack knew from before his change. *Master Shingdu.*

Jack ripped his sword from its holster and greeted the approaching blade quicker than a cat against the bite of a dog. The two blades clanged against the Grey, echoing out beyond the trees and into the sky like thunder. The old man's eyes looked frail and forgotten by the world.

'Penance', Shingdu said, with the biting tone of a curse. 'The whispers are true. You are the Unseen Enemy.'

'You were never one to take drastic actions like this, Master. What has changed?'

'Nothing has.' Jack pushed his blade against Shingdu's, but the Master refused to tire. 'Only you. Did you not listen to my warnings? What caused you to fall so far?'

Jack tried to strike Shingdu in the chest with his foot, but the metal point of his boot only kicked the dead air. He felt Shingdu's presence to his rear and turned to throw the full weight of his amour and sword at him. The Master blocked the blade just in time. He twisted his body twice as fast to the left, lifted his foot again, and this time managed to elbow Shingdu's right hip. Shingdu stumbled backwards with a wail, fretting against the blow as his hand clutched his stomach.

'I did listen.' Jack strode forward, swiping through the

air. 'You just never warned me about them – about the Hatred.'

Shingdu moved again, this time to his right, but Jack greeted him with the ankle of his right foot. The slowing, old fool winced and cried out, but did not falter. Every slash of Jack's sword was blocked in a chant of clangs and screeches. He only needed to score one other strike and he would take down the man for good.

'You were never this selfish', Shingdu peddled, 'It would have been pointless. It isn't possible for a Morre to be felled or bewitched – the idea of it goes against nature itself.'

'Nature?' Jack roared through a strike, as he knocked the master onto his back. 'Was it natural for me to watch my family be butchered?'

He struck the base of Shingdu's katana just above the handle, stealing it from the old man's grasp. Before he had a chance to rescue it, the blade was pressed against his throat.

'Is it?'

Jack's growl carried across the landscape. His rage blinded his ability to see Shingdu's thoughts, and he could only climb further into the pit of his family's blood.

'No', the master answered. 'It isn't right. It's never right.'

Jack knew he had to kill him but, with every attempt at a thrust, his arm refused to comply.

'What is this', he asked. 'A trick? The old Magic?'

Shingdu seemed unaware of the source, but he took this chance to kick the blade out of Jack's grasp. He rolled himself away into the night, using his powers to vanish, reappear behind Jack, and give him a swift kick onto his knees. Jack tried to retaliate, but the slippery bastard had vanished again. As he struggled to push himself up Shingdu re-appeared. He thrust the Katana into Jack's pelvis with a fleshy crunch.

'Torre be with you', he said as he pulled out the blade

and let Jack fall to the floor. He wielded the sword above his head, preparing to seal his victory once and for all. However, before the sword could pierce Jack's neck, a black tendril had caught hold of the blade. Its owner, a four-legged floating serpent birthed from the energies of the Fallen's souls, let out the loudest roar he had ever heard.

The Hatred – praise them.

For the first time since he showed himself, Jack could feel that Shingdu was afraid. The beast tore the blade from his grasp, and he stumbled backwards in shock. After a poorly timed swipe from their razor-sharp tail, their front claw landed a bone-crushing stomp on the Master's hip. He had no choice but to retreat, so he closed his eyes and vanished into the night.

The Hatred clawed at the ground, disgusted that a feeble human could have escaped their grasp.

'Get up, you pathetic fool', they barked at Jack.

'I can't! He severed my spine!'

Their tentacles lifted him to his feet as the souls delved into the void left by Shingdu.

'Your old master is causing more deviations.'

'No he isn't!' Jack rubbed the pain from his body as he searched for his sword. 'After we vanquish the Great Father, and take his son-'

'The Dragon Blood Prince will soon no longer be in Joanas. He is already out of our reach. Out of our plans. A deviation that was caused by your Master, Jack.'

'It is a minor deviation, it just needs a correction.'

'That is the problem. Corrections waste time.'

'Even if we had killed him, we'd have had to confront his mother, and the rest of Centra.'

Jack found his sword lodged into an oak standing just outside of the old wood. It was a short walk away, but the pain was all but gone. To his disappointment, the Hatred obliged him their company.

'She will come for the Great Father and beckon the

Prince to remain home. She will separate them all, and Centra will be disorganised under Drake, I know it. This correction will, if anything, give me more time.'

'No. He remembers, Jack. He remembers everything.'

Then that is your failure.

'How unfortunate. But hardly something that needs a large correction. Perhaps instead of just facing Centra, we should consider facing the Centra in the Grey?'

'But it is still a further correction. A correction we are too weak to provide for.'

'Then stay out of my plans. I am a being of ingenuity and I do not need you hassling me about every deviation.' Jack pulled at the sword's handle, but the oak held strong. 'The scrolls will provide me the solution. Their power is plenty.'

With an impatient kick to the old bark, the sword was free. For a moment, the Hatred froze, and Jack was unsure how to react. Suddenly, without warning, they turned and squared up to him.

'We did not grant you this power to run a dominion of your own. Remember that, Jack. Remember that on the shores of Navuro. Remember that when you finally take the Dragon Prince's life. We grant you this silence. But remember. Always, Jack. Always.'

The Hatred roared at Jack's face before vanishing. He shook away his worries, and checked his sword, which had several fresh scuffs from the encounter.

It is easy to sharpen a dull blade, he considered, *but it is not easy to sharpen the loyalty of a man whose children sit at the edge of one's lines.*

'In the end', he spoke aloud to himself, 'it will be all part of the final design.'

The Promise of Joanaria

'Tell me, Lord Aldwin', Sepherance began, cleaning the *Spirit of Alcadia*'s blade as he enjoyed the caresses of the cool midnight breeze. 'What are your feelings about all of this?'

'It was nothing worse than Forecourt, my King', Aldwin replied, watching as a group of Morre threw bodies of mud goblins onto a pile. 'Better this than a Lorre.'

Aldwin was never usually one to hide his feelings, but today he was visibly spooked. He and Sepherance had been visited by a mystery caller the night before, who seemed strangely familiar, and he'd given them a warning about the army of dirt and flesh waiting to ambush them. The moment they rushed the goblin position, any concern the King had of the stranger disappeared. Everything Sepherance thought he knew was laid to bare at that moment. Now he was just grateful a wineskin was approaching, being passed between his jubilant subjects.

'Please, old friend?' Sepherance encouraged him. 'What's troubling you?'

'With respect, your Grace, but how could he have possibly known?' Aldwin asked, also watching the wine's approach. 'They were right on us- like ghosts.'

'You forget you're speaking in an age where messengers can be intercepted and, apparently, Morre can be turned.'

'That is another issue', Aldwin said, spitting with disgust. 'All this time, swearing by the Torre about Forecourt. Now that it might be true, I can hardly believe it. '

Sepherance agreed. *There are so many legends in Alcadia. That is one I dare not think true.*

'Since he was right about them, maybe he was right about this also.' A sour taste greeted Sepherance's mouth. 'It would be a terrible thing indeed.'

'Not far wrong, my King', Aldwin returned, 'Is the memory troubling you again?'

'Not as badly as it used to', Sepherance answered. 'Enough about our friend. I value your counsel more than I do your suspicions. Tell me, who do you think is behind it all?'

'It's too soon to tell'. Aldwin eagerly received the wine-sack and poured the scarlet liquid into a small mug for Sepherance. 'But I would wager this is all just a ruse by Thias Doncaster.'

Sepherance sheaved the *Spirit of Alcadia*, He'd dare not spill the wine- they may not taste such sweetness again for a long time.

'I heard he came out worse than Drake.' He thought back all those years to when the boy got himself into a cult and resisted the temptation to wince. 'Whatever they did to the fool, must have done it for Thias. Penance too.'

'Much good that did him- for the entire clan', Aldwin noted. 'Once we are done here my King, I think it will be safe to start the search.'

'If you think it wise.' Sepherance gulped down the last of the wine and hissed away an old pain tickling his hip. 'I put a great deal of trust on Edward Gromwell's shoulders, Aldwin. I trust you won't fail me as he did.'

Aldwin barely reacted to the comment. It was out of place, and he may never have the same responsibilities, but he was the only one Sepherance could trust now.

'Are you sure this is the right path, my King?'

'Not you as well', Sepherance barked. 'I can easily demote you, you know. Clearly the last age wasn't enough for you to see sense.'

'You know I would accept the honour of shovelling after your horse, Sepherance.'

'I know', Sepherance said, sighing away some of his rage. 'Too many of my Morre tell me this is a 'bad idea.' Torre damn me, I know my Kingdom! I know what is good for it, and the boy. But yes, I know he is my only son. I alone saw the worst in Muriel before she took her life, and it *does* scare me that he might fall to the same fate.

The future of my Kingdom and my Clan hang in the balance, Aldwin, and it *does* keep me awake most nights. That is what you all fail to see.'

The old Morre placed his hand on Sepherance's shoulder and he looked up at him with a grateful smile.

'My King is not alone', he assured him as he tightened his grip. 'I hear you, as I did when you first discovered what was happening to Muriel. As I did when you first danced with the Queen. It is for you I fear, not the boy or the Kingdom. If you do not settle this dilemma, think of what will happen should you fall-'

'Impossible!'

'The Lorre still flew my King.'

The words cut into the King's coming rebuttal, silencing him. Ever since that day Aldwin swore the winged beast had been raised by the spilled soul of a lost Morre. It must have been true. They were all dead and buried by his fore-fathers.

'The Lorre still flew.'

He was right. It must have been a Morre. *So, who could it be? Sirius? Jack himself? No- he did too much good in Joanas to willingly destroy it. Stanley? Maybe. Fool enough, but still a loyal Morre.*

This dilemma would be the end of him, and he was convinced he would never know peace again. Worse, he was now sure he would become one of the Fallen, forced to watch both Drake and Emelye fall to the curse. *All to keep up appearances with a race half our strength,* he thought bitterly. *Piss on them all!*

'Thank you, Aldwin', he said with a sniff. 'I am grateful you were there and are still here now. Help me, then. What should I do, how can I save myself?'

With an approving nod, Aldwin produced his pipe and proceeded to light the Hinterland's Grey within. Sepherance refused the offer of sharing, as he always did.

'Order them wed.'

'Marry them?' Sepherance scowled at him. 'Is there no

other way out of this?'

'It will not come to war.'

'I want to believe that. Don't you think I want to?' Sepherance tossed his cup onto the cookfire. 'Those barbarians would execute their own children if they learned they were courting outside of marriage.'

'But their children *are* courting. And Navuro has come a long way. Besides, why should they have any say in what we do? After everything the Morre has done for them-after everything we've lost?'

'But the Torre's decree-'

'Fuck the Torre! Who discovered the Sea of Souls, and brought Alcadia to her knees? Who hunted the Lorre, the Sorre and even our ancestors? Who decided to enslave their own kind? It was never us, but we were always the ones to clean up. If the decree was worth its weight in stone, we needn't have intervened at all, and sacrificed so much. We will gladly clean up the mess their marriage would make, because we would know it was for us, and for you.'

'My father would never hear the end of it.'

'True, but your father is also long gone.' Aldwin drew in a long breath of the Grey, and the embers in the funnel shimmered in the dark. 'Moreover, I suspect Emelye has already sought assistance to this very problem in your absence. Tiana is a very persuasive Dragon Keeper, after all.'

'That is a truth.' Sepherance said with a sigh. 'She'd likely have gone to that brother of hers. I should try them both for treason.'

'And we'd love you all the same. But neither Drake nor Emelye would ever forgive you for it and your soul would still be at risk.'

'Then, the only way is to allow it?'

'Either decree the marriage or wait for the Queen to manage the same. In fact, maybe waiting is better.'

The Morre inhaled another long breath of the Grey

before saying another word.

'My King, there's a small story to this', he began, lowering his voice. 'During my time of learning, I worked with a trader near the old Thurston salt mines in Navuro. Despite the mines, my Master told me never to hope for success in the salt trade. I was surprised, because it was everywhere, or at least I thought it was.'

'That's ludicrous', Sepherance croaked. 'Was it not then?'

'No, it wasn't there. It was a mirage. Some were saying the first revolts were caused by it. Their Masters were pushing them too hard, and the enforcers couldn't take it. And there we were infiltrating the slavers, trying to do the same thing.'

'So you're saying that revolt we encouraged back before Sanctity – It was going to happen anyway?' Sepherance queried with a shocked look.

'Exactly. Treat this situation exactly like that. Because it will happen anyway.'

'Support a marriage, because it will happen anyway.' Sepherance repeated. As it began to stir thoughts of redemption, he quelled them with a clap on Aldwin's shoulder. 'Forgive me for not settling your concerns tonight my friend. I need to think on it.'

As Aldwin nodded, they both noticed the red hues on the Eastern horizon. Calling for the nearest Commander, the army was alert and standing in moments. Aldwin spilled out the spent Grey, whilst Sepherance pulled out *Spirit of Alcadia,* her blade shimmering as it reflected the distant fire.

It's time, he thought, preparing to begin his march. *I will end this.*

***

'Take a good look at it', Weir said, clapping Drake's shoulder as they looked out over the docks. 'The next time we see this place, there may be peace again.'

Drake looked up at Castle Halos, and the torrent of bodies moving through the camp. It was peaceful, despite the endless toil of Smithies' hammers. It seemed strange seeing it like this, especially after the events of the past few days. Discipline was maintained throughout, and there was no sign of the injured wailing through the night.

However, those Morre were staying behind, while he returned home. Anxiety filled his thoughts, especially of the enemy. Then they drifted to the assassin, and the nights following. Finally, as ever, they settled on Laura.

'I can't help but feel they are in danger', he said, resisting the Captain's gaze. 'As if me leaving here fails them somehow.'

'Would you rather risk going home in chains?'

Drake had to look at him then, and the Captain's expression told him enough. He quickly looked away and shook his head.

'I thought as much. My Last Captain spoke of honour, duty and self-sacrifice on the day before he was killed. It would suit well for this moment, and I'm sure it'll settle your nerves. But for the life of me, I can't remember it.'

'You're a unique kind of Living Legend, Donald', Drake said. 'You know that, don't you?'

'I like to think myself as a simple Morre', Weir reminisced, pausing as two sailors lumbered past with a barrel. 'Stories and fancies about heroes long gone don't do the true weight of honour justice. Everyone expects so much of me, sometimes it feels as if I'll lose my station if I don't act like the Legend they keep hearing about.'

'But that doesn't happen. You got us here on your Legend alone.'

'Don't be so sure of that', he replied, crossing his arms. 'And don't underestimate the newfound respect these Morre have for you. You're becoming a Legend of your own, my Prince.'

Drake should have smiled at that, but the last thing he

wanted was to look a fool in front of a Legendary Captain.

'Why does it feel as if we've achieved nothing then?'

'It's the curse.' Weir found his personal cask of nectar, tucked between spare boxes of cloth, and pulled out an accompanying pair of cups. 'The sense of loss overtakes everything good we have achieved.'

'I thought we weren't to use any of that until we were in sight of Centra?'

'Only the Torre need know that. Besides, you clearly need its sugar', Weir said, pouring the sweet juice into one of the cups. 'And it is *my* personal cache, not theirs.'

Drake wasn't keen on nectar. It felt like swallowing a jug of syrup from the Gaulian Pines, let alone the oversweet taste.

'Try it' Weir insisted, handing him the cup. 'It's mixed with orange and lemon. They loosen the texture and give it a better taste.'

Drake accepted the cup and sipped at the liquid. To his surprise, it was better than he expected. At least it didn't lather the roof of his mouth like the last nectar he forced down.

'Not bad', he said, returning the empty cup. 'But I feel no different.'

'That's because you need at least three before it works.'

'And for me?' Asked a new voice. Gromwell was walking towards them, carrying his bundle for travel just as he did when they departed Joanas-Sorrow. 'Is there enough for the three of us?'

'There is enough for five if needs be', Weir answered with a smile. 'I wondered when it'd be done. Show me the sword?'

When Gromwell reached them, he took out his personal metal mug and clapped it on the box beside the others. Then, he pulled out *Walter's Wrath*, looking as sharp and pristine as ever. Weir gladly took it with a gentle hand, before passing the full mug to the Morre.

'Whose work is this?' Weir asked, marvelling the

freshly-honed steel. 'Good rapier forging skills are hard to come by these days.'

'It was Master Yushin'. Gromwell pointed to a blacked-out tent leaning against the Eastern wall, spewing grey smoke. 'From Iliad. He has several rapiers for sale if you're interested.'

'Maybe I would be.' Weir poured and quickly drank some of the nectar, before handing *Walter's-Wrath* back to Gromwell. 'There's plenty of time before we depart. But first, Drake needs this.'

Drake received the next cup willingly and emptied it in seconds.

'Trying to drown your sorrows, hey lad?' Edward jested. 'It'll work out, just you wait.'

Drake was beginning to feel nauseous around the two Morre. Despite their manners and smiles, they insisted on telling him how things were, and the way they ought to be. *I'll show them. I'll show them both, curse or no.*

'Hold that thought, Edward', Weir interrupted, pointing to a figure limping onto the dock. 'Isn't that Shingdu there?'

Drake followed Weir's pointing finger to a hobbling man. Before he could make him out, however, he collapsed. The three of them ran to his aide. *It was Shingdu.*

'Drake', Shingdu sighed. 'Thank the Torre. I came as fast as I could.'

The old Master let out a scream as Weir's hands touched his stomach. Convinced of something serious, the Captain rushed off calling for a doctor. Despite struggling against the pain, Shingdu reached up and pulled Drake closer.

'Drake. Listen to me. It's important.'

'Stop straining yourself, you fool.' Gromwell ordered. 'You need to stop talking.'

'No.' Shingdu pulled Drake closer towards him with a strength no injured man should have. 'Your father. The enemy he is facing. He needs to know. *You* need to know.'

'What is it Shingdu?'

'Not what Drake. It's a Morre. It's-'

Shingdu let out a piercing cry as he doubled over.

'Who, Master?' Drake tried to comfort him, but the man flinched from every touch. 'I don't like this Edward- I don't like this at all.'

'Hush boy', Gromwell snapped. He ripped open the master's shirt to reveal his stomach, which was a deep hue of purple.

'Donald! Get that bastard doctor here quickly!'

'He's here!' Weir returned, running with a middle-aged Morre. 'Step back; the both of you.'

'Oh dear', the Doctor exclaimed at the first sight of the Master's stomach. 'Not good, not good. I need my other satchel. Quickly!'

Weir was away in a flash. The Doctor comforted Shingdu, feeling around his body despite the quick movements and gut-curdling wails. Before he had examined his whole body, he discovered the source of the bruising; the man's hip had been shattered. The Doctor's disbelief that he walked here fell on deaf ears, for Drake and Gromwell were looking at each other in worry.

'The enemy is a Morre?' Gromwell asked Drake. 'What does he mean it's a Morre?'

It's not possible. But if it were a Morre, then he'd know our secrets. He'd know how to stop us. Stop an army.

'I don't know. But Edward, Father and his army are in danger!'

'You're right.' Gromwell began to pace, shaking *Walter's Wrath* in frustration. 'We have to warn him – but how?'

Between Gromwell's mumblings and the hurried talk between Weir and the Doctor, Drake began to delve through the dredges of his slowly repairing memory. He found dozens of lessons, drills and even exercises, before he stumbled on one such memory that might work.

Shingdu let out another wail. Drake waited until

Gromwell stopped pacing before beginning his plan.

'Don't follow me', he whispered.

'What-'

Drake was humming to himself before he could hear Gromwell's final words. Closing his eyes, he took the final step. He focused all his emotion, especially his rage, into a tiny spot he imagined before his eyelids. Silence soon followed, and the wind died. To his surprise, he found himself exactly where he needed to go.

It worked, he thought. *I'm in the Grey.*

Turning to the group huddling around Shingdu, he found statues of the Morre and the Master. The only sign of life was a pale glow in each torso, including Shingdu's. He felt a strange presence to his side and turned to face it.

It was the soul that sang to him before. It hovered over the water with no accompanying statue or grave. Its greeting sent shivers down his spine, but he could not back down now. He was not even sure if he knew how to go back.

Turning to Gromwell, he snatched the sword from his frozen clutch, and allowed one look before setting off. *I'll bring it back, I promise.*

***

Jack stepped closer to one of the bigger trunks, one that could hide him from the prying eyes of the Morre, and peered into the camp. No sounds came from the tents, despite the silhouettes against the lamp lights. *Perfect. Just as we planned.*

He unhooked his helmet from his belt, slipped it on and turned to the regiment of Fallen waiting behind him. He could see all manner of diabolical weaponry hanging from their claws, many of them far too impractical for serious use. But it was exactly as intended.

The Commander walked into view – a beast no different from the others except for a mass of hair growing out from the base of his helm. Jack exchanged a nod with him and watched as the collective roved towards the camp at his signal.

'I still disagree with this plan', whispered Sirius, as they crept closer to the clearing. 'We will need everyone.'

'Hush, Sirius', Jack soothed him. 'Trust me. We will not, when the time comes. Just be still and stay very silent.'

Sirius gave a dissatisfied sniff, crossed his arms and turned to the lines forming behind him. Not a sound was heard but the low patter of feet as the first group approached the clearing. Jack let himself fall to the ground, onto a sheet of leaves and dried mud.

The line reached the clearing and broke out into a loud sprint. They let out hungry squeals and roars, with weapons held high. Ripping through the small barricade, they roved through the entire camp as if scouting for lives. The fools did this for what seemed like an eternity, before deciding to whip and destroy every tent.

'Why aren't they fighting back? They're killing them!' Ouster whispered, sounding concerned for the Morre. Jack peered back at him. 'Unless – it's a trap?'

'Yes, Commander Ouster.' Jack said with a smile, before turning back. 'They are not there.'

'But why waste good Fallen?'

He was cut off with a screech from one of the Fallen. Although he missed the beast tumbling to its death, he managed to locate its neighbour, who had started at its fellow's demise. It let out its own scream of pain as a night arrow pierced his back. Another, leaping from a collapsing tent, peered around frantically for the shooters. It too was taken by a bolt, and this time Jack had found the source.

Once he located the Morrc, he signalled a readied bowman, relaying the direction. The first shot was lit and fired at a low angle at a seemingly innocent crate sticking out of a felled tarp. It exploded in a mass of flaming debris, sending off a chain reaction within the rest of the false camp. The second shot was fired during the chaos, but this time it was aimed high, and reflected the direction of the Morre. *That fat, greasy fool had better see it*, he thought angrily.

Jack felt dread overcome Ouster, but he dared not speak a word under his gaze. A ballista bolt from Grigor's division flew into view and impaled a tree not far from the burning camp, whooping at the air as its tail rocked side to side. It had mimicked the intended direction perfectly.

'Down!' roared Sirius.

Jack's forces under the cover of the trees fell to their bellies, pulling their shields up their backs. However he was still looking in the Morre's direction, smiling through the sounds of distant twangs coming from the south. *Thank the Hatred! Good Grigor.*

The main force of Morre were running into the clearing when the long, low-pitched squeals began to fill the air.

BOOM! One shot struck paces from the leading Morre. BOOM! The second poured its flaming, oily contents right onto the canopy. It showered down onto the ranks below in a mess of screeching and wailing.

BOOM! Another smashed and rained its hellfire onto the below mass of panicked soldiers. More went off, lighting up the northern treeline like an aggressive wildfire, revealing the entirety of the Morre's position, and their panicked army baulking in an all too familiar scene. Grigor delivered six more rounds, one of which missed its mark and took out Jack's leftmost flanks. It was a minor loss, because the Morre was no longer charging. *Good. Now, it is our turn.*

Hurling his shield away, Jack leapt up and called the attack. Together, in a discipline matching the Morre, his army stood and sprinted for the fires. He, Sirius and Ouster were left alone on the jungle floor.

The army enclosed the Morre position, forming an impenetrable wall that fired arrows and threw spears into the killing. They did not feel heat, nor did they fear death. Unlike the Morre, who screamed in desperation as, one after the other, they failed to breech the wall of bodies. It was beautiful.

'A fine strategy', Ouster commented, his thoughts betraying him at every word. 'How would you know where and how they'd spring the trap?'

'That's a very good question, my friend', Jack said, keeping his mind on the fool's growing fear. 'Sirius, fetch our guest.'

Sirius slipped away into the night, leaving the two of them alone.

Jack turned to Ouster, eyes alight as he rumbled his deception. He began to close the gap between them, with a slow and tantalising pace. Ouster knew what was happening. His fear was a scolding mess and his thoughts were laid bare, just like the thousands of humans that fell before him. And yet, it was only a presence. His resolve was to remain true, and brave.

His sword was quickly out, pointing at Jack's neck.

'Stay back – not one step closer.'

'We need to talk, Ouster', Jack said, still closing in. 'We need to talk about you, and what you have been doing of late.'

'I have remained loyal.'

'Oh really?' Jack said, turning to make sure they were there ready for him. 'Then explain that.'

Sirius pulled the newcomer into the light of the fires. His claw dug into the man's shoulder so tightly that a little blood was seeping out. He was old, but he knew Ouster knew him, despite being badly beaten and gagged.

'Edgar', Ouster whined.

Sirius pulled away the gag, allowing Edgar to speak.

'Forgive me, my Lord.'

'It's all right', Ouster said. 'The Morre are coming. They'll save us. They'll get us out of this.'

'But they are not coming', Jack said, pointing towards the firestorm. 'Edgar, tell Jonathan what you told me.'

Edgar looked up at Sirius, as if expecting an approval.

Instead, he was met with snarling teeth.

'Sepherance's force isn't enough. He sent them all here.'

Edgar looked at the fires, roaring against the muffled screams still bellowing from the trapped Morre. He seemed to wince at every wail, and every felled solider.

'I didn't know about Jack's weapons. I'm sorry.'

'So, this is how you knew?' Ouster asked, gulping. 'And the weapons – How did you keep them secret? Why?'

'Why, why, why', Jack mocked, with a great, echoing laugh. 'That's all it has even been with you, hasn't it Ouster? I admit, I noticed later than I should, but how could you have been so foolish *not* to think I would figure you out?'

'Stay back!' The traitor wailed in response to Jack's advance. 'I have done all that you have asked of me, I told you everything I knew.' He kept his sword still, holding it at Jack's throat. 'It's me you want. Release him. Release my children. Please.'

Jack looked at Edgar, who had soiled himself from the beating.

'You have your victory. The Dragon Bloods are finished!'

'I say when they are finished!' Jack snapped, snatching the sword from Ouster's grasp. Sirius pushed the captive straight at Ouster and, before the two of them could embrace, Jack had slit the man's throat. Much to Sirius' satisfaction.

'There, he is released.' Jack watched as the old fool whimpered and gurgled up at a sobbing Ouster, who was covered in blood. 'He told me many things about you. He told me about the horses and the people you had hidden from me. I don't suppose you noticed how fat Grigor and his minions were before we parted…?'

'Bastard!' Ouster grumbled, watching as his final friend fell limp.

'Seize him.' Jack shouted at the canopy, making a dozen

Fallen drop to the floor, surrounding the traitor.

Ouster didn't fight and allowed himself to be feebly dragged before him. But, to Jack's surprise, as soon as they stopped, the man found a sudden bloodlust. He knocked the guards from their feet and lunged straight at Jack, a dagger in his approaching hand. Instead of striking flesh, it impaled the ground as its master was taken. Jack had pierced his belly in a single stroke and roared as he pinned him to the tree.

'There. Another mercy. Here you shall die. But know this, Tammy and Louisa will not be so lucky.'

Ouster, despite struggling against the pain and bringing up saliva diluted with blood, was overcome in a mad-like hysteria. He gave a calculating smile, before erupting into a long, wet cackle. Jack looked at Sirius, who merely shrugged.

'What's so funny?'

'It's a fine thing, that', Ouster began with a blood-spewing giggle. 'But Thias and I went a long way back. So far back, Jack. Before his injury. Before he met you.'

Jack understood. *The children. The fucking children.*

He ran for them, as Ouster cackled loudly at his back. The cart was still safe where he left it, out of sight and hidden under a roof of steel. The horses, however, were unnaturally silent. He looked to the sides, where he left them, and found them missing.

'Children!' He called as he approached the cart's doors. 'Tammy! Louisa! Are you there?'

He ripped them open and found it as Ouster had hinted. Empty and deserted. *Foiled. Foiled by a fucking man.*

***

Drake's first view of the area was the orange glare of a raging fire. He wasn't sure of the whole plan but, knowing his father, he'd have set an ambush. But something was terribly wrong. Stepping closer to the frozen licks of flame covering the mass of tree trunks, he began to make out shapes that were not trees. They were Morre.

The developing scene became clear. His father's trap was sprung, but the enemy had control. They had used the fire to pin the Morre, and they were winning. Dozens of souls clinged to the air, many paying him no mind, but some were telling him to run. Looking beyond them, and beyond the fires, he made out a wall of glowing statues. It was the Fallen, standing behind shields as tall as themselves, some even in the process of cutting through a Morre. Drake's rage began to boil.

'Look, Great Father', called Drake's soul friend. 'To your left.'

When he turned, he found a wall of thick, black smoke on the edge of the opposite clearing. It looked like thunderous clouds, except it had an ominous feel to it, intensifying as he moved closer. *Could this be the source of the Corruption*, he wondered.

He stopped paces away, and swore the wall was whispering. Leaning an ear toward it, he began to hear cursing, promises of destruction, and even a song about torture. The more he listened, the closer his nearest hand was to touching it.

'Stop, Great Father', cried the soul's voice from behind.

Drake spun to face it.

'What is it?'

'Nothing good.' The dreaded whispering was intensifying. 'It is a sickness. He uses it for his power.'

'The Unseen Enemy?'

'The Unseen Enemy', the voices whispered between curses. 'Dragon Slayer. Traitor. The Hatred.'

At those final words, Drake was overcome by a familiar chill. Instinctively, he reached out his hand to the soul, finding it encased with tendrils of blackness.

'It's him.' The whispers spoke with a satisfied sneer, as if a group of hungry children. 'It's the Dragon Prince.'

The soul sped through the distance right at him. As

soon as it touched him, he was catapulted straight back into the Bright. Landing against something hard, he barely had enough time to take in a breath before being sick. It was over quickly, but he soon found himself confronted by two towering figures clad in black armour. In a panic, he reached for his belt, where he put *Walter's Wrath*. To his horror, the nearest of the two held the sword before he even reached the scabbard.

'Well this is a pleasant surprise', he said, pointing the rapier at Drake's neck. 'It appears we will finish the plan sooner than we had hoped.'

***

'Traitors!'

Jack looked around just in time to face an arrowhead of charging Morre. Their silver armour embossed by Golden Dragons twinkled against the fires. The one at the head had a single gold ringlet in the clutches of his helmet's Dragon. *Sepherance!*

The King flung himself shoulder first into Jack, winding him and pushing him several feet back into the underbrush. Within seconds of his recovery, the Morre had discovered Drake and had surrounded him. Sepherance and Drake were shouting at one another, but it was difficult for Jack to hear what about.

Sirius, who had landed not far from Jack, was quickly up and snarling in a rage. He flung himself at the Morre and was greeted by the well-timed swipe of a sword. They disabled him by stabbing him under the breastplate. Jack looked up at the Fallen waiting in the trees.

'What are you waiting for, you fools?' he barked. 'Attack!'

They answered, and quickly engaged the Morre. Jack stood and proceeded to march through the duellers, barging through the Fallen and grabbing a Morre by his sword arm.

Confused, the Morre tried to fight him off, but Jack was already drinking the power of the Hatred. His grip crushed the Morre's gauntlet, hand and pommel into a bloody mush, and he shrieked out in agony. With his last lap of power, Jack punched his breastplate, forcing it to cave in on his chest. With barely a wince or a grunt, the Morre collapsed.

That left only the Prince and the King. The younger of the two was the first to greet him. However, this time Jack had his bloodied gauntlet ready, blocking the fool's hit. He countered by punching the boy's eye. The weakling's scream was music to his ears, and he could not help but smile when the Prince tried to fight back. Tossing the rapier away, he grabbed the Prince's neck, and rose until he was standing on his toes, struggling to breathe.

The King soon followed. Jack caught his sword in the first attack, stealing and tossing it in the same direction as the rapier. He was up in the air and at his son's level in little time. Drinking the Hatred, Jack prepared to crush both of their necks. *Like father, like son.*

An unexpected blade suddenly stole his victory. The power trickled away through a burning hole in his stomach. The Royal Morre fought their way free, giving Sepherance ample time to pick up *The Spirit of Alcadia* and thrust it in Jack's unhurt side. *Bastards,* Jack thought as his leg gave way. *How could I not see this?*

Looking up at the saviour, he found a face covered in soiled cloth, with charcoal black hair. The last thing Jack saw was a leather jacket hanging open to reveal a scarred torso. *Foiled again!*

To everyone's horror, the Hatred had decided to intervene. They appeared right between the Morre and flung everybody in opposite directions with a curdling roar. Then, they began to hunt the Morre, starting with the dozen still standing and fighting.

'It's you. You can get him out of here!' Jack heard Sepherance shout above the screaming. 'You have to!'

The stranger's mumblings were too low to hear, and the Hatred's reaping far too loud.

'No!' Jack wailed, unable to move. 'Don't you dare take my victory away from me!'

The Hatred stopped mid-reap, sipping at their prey's soul as they looked straight at him.

'They're getting away. Do something!'

Flinging the lifeless body away, the Hatred turned to the three figures. The stranger already had Drake on his shoulder.

'Go- Get out of here!' Sepherance ordered, noticing the Hatred coming right for them. 'Now, damn you!'

Just as Sepherance screamed the last order, the creature smashed through him to get at Drake and the stranger, but they were greeted by dust. The Hatred looked this way and that, but the two figures were gone. Jack knew where, and he knew how. He was surprised to see anyone except Drake perform such a feat.

The Hatred turned back to Sepherance.

'No!' Jack cried out, right as the beast reached for the King's soul. 'Not that one. I can use him- I *need* him.'

***

Drake gave up trying to sleep. It gave him a headache, but his eye was getting better. He peered over at the desk. The letter he wrote just as the ship was setting off still lay on the table beside Laura's handkerchief. He remembered where he'd stopped. *It'll never work,* he thought. *Maybe Gromwell can help.*

Getting up and dressed was still difficult. But he'd refused help from the doctor and Gromwell too often to start looking like a weakling now. It was a slow and painful process, but he was soon wearing his chosen outfit with Laura's handkerchief and letter in his pocket. He slowly made for the deck.

Before he reached the open air, he heard singing. When

he arrived, to his surprise, every soul was on board listening to the music. They were surrounding two girls, the eldest of whom was the singer. To his relief, Gromwell was by the stairs, and had already noticed him.

'What are you doing here?' he chided. 'You're supposed to be resting.'

'I couldn't sleep.' Drake replied, still paining from the sunlight. 'Besides, I need some help.'

'With what?'

'The letter.'

'Fine, but not now', he said, pointing to the girls. 'Do you know who they are?'

Drake glanced at them. They looked like regular human girls. One was barely old enough to stand, and the other likely several years from maidenhood.

'They're Ouster's girls.' Gromwell explained.

'Really? How did they get here?'

'Just as you and Shingdu did – appeared out of the night. Healthier, mind, but still shaken. I'm surprised Tammy is singing.'

'It helps her forget what has happened.' Weir interrupted, joining the ovation when she finished singing. 'How is your eye Drake; may I see it?'

Drake let the Morre pull up the bandage, causing him to flinch. *Maybe not so healed yet.*

'Good. It's getting there', Weir said with a grin. 'And in general? High spirits?'

'Higher, thanks.'

'That's good news. Are you up for meeting me in the cabin later? Say- tonight? I must discuss a few things with you, and Edward. Pressing things.' He waited for an acceptance from them both before walking over to the elder girl. 'Do you feel like one more, Tammy?'

Bravely, and with a shy smile, Tammy nodded. She took in a deep breath just as Weir started walking away towards the foredecks.

'Come ye all whom fallen,
To life's bitter fate,
Open arms on an endless lake,
To the Promised Land,
Where the Children of Joanaria,
Rest their spirits make.'

'In trees of scolding blue,
And blossom of spirits anew.
The hope and dreams of Kingdoms true,
Against the spirits take.'

'Come ye all whom dare,
To death's twisted stare,
Endless breathes and endless tears,
What lies beyond at Sea,
Is little more than misery.'

The deck cheered as she finished.

'Very good', Gromwell said. 'That is a fine voice you have Tammy. I'm sure it will carry well in the Dragon Court.'

Tammy smiled away her fright and made her escape along with her sister. The shift change bell rang into the sky, and the deck erupted into organised chaos. Both girls quickly disappeared between the roving Morre, likely headed below deck.

'Edward, can you help me now?' Drake asked the old Morre, showing him the half-finished letter.

'It can wait', Gromwell said, waving him away. 'We're making good speed and you haven't healed yet.'

Drake pulled Laura's handkerchief from his pocket. If he could make amends, there might still be a chance. Together they could raise lots of children and teach them to be good Kings and Queens. But then there was the expected future, the future where he married one of the nobles.

Drake looked up at Allora, her green hues barely visible against the day.

I am thankful – I really am. I just wish it could be different. Not with a stranger – please?

The green and blue living moon seemed to smile at him with her reflection. He knew it was just the water, but there was no harm in hoping for the better future. For a better tomorrow.

'Are you sure you are doing alright there?' Gromwell asked.

'I'll be fine', Drake said, looking towards the wind. 'Why?'

'You look a little distracted', Gromwell replied, 'I don't blame you; so much has happened. It's good to be going back home after all that.'

'It isn't so much a good thing as a punishment.'

'Oh, come on now', Gromwell said, 'it isn't so bad.'

'What makes you so happy? You've lost your estate – your title. How do I know you aren't going to kill me?'

Gromwell laughed, taking a moment to reflect on Drake's words.

'My estate has been abandoned for seventy years. My home is the castle – as it always has been. So what if my title isn't 'Lord' now? It's easy to get that back – just need to get into some more battles and maybe save your life! Still, come the Dance of the Skylarks I'm sure it won't be too long until you are King. That means you could reinstate me.'

Drake smiled at the thought of revoking Sepherance's judgement.

'I'd undo a lot of things, Gromwell. Your Lordship isn't one of them though.'

'Hah. I may reconsider not killing you then.'

'Don't be stupid, of course I would reinstate you. It's just… I wouldn't know where to begin with it all.'

'I think the key is to not think of it too much. Most affairs of state are handled by the Council, anyway. I'm sure they'd be happy to reinstate me themselves.'

'What about Jefferson and Bartarian?'

'They'll be fine', Gromwell said, letting a sly smile grow. 'Just beg the Torre we make good speed to Joanas-Sorrow.'

'Joanas-Sorrow? What are you up to?'

'Oh, nothing. I just might avoid the galley if I were you. Until we reach Joanas-Sorrow, at least. Maybe stay in your cabin too. Don't want you seeing Laura again and all that.'

'You didn't-'

'Look, it was either leave them feeling sorry for themselves or giving them a lift to Joanas-Sorrow. What was a Morre to do, with so much debt hanging off his arse?'

'Debt for what?'

'Convincing those two idiots to follow your Command. It was Jefferson's idea. Weir was standing there listening to the whole thing. Do you know who the first to agree was?'

'Weir?'

'Mr Loyal-to-the-end Donald bloody Weir.' Gromwell glared in the direction of the command deck, where Weir was standing with his first officer. 'He even suggested taking them as far as Navuro, but Bartarian wouldn't have it. He said he'd rather die in Joanas than put up with us for that long.'

Drake couldn't help but smile at that notion. *Classic Bartarian.* It may have been sneaky, and treason, but it was the least of his problems. Besides, he could claim ignorance to the whole thing, and pretend he was an innocent. But, thinking on it, the odds looked very good for Bartarian and Jefferson. All that was left was Gromwell, who, regardless of whether he felt content with his punishment, deserved a little more than that.

'I'm sorry, Gromwell', Drake began, letting out a long sigh, 'I'm sorry for everything I have put you through. And your sword.'

'Ah yes, the sword.' Gromwell gave him a serious look.

'That one will be costing you when we're safely back in Morkor.'

The following silence did not help the mood. He soon rectified it however, with a friendly slap on Drake's knee.

'It's alright lad', he said. 'Just a bloody sword after all. Shouldn't be too hard to get it remade. Besides, it's my job to put up with your lunacy.'

'But I mean it about everything', Drake insisted, brushing away his hand. 'Come tomorrow. I'll be different, I promise.'

'Sit on that for now, boy', Gromwell reached over and examined Drake's eye. 'The swelling is indeed better. Can you see out of it yet?'

'Almost. It's a little blurry though.'

'As I could imagine', Gromwell said with a sigh. 'You bloody idiot. Why did you have to run off like that anyway?'

'I was right though, wasn't I?' Drake moaned. 'It wasn't just one of them – there were *two!*'

'To be fair, Drake, I was surprised you let them.' Gromwell playfully punched Drake's shoulder. 'We'd need to train twice as hard now.'

'I will, I promise.'

'Promise, hey? Are you up for trying a bit now?'

Drake nodded. Gromwell waved Weir down as he marched past on the other side of the deck.

'Weir – Can we get some swords please?'

'All right', Weir turned to the nearest officer. 'Markus, some swords for the Prince and Lord Gromwell.'

'Aye, Admiral.'

Drake and Gromwell exchanged a surprised glance.

'Admiral? How curious', Gromwell said with a grunt. 'It seems the Promise of Joanaria isn't *just* at work for us…

Alcadipedia

Afterlife Time has Remembered, the – See: *The Dark.*

Afterlife Time has Forgotten, the – See: *The Grey.*

Alcadia – The planet, home.

Allora – Also known as The Living Moon. Nearest and brightest of the 3 moons of Alcadia.

Astoria – City in North-West Centra.

Benson & Crandle – Main banking firm of Alcadia. Formerly headquartered in Joanas.

Bird Tongue, the – Language utilising a bird's talons, beak and songs. Traditionally used to deliver messages and cite reports.

Black Forest – Large, wild forest in Joanas.

Black, the – See: *The Dark.*

Bright, the – Existence as we understand it.

Carpathia – City in South-West Centra.

Centra – Also known as The Dragon Kingdom and Lands of the Morre. A Kingdom, with direct links to Draberia.

Citadel – City in South Centra upon a lake, fed by the mountains of Gaul.

Named Clans of the Morre – Entire families whose duties are recognised by the Dragon Council and/or the crown.

Collas-Firtheria (The United Kingdoms of) – Formerly two Kingdoms, now united as one country. Neighbouring Joanas.

Dance of the Skylarks – Traditional engagement ceremony for prospect Morre from the Elite Clans.

Dapple (-Morre, -Heim, -Thor, -Salle, -Wood, Kingdom of) – Five City States that used to be a single Kingdom in Joanas. East of Negura, touching the north and south beaches of Joanas.

Dark, the – Also known as The Black, and The Afterlife Time has Remembered. A plane separated from existence, yet still bound by time and touched by the Sea of Souls. Unlike the Grey, existence continues to move here, so any visitors within The Dark merely appear distorted to those remaining in The Bright.

Draberia – Country situated between Centra and Navuro. Governed by a Priest or Priestess.

Dragon Bloods – See: *Morre*

Dragon Council, the– Representatives of the Morre within Centra. Elected by the populace or by the elite status of their Clan. See: *Elite Clans of the Morre.*

Dragon Keeper – Morre trained and stationed in human nations to advise and oversee affairs on behalf of the crown of Centra.

Dragon King – Term for the King of Centra. See *Centra* for further details.

Dragon Kingdom, the – See: *Centra.*

Dragon Tongue, the – Main language spoken by the Morre.

Dunfife – City in North Centra on a bay, otherwise landlocked by mountains.

Elite Clans of the Morre – Entire families of Morre recognised by their honour, nobility and popular vote amongst the human Kingdoms.

Fallen – The souls of the dead who cannot move on. Also used to reference the creatures that spawn under the power of the Fallen.

Father, the – Deity to the nations of the East. Similar in many aspects to The Mother.

First Division, the – Centurian military, normally the front line.

Firth-Wrights – The people of Firtheria. Also used to refer to people from the United Kingdom of Collas-Firtheria.

Forecourt (The City of, The Cathedral of, the Field of) – Famous city in Fugula for its part during the War of Sanctity.

Forgotten Kingdoms, the (The City of, The Mountains of, The Capital of) – A united set of City States located in Western Joanas.

Free Countries, the – Nations under democratic rule, either fully or partially. Predominantly Fugula, Navuro and Titeria.

Fugula – Island nation directly south of Navuro.

Gaul (And the Forests, Mountains of) – City state guarding the southern pass of Centra.

Gaul-Hon (The Fortress of) – Castle located on the border of the Morkor Hinterlands and Gaul.

Grand Duchess, the – Centurian ship that was sunk during The War of Sanctity.

Grey, the – Also known as The Afterlife Time has Forgotten. In the Grey, existence does not move from the point where the visitor enters, granting the user the ability to vanish and reappear in The Bright at the same moment.

Halos (-Salle, Kingdom of) – Two city states in Joanas that used to be a Kingdom. Shares the Eastern beaches with two other past Kingdoms.

Hatred, the – An ancient collective, their power comes from the darkest pit of the Sea of Souls. Jack Penance's Masters and source of power.

High Lord (or High Lady) – Morre political rank. Normally given to the Patriarch or Matriarch of a Clan of the Morre.

Hobsythe – Also known as the Scale and the Lizard Men. A type of Sorre. Walking, talking two legged reptiles slightly larger than an average man.

Iliad – City on the East coast of Centra.

Joanaria – Former Kingdom, now known as Joanas.

Joanarian March, the – Main battle pace on drums used to push and lead the Joanarian Armies.

Joanas – City states and lands previously known as Joanaria. Lorded over by Knights of State who convene as the Knights Republic.

Joanarian Straight – Heavy traffic water route used by traders and the military of Alcadia. Starts at a central seafaring point near the East Joanarian shores, passes just above Joanas-Sorrow and finishes at the Western Beaches of Navuro, not far from the Northmost tip of Titeria.

Joanas-Sorrow – Island City State independent from Joanas. Overseen by a governor, voted into power by the City Council. Situated almost dead centre between Joanas and Navuro.

Jonte (-Salle, Kingdom of) – Two city states in western Joanas previously known as Ponte-Wood and Ponte-Haem, formerly known as the Hobsythe Lands.

Knights' Republic, the – Central Governing Court of Joanas. Formed of Lords from the main City States.

Lands of the Morre, the – See: *Centra.*

Legend (Living or Dead) – Morre and men honoured by Centra for deeds that changed the course of a major battle or feats of incredible courage and valour.

Living Moon, the – See: *Allora.*

Lizard Men, the – See: *Hobsythe.*

Lord / Lady – Morre and Human political rank. Granted to highly stationed members of Clans below High Lord or Lady.

Lorre – Descendants of the Torre. Hellish, winged beasts who use the Sea of Souls to cast destructive magic.

Maiden of Gaul-Hon, the – Centurian support craft sailing with the *Vengeance of Dunfife.*

Maiden of Shauna, the – Centurian support craft sailing with the *Vengeance of Dunfife.*

Mother, the – Deity to the western nations (Except for pockets of Collas-Firtheria and Centra).

Mobius – Second furthest moon of Alcadia.

Morkor (River, Castle, City of) – Capital City of Centra. Its northern boundary and castle sit on the River of its namesake.

Morkor Hinterlands – Grassy plains just south of Morkor. Their boundary ends under the eye of the Fortress of Gaul.

Morre (Dragon-, the) – Also known as the Dragon Bloods. Beings like man in almost every way, however, they are believed to be the direct descendants of the Torre, charged by their gods to watch over man. They live longer than men, are stronger, and their mortality is tied to their state of mind rather than their health.

Mud Goblin – A type of Fallen made mostly of flesh, bones and mud.

Navuro – Industrialised nation of the East. Democratic Republic, under the Council of Navuro and its High Councillor.

Necromancer, the – Last tyrannical Emperor of Joanas. Elected by the Knights Republic during the time leading up to the War of Sanctity.

Negura – Capital of Joanas. Separated into two districts.

Nukuoro (The Fields of) – Fertile plains in northern Fugula.

Pace – Favoured unit of measurement for distance. Two strides of the average-heighted person.

Ponte (-Puris, Former Kingdoms of) – Two disgraced northwest Joanas city states separated from one another and vassal to their neighbours. Were formerly part of the Hobsythe's Kingdom.

Rest, the – Also known as The Passing. Timeless plane of existence that stretches across the cosmos.

Scale, the – See: *Hobsythe*.

Sea of Hope – Water mass sitting between Eastern Navuro and Northwest Collas-Firtheria. Larger than the Sea of Sorrow.

Sea of Sorrow – Water mass sitting between Eastern Joanas and Western Navuro.

Sea of Souls – The combined definition for souls that have yet to pass on, lingering or waiting in the Afterlife.

Sea Worms – A water-bound species under the order of the Sorre. Found primarily in the waters between Northern Joanas and Southern Centra.

Segura – Central city state in Joanas bordering the state of Negura.

Severed-Salle – City state in Joanas previously known as Ponte-Salle; Former Hobsythe Kingdom.

Silver Tail – A breed of Falcon. Chosen for their stamina by the lower courts of the Morre and Human Kingdoms.

Snuggle Tail – A breed of Falcon. Chosen for their dependency and long range. Very agile and intelligent, hence, are a favourite among the high courts of the Morre

Sorre (Dragon-, the) – Believed to be the descendants of the Torre, who chose the land and sea as their Kingdom. Multiple known races in existence and unlike the Lorre, they cannot fly. See also: *Hobsythe* and *Sea Worms*.

Soule (the Mountains of, the Forest of) – Centurian City located at the base of the Soule Mountains, just off the southern pass; leading to Citadel from Gaul. Halfway rest point for most travellers on the pass.

Sprint – Favoured unit of measurement for distance. Roughly the distance a person would be able to sprint until they became tired.

Storm Trotter – Breed of Horse. Found mostly in Joanas, but some have been seen as far as Navuro.

Titeria – Island nation northwest of Navuro.

Titus – Furthest moon of Alcadia. Rarely seen.

Torre (Dragon-, the) – The creators of Universe, their last act was known to be the creation of Alcadia. After finishing their work, they chose one of three paths of Mortality either to become the Lorre, Sorre or the Morre. Revered as Deities by the Morre and some parts of Collas-Firtheria.

Venom Fire – Spitting poison of the Lorre. Both toxic and flammable. Normally set alight by the Lorre's magic for maximum effect.

War of Sanctity, the – Last major planetary-scale war. Started by The Necromancer opposing the Morre's involvement in the sabotage of the slave trade.

Westerlock (Port of) – Small fishing and trading town in Jonte, Joanas.

Winter (-Haem, -Salle, -Puris, -Wood, Kingdom of) – Four city states. Ex-Kingdom of Joanas.

Vengeance of Dunfife, the – Centurian Warship that carries the crown.

ABOUT THE AUTHOR

NR Kamper is the architect of the Fortresses in the Hereafter series. Working with his wife Katerina as editor, he has built upon an existing novel he wrote many years ago, and moulded it into the series you are reading today.

He works in London and generally fills his spare time either working on his model railway, playing video games or writing the next instalment of the series.

He lives in Essex with his wife and beloved pet cat.

95306179R00137

Made in the USA
Columbia, SC
10 May 2018